"The Creep's Got Me!
The Creep's Got—"

Brina screamed, but the man's strong hands covered her mouth.

"Be quiet now, little girl," he said, in a soft, whiny voice that sent fear down her back. She kicked out at him and made contact with his kneecap. But the childish shoes weren't strong enough, and she only hurt her foot.

Where was everybody? Why didn't they come? The creep kept murmuring, "Sweet little girl —so pretty."

Then he had her inside the hut with the door shut. . . .

Where was Wallace? Grandad? Perky?

She opened her mouth to yell. . . .

THE CREEP
SUSAN DODSON

AN ARCHWAY PAPERBACK
POCKET BOOKS ● NEW YORK

With special thanks to Detective Warren J. Broz of the Youth and Sex Assault Section of the Pittsburgh Police for answering my questions and for helping me form a picture of a concerned police department which sincerely cares about the victims of one of the worst of all possible crimes, rape.

POCKET BOOKS, a Simon & Schuster division of
GULF & WESTERN CORPORATION
1230 Avenue of the Americas, New York, N.Y. 10020

*To my family, with love,
and to my teacher, editor, and friend,
Barbara Lalicki*

1

Sometimes, looking back, I wonder where I'd been all my life, before last summer changed it so much. But then, I read somewhere recently that you never hear new ideas about yourself and your world until you're ready to. I guess I was ready to. Some people would call it growing up—I like to call it growing out.

It all started with an argument with my mother. School was out and summer had begun. It was the first Saturday in June, and we had been fighting since early afternoon. Grandad tried to referee, but Mom and I kept pulling him into the fight, expecting him to take sides. He wasn't about to. It beat me how three people in one house could seem like three hundred. We usually got along real well, but we had been bumping into each other for hours.

The argument had reached the point where we were going over and over the same ground. Suddenly, I had to get out of the house. I was sick of arguing and I wanted to be alone. To think things out.

I was headed for the front door, when I heard Mom ask, "Where are you going, Brina?"

"None of your business!" wasn't the way to handle Mom, when (as Grandad put it) she had a bug up her bonnet.

I answered quietly, "Over to the Duvalls' to baby-sit for Annie." I even managed not to slam the screen door on my way out.

I ran across the front porch, down the steps, and toward the woods to the left of the house. It was true that I had to baby-sit for Annie, but I had at least an hour before I had to be there. I needed that hour to get myself together.

I ran past Grandad's prize rose bushes and into the woods. They weren't very big—just about four square blocks on this side, and then some houses started up.

At one time my dad's family owned and farmed the whole area around us, but it had been sold long before I was born. When I was younger, our house had been the only one at the end of a dirt road. But now, creeping suburbia was catching up to us and a new housing development was slowly being built on the land I used to roam freely. The dirt road was gone and now the house fronted on a real street. Some enterprising soul had named it Larchmont Lane. It went through the woods on both sides to other, more populated streets, but we were still the only family actually living within an eight-block radius.

Our house is the old farmhouse, surrounded by about an acre of land, and it's a nice old thing. It has a front porch, with green-and-white-striped awnings, a back kitchen porch, high ceilings and an old-fashioned atmosphere—a comfortable house, set back far enough from Larchmont Lane to insure us privacy even after the new houses are built.

I was sorry to see most of the woods around us cut down. I was even sorrier to lose a lot of my brooding places. But my favorite thinking and brooding place was still there. A big old tree stump in the middle of a clearing in the woods. I had been coming to it for years, every time I had a problem to work out. Now that I was fifteen, almost sixteen, it seemed that

I was spending half my life on the tree stump in the woods.

It was a lovely late spring evening, and the trees above me were getting so bushy that I could barely see the sky through them. The spring flowers were all gone. I used to love to sketch them and identify any new ones, but this year they blossomed out without my even noticing them. I had other things on my mind.

I sat on the tree stump and tried to work out my feelings of anger. Even though Annie Duvall was only ten years old, she was smart enough to figure out when something was bothering me. I knew she would ask me questions that I didn't want to answer.

I thought about the fight. I tried to see Mom's side of it, even though she wasn't seeing mine. She'd been absolutely paranoid about my growing up lately. She'd always treated me like I was older. She'd shared things with me and taught me to be independent. But now that I really was growing up, she sometimes treated me like a baby.

My Dad died in an auto accident when I was five and Mom has been working ever since. She has her own interior decorating business, with an office in downtown Pittsburgh.

Grandad says she's real smart and has worked her business into a real money-making proposition. He's lived with us ever since he retired from being a railroad engineer. He's the only sixty-seven-year-old man I know, or have ever heard of for that matter, who wears a jumpsuit all the time. He always wears a gold pocket watch with a long, heavy antique gold chain. Since all of his jumpsuits have different arrangements of pockets, you never know how he'll loop the chain, but my favorite is when he stretches it across his middle. He always has a red bandana handkerchief in one of the pockets, too, and sometimes he tops the whole thing off with his old railroad cap. I love him dearly and I'd hoped he would side with me in the argument with Mom. False hope. But then he hadn't exactly sided with her either.

I sighed aloud. The anger was beginning to go away. I never could stay mad at Mom long. Grandad always said she was doing the best she could with a business and a kid to take care of. I figured, since he was her father, he knew what he was talking about. But it was so frustrating to want something so much and be turned down. I wanted to go to a camp that specialized in the arts, especially painting, for the summer. I had made at least half the money I needed for it by baby-sitting. But money wasn't the problem. The problem was Paul.

Mom claimed that Paul was too old for me and that I was getting too hung up on him. She wanted me to be interested in boys my own age. But I had nothing in common with them and I had a lot in common with Paul.

It was true that Paul was nineteen, soon to be twenty. Our birthdays are on the same day. Maybe that's why we were so much alike. We met at day camp four summers ago. He was teaching an arts and crafts class and I worked very hard to become his favorite student. I'd never met anyone like him before. He was tall, skinny, red-haired and freckled— and the most sensitive, alive, interesting boy on earth.

We'd stayed good friends, even after day camp. He was apart from most kids his own age, because his love of painting was almost all-consuming. It was something he shared with me, because I felt the same way. We sketched and painted and went to museums, art galleries, and exhibitions together.

Mom never said a word, even after Paul graduated from high school and went to college. His first year was spent at a college downtown. He lived at home and I still got to see him. But suddenly last year he transferred to an out-of-state school. He said he felt the need to get away and, Lord, I had missed him. It had been such a lonely year and I wanted to be with him again. Then he got a summer teaching job at a camp and I wanted to go, too. But Mom was doing everything she could to stop that. I had the feeling she thought best friends might become best lovers. And she wasn't far wrong. The thought had occurred to me that if we were away together all summer, I could convince him to be more than a big brother. We had already experimented with so many things: booze, which made me sick, grass, which didn't mean anything to either of us, Yoga and meditating—right in the woods where I was sitting. And this summer I thought we would become more than good friends.

I got up from the stump and dusted myself off. Time to face Annie. As I left the woods, I realized I'd forgotten my sketch pad. I ambled up the street, kicking stones, thinking about going back to my house for it. But then I'd have to face Mom again and I wasn't ready. I had to think of some other way to keep Annie busy.

She was really pretty for a ten-year-old, with dark curly reddish-brown hair and huge brown eyes, almost the same color as her hair, a little pink rosebud mouth, all in a luminous pink-skin setting. Someday she would be gorgeous, but right now she was a busy ten-year-old actress. She was going through a story-telling stage

—not exactly lies but just little stretches of the truth. She liked a lot of attention and I cursed myself for forgetting my sketch pad. One of the ways to keep her quiet was to draw her.

I needn't have worried. I was halfway up the Duvalls' walk, when the door flew open. Annie stood there hopping up and down.

"I've been waiting for you, Brina—I got a new paint set. My uncle sent it from New York. All colors and paper and pencils and everything. You can teach me to paint just like you."

"Fat chance!" I thought, as she dragged me into the house. Why does everyone think it's so easy to paint? She kept babbling on and on, while Mr. and Mrs. Duvall gave me last-minute instructions, and left.

Finally, Annie and I settled down at the kitchen table. Soon she was happily painting away, ignoring any and all advice. Her paper had fingerprints all over it, and she soon had paint all over her. She was painting what looked like an abstract cat. Purple. I decided to keep my mouth shut and let her go her own way. Paul always said to let everyone find their own level—whatever that meant. Paul again. I sighed. Annie looked up immediately, "What are you thinking about, Brina?"

"Drawing you." I smiled winningly, and borrowed some of her paper. I got busy with a pencil, but my thoughts were still on Paul.

After a while, I thought I heard her say something. I looked up from drawing her eyes and glanced into her real ones. She had the funniest look on her face. She was trying to make up her mind about something.

"What's up, Annie?" I asked.

She looked down at the purple cat and added green whiskers. A stroke of pure genius. She mumbled,

"A man said something to me yesterday . . . outside the library."

I sort of grinned, "Someone you know?"—thinking it was another Annie-type story.

"No. I never saw him before."

"Well . . . what did he say?"—still waiting for the punch line.

"He asked me if I wanted a ride home. He called me Ann. Nobody calls me Ann," she said a bit proudly. She was always correcting people when they made that mistake. She would say *Ann-ie!* loudly, and get louder if they continued with *Ann.*

"What did you do?" I asked, looking back at my sketch and correcting an eyebrow.

"Nothing. I saw some friends of mine and ran to catch up to them."

"Well—be careful. You know there's a"—I paused delicately, not knowing how to put it—"bad man around here. If you see him again, just ignore him. And tell your mom and dad about it. You see, Annie, some people aren't very nice and they could hurt you."

She nodded as if she understood, and I felt real pleased with myself for handling a difficult situation so well. "Just be careful from now on."

I let it go at that. After all . . . everyone in the Pittsburgh area knew there was a guy going around molesting little kids. We'd all been warned. Our police had made the rounds of all the schools in our suburb, Mount Hope, in May. They told us not to accept rides from strangers, to report anyone offering candy or special treats. To run if someone was following us. There had been at least five cases in and around Mount Hope alone. Three little girls had been raped and beaten and another two had gotten away.

Even though the police had a composite sketch of the man, which interested the budding artist in me, they had not caught him.

I didn't take Annie's story too seriously. She loved attention too much and could make up wonderful stories to get it. Besides, I was sure she'd already been warned about strangers.

She added an orange tail to the purple and green cat and said it was finished. I breathed a sigh of relief, about both the conversation and the painting.

I looked at the clock and saw it was almost ten. "Time for bed," I said.

Annie gave me one of those charming little begging looks, meant to melt my heart. "Oh, Brina. Just a little while longer. Till you finish your drawing."

"It's no use, Annie. I'm finished." I put a final shadow on her hair, signed it, and handed it to her.

I shooed her on upstairs, got her bathed, brushed, and into her favorite pink elephant pj's. I settled her down in her pink-and-white canopy bed, in her pink-and-white ruffled room. An excess of pink and white, but it suited Annie. I told her a quick story and watched her lids flutter down over her brown eyes, until they were finally locked in sleep. I looked at her fondly. I'd been baby-sitting for a lot of the neighborhood kids in the past three years, but Annie was sort of special. I thought about her story again, as I kissed her sleeping face good night. Then I remembered all her other stories. It was a phase I hoped she'd grow out of soon.

I switched out the light, half-closed the door, and went back downstairs. I knew the Duvalls wouldn't be back until twelve-thirty or one and the rest of the evening was mine.

I prowled around the house, picking things up and

putting them down. Even after all of those years of
baby-sitting, it was still a strange feeling to be alone,
except for a sleeping child or two, in a house that
wasn't mine. I looked at the *TV Guide*. Nothing on
that I wanted to see. I helped myself to some cookies
in the kitchen and thought about Paul again. He
would be packing frantically now. He was leaving
early Monday morning; he had to be in camp at least
a week before it opened.

I knew I had to talk to him. He still didn't know
for sure that I wouldn't be going to camp and he was
holding a reservation open for me. I postponed the
call as long as possible, then went to the phone in
the Duvalls' living room. I dialed his number. He
answered on the first ring.

No sense beating around the bush. I didn't say
hello, how are you, or any of the other niceties. I
got straight to the point.

"I can't go."

"I know. Your mother called to explain."

"She what? What did she say?" How could she!

"Don't be mad at her, Brina. We had a long talk."
I couldn't say anything. I was very hurt that they
would discuss the whole thing without me. "Brina?
Are you there?"

I took a deep breath, "I'm here. What was your
long talk about?"

"Now, don't get sarcastic with me. She feels we're
too involved and you're too young for me."

"And what did you say?" I wanted to hang up
right then and there. I knew I didn't want to hear it.

"Brina—I agreed with her. You are too young for
me right now. In a few years, maybe it will all work
out. But not right now. You have a way to go and
so do I. I knew if I stayed around Pittsburgh I'd

9

never make any new friends. I've made a lot of new friends now, and in particular, a girl my own age. I've found it easier than I thought. I've also been doing a lot of thinking about you, and I realize that as long as you think you can rely on me to be around, you won't give boys your own age half a chance."

"I don't want to hear this, Paul. We've always been such good friends. . . ."

"That's exactly what I'm saying. I'm your only friend except for Ella and that's too isolating, too. You have to let other people into your life. I won't be—I can't be anyone's whole world."

"Don't be so conceited! There are a lot of other people around."

"Sure, they're around, but you don't pay any attention to them. I'm sorry Brina—but we've always been honest with each other. You have to learn to reach out to others and to stop leaning on my friendship. I really do care a lot about you . . . but don't you see? It's more than time for you to grow up and learn about yourself and others. You'll always mean a lot to me, but it's time for me to have my own friends, too." He paused and then said, "I know you don't believe this but it really isn't hard to make friends. All you have to do is let them know you're interested. I'll come over tomorrow to say good-bye and we can talk some more. . . ."

I couldn't take any more. I was choking back the tears as it was. "Don't bother coming over!" I shouted. "I don't want to see you!" I hung up before I started crying.

I remember throwing myself on the floor and shaking all over, before I actually felt the hot tears on my cheeks. I seemed to hurt all over and I couldn't stop shaking. The oddest thing was—I wanted Mom.

I'd been so angry with her before, but now I wanted her there to put her arms around me and tell me everything would be all right. And then I wanted Grandad to come and wipe the tears away and make me blow my thoroughly running nose in his bandana. I wanted to be a little girl again.

I finally got up shakily and went into the kitchen. I always get hungry at the strangest times, and I was starving. I had a Coke and gobbled up the rest of the cookies, while sitting at the kitchen table. I stared at Annie's cat and thought about my life. I had an endless summer ahead of me. It was too late to get a summer job—all the good ones were gone—and my best friend Paul had deserted me.

I thought about my only other friend. Ella James and I have been friends since about the year one. She is an only child—like me. We went to grade school and junior high together. When we were younger we had to take a lot from the other kids. The black kids thought that Ella should be best friends with one of them and, of course, the white kids thought I should be best friends with one of them. Now that we were in high school, everyone pretty much left us alone.

Paul knew that and I had to admit he was right about being isolated. But Ella was the only friend I had left now that Paul was gone. And she would be busy during the summer. She had her music, her church choir, and her new boyfriend, Howard. He was a senior at our school and played the guitar. I was happy for her that she liked Howard so much, but at the same time I was jealous. We had been so close because we were different from the other kids— she with her music and me with my painting. I was going to be a famous artist and she a famous singer.

"Friends. . . ." I sighed aloud. Paul said I had to go out and find new friends. It was easy . . . he said. I almost started crying again. It wasn't easy for me. I was terribly shy and even when I met someone I liked, I'd screw it up somehow. I'd get sarcastic or say something dumb. Or worse—not say anything at all and lose out.

It didn't help to have a beautiful and charming, socially-correct-at-all-times mother. I loved her—but I envied and resented her at the same time. I used to hope I would grow up to look like her—but no way! She has reddish-blonde hair and big green eyes. I have light brown hair and blue eyes. She is tall and sort of well-rounded slim. I am short and skinny. She says I will probably grow some more. She didn't reach her full height of five foot nine until she was seventeen. She is even taller than Grandad, by an inch. But from my height of barely five feet, they are both giants. She has always said that no one is happy about their looks until they grow up, find out they like themselves and that they are unique because they look the way they do. I wasn't sure that would ever happen to me. It was easy for her to say. I saw a print of a painting once that looked just like her. It was called *Diana Bathing,* by François Boucher. And since her name is Diana, too, the likeness was amazing. I'd never seen any painting that looked like me—who ever wants to paint a skinny little runt?

Mom isn't like any other mother I've ever met. She always lets Grandad take care of seeing me off to school and he is usually there when I get home. He's a great cook and fixes most of our meals. Mom doesn't care at all about cooking, but she does her share of the housework, even though she doesn't like it. I don't care for it much myself, but I always take care of my own messes and clean my room. Grandad says that Mom decorates, he cooks and cleans, and I watch.

I sat there for a long time feeling sorry for myself. I knew that Paul had a point, but that didn't make it any easier to take. The Duvalls got home around twelve-thirty and Mr. Duvall drove me right over to my house.

I arrived there richer in pocket, but poorer in spirit. Mom had gone to bed, but Grandad was waiting up for me. I told him all about Paul and my feelings. He listened all the way through, was quiet for a moment and then said, "Brina—Paul is right. Diana is right. And in your own way, you're right."

I had to laugh. Grandad can always make me laugh. "I suppose you're right in saying that everyone is right?" I asked.

"Well—I am right," he grinned. "You see everyone has an opinion and everyone is entitled to that opinion. What you're going to have to do is sift through all the information you've been given—all the opinions—and then pick out what's important to you. You have leaned on Paul and Ella for friendship. Paul is almost grown up though and Ella has other interests. And you've been alone too much this past year. I'm not saying that's totally wrong—you are a little different from other kids. You've already decided to be an artist and you've made a good start. Most kids of fifteen are still looking around for something to do with their lives."

He sighed a little. "Lord knows—I don't have all the answers. No one does. I know you're shy, but you have a tendency to hide behind that shyness, to put people down before they can put you down. You feel deserted by Paul and you resent Diana's interference. I understand that, but you can't live your life by yourself. No one can." He shifted around in his favorite over-stuffed chair. "You'll have to force yourself to get involved with others. Instead of drawing a face—find out what's behind it. Maybe that will bring more life to your drawings."

"Is there something wrong with my drawings?" I was startled, really upset that there might be something wrong with the one thing I could do well.

"It strikes me that an artist is one of the few people in the world who keeps on improving and improving. For the rest of your life, Brina, you'll be getting better at your work. That's a good way to be. By the time I was twenty-five, I knew all there was to know about driving a train, except for changes and improvements in the engines. But they came gradually and made it easier instead of harder.

Grandad leaned forward in the chair, speaking slowly, forcing me to listen to every word. "It's not that there's something wrong with your drawings—it's just that you haven't experienced enough of life to put it in your drawings and paintings. You can know how to draw something . . . but if you don't feel it—you can't show it. You'll have a pretty picture, but not something that will bring feelings of pain or joy to someone else. In order to do that, you have to have the feelings of pain or joy yourself. And you won't do it by isolating yourself."

I studied his face—his wonderful, kind, beautiful face. All of a sudden I wondered if he was happy. I'd never thought of it before. I couldn't take in all he said. Not yet. But there I was—wondering what was behind the face that I had seen all my life. Was that what he meant?

I remembered trying to capture the look of him

just a few weeks before. I'd struggled for ages with the drawing and still had not been pleased with it.

I kissed him good night then, and went upstairs to my room. I took out the drawing and studied it. He was right. I had a very nice drawing of a youthful-looking sixty-seven-year-old man. His white hair was standing up in the spikes caused by cowlicks. There were the kind blue eyes, with all the crinkles and laugh lines around them, the weather-beaten skin, the hook nose with the tiny bump—the result of some accident in his youth. I didn't know what the accident had been—was that important to the drawing? His fingers crossed over a slight pot belly. He had made a great Santa Claus for me when I was little.

I wished I were little again. In a rage I tore up the drawing. I hadn't caught the real spirit of Grandad. But I didn't really know what made Grandad the way he was, so how could I put it down on paper? Then I realized—that's what everyone was telling me. I was so tired then. I had done enough crying, fussing, and did-I-have-the-answering. I went to bed.

2

Sunday was a real bummer of a day. I hung around the house hoping Paul would come over after all. I was beginning to understand what he was trying to say and I wanted badly to talk to him about it. But he must have taken me at my word. He didn't show. And I wasn't going to call him.

Mom and I tiptoed around each other all morning. It was a silent truce. In the afternoon, she went to her workroom over the garage. Grandad retreated to the garden and his rose bushes. I sat on the front porch and thought about Paul and other, nicer summer weekends.

We usually had so much to do on weekends. Mom never went to the office, but sometimes she would have to entertain her clients, and we would have a barbecue in our huge backyard. Grandad would invite some of his cronies from the small park nearby where he spent every summer weekday afternoon playing chess. I would usually invite Ella and Paul. I didn't know what I would do now that I didn't have them.

By dinnertime, I was so down in the dumps, I was just sitting there staring into space. Grandad came over from his rose bushes and said, "Why don't you call Paul and we'll all go out to dinner?"

"No. I don't want to."

"Then let's get Diana and we'll go."

"I'd rather stay home. Why don't you and Mom go?"

He sat down heavily on the glider beside me. "You're hoping Paul will come over after all?" I nodded. "If you want to see him—call him. Your friendship isn't ending—it's just going to be a different kind of friendship. You're not still mad at him?"

"Yes and no. I want to talk to him, but I don't know how." I felt a lump in my throat.

"Are you still mad at Diana?"

"Yes and no. I just don't want to talk to her."

"Well . . . good Lord, Brina . . . you live in the same house. You can't go on not talking to her. I can just see you ten years from now, writing notes

16

to each other." It was a feeble attempt at a joke, but I smiled anyway. It was better than crying.

"It's not that I won't talk to her. I'm just not ready to talk to her."

"Hmm. Believe it or not . . . that makes sense to me. But there are a lot of yeses and nos to you this evening. If I offered to go for Chinese food—would you say yes and no to that?"

"No! I'd say yes to that!" We laughed. He knew I couldn't say no to Chinese food and when I was nervous or upset, I ate like a pig. I never put on any weight. Worse luck—I was as underdeveloped a fifteen-year-old as the world had ever seen. I looked more like a ten-year-old. Even Annie looked better than me.

"First positive words I've heard from you in a dog's age!" He patted my knee and got up. "O.K. I'll go get the works. You run over to the garage and tell Diana. She'll need time to clean up. Let's make it a picnic—you set the table in the back yard. And don't be afraid to face Diana—she's only trying to do her best by you." He went on out to his car, parked in the street.

I sat for a moment after he pulled away. He was right. I had to face Mom sooner or later. I got to my feet and went through the house, picking up plates, silverware, and napkins on my way. I went out the back door, down the kitchen steps, and dumped them on the old redwood picnic table.

I crossed the driveway and went around to the side of the garage, where the steps led up to Mom's workroom. I gave a longing glance at the old apple tree and the swing where I had spent so much time in my youth. I certainly was being nostalgic, moving up the steps slowly, as if I were going to a hanging. Then I reminded myself not to be so dramatic. Mom wasn't a henchman. Or even a henchwoman—if there was such a thing.

I always knock before I enter her private places, just as she always knocks on the door of my room if it's closed. She laid down the rules of privacy early in my life . . . hers and mine.

I knocked and heard her say, "Come in." I went on in.

I found her struggling with the drawer of an old, rather small Victorian dresser. We'd found it at a garage sale a few weeks before. She'd been meaning to strip it and restore the oak finish. We bought it in such a hurry, we didn't realize until we got it home that one of the drawers was stuck. Grandad was supposed to work on it, but he hadn't gotten around to it. Now here was Mom, tugging furiously at the drawer. Her blonde hair was escaping from the knot she wore on top of her head when she was working and she had strands of it in her mouth. The oval mirror above the dresser was tilting dangerously and I moved quickly to grab it.

She looked up from her cross-legged position on the floor. "Good . . . hang on to it. I'll pull." She spit the hair out, took a firmer hold on the carved knobs, and started tugging. I held on to the dresser, with one arm around the mirror. It startled us both when it suddenly gave way and she ended up lying on the floor with the drawer on top of her.

I helped untangle her and held the drawer, while she scrambled to her feet. "Are you hurt?" I asked.

"Not really. Is the drawer?" She looked a bit ruffled.

I held it up in front of me and checked it out. "Nope. Looks O.K. to me."

She sat down in her old desk chair, by another one

of her finds. An old-fashioned roll-top desk, where she did her paper work.

"I spent an hour trying to get that dumb drawer open . . . and then it attacks me. Whew! I'm exhausted . . . but at least I worked out some of my tension."

"Tension?" I asked innocently as I sat down on a purple-tufted stool.

"Don't hand me that . . . of course I'm tense. I don't like it when anyone is angry with me, but I especially don't like it when you're angry with me. I suppose I shouldn't have called Paul. . . ."

"Then why did you?"

"I don't exactly know. . . ." I was glad to see her looking guilty. "But I thought if I explained my feelings to him, he would understand and help explain them to you. He'd already figured it out, but he hadn't figured out how to talk to you about it . . . you know, about your finding other friends. He said he thought camp was a good idea, because he could try to get you involved with kids your own age."

"So why don't you let me go after all?" A faint hope rose in me.

"Because you're stubborn and you'd probably just follow Paul around all summer long, get your feelings hurt, and end up feeling worse than you do now."

"I'm not all that stubborn. I mean to quote Grandad—'A barn door doesn't have to fall on me.' "

"Yes, it does! You think I'm treating you like a child because I won't let you go away. You think I'm trying to stop your relationship with Paul. I'm not. I just want you to put it in its proper place. He's your friend . . . Brina . . . nothing else. And now you need other friends. Look—this is probably all my fault, because I've let you go your own way for a long time and your way isn't working. We haven't really talked for ages, so try to relax and let me explain something."

I tried very hard to look relaxed.

"When I was your age . . ." she went on, "things were black and white. If you smoked or had a drink, or even swore a little . . . if you had too many dates . . . you were labeled a Bad Girl. You had a Reputation. We were all under so much pressure to conform. If there was something different about any of us . . . we were left out. I didn't have any friends because my mother was sick so much. I couldn't have anybody over to the house. I couldn't have slumber parties or birthday parties, so I was left out of the group a lot.

"I thought when I grew up and had my own family . . . I'd let my kids have parties all the time and have an open house to everyone. It didn't turn out that way. I only had one kid, you, before your father died. And then I had to go to work. You know I love my work. But with me working, I couldn't be the kind of mother that gets involved with other mothers. Car pools, P.T.A., whatever. So I couldn't help you make friends. Things have changed a lot since I was a kid. I know there's the pressure of drugs and sex, and believe me . . . I'm glad I'm not your age. I could never have handled that. When it comes to those things . . . you seem to be pretty level-headed. I'm sure I can thank Paul for that."

I moved a little uncomfortably on the stool. I didn't know how much she'd guessed about my experiments with Paul and grass and booze. I wasn't going to tell her about them . . . at least not now.

20

"But Paul is going his own way and it's time for you to expand . . . to open up to other people." She paused. "I'm probably going to put this badly, but as long as we're talking, I want to be absolutely honest with you about my feelings. You know I love Ella and I certainly don't want you to stop being friends with her. But in many ways, Ella is much more grown-up than you. Maybe it's because of being black, she's a stronger person. Maybe it's because she's performed in front of people. Remember that last concert we went to, at her church—she's as polished an entertainer as I've ever seen. In any case, she's light years ahead of you in dealing with people.

"I want so many things for you. I'm realistic enough to know I can't go out and get them for you, but as your mother I can at least point you in the right direction. I do want you to enjoy yourself, and you can't do that by being lonely all the time. And I know you're lonely. I've taught you to be independent and self-reliant. Now you're too independent and self-reliant. You don't even know how to reach out to other people."

I sat there listening to her talk on and on. I understood most of what she said. And I agreed. I had been pretending I didn't need other people, and, as Grandad said, hiding behind my shyness. But I wasn't ready to admit it to her yet. I still felt on the defensive. When she stopped talking, I had to say, "But Mom . . . you don't have all that many friends now . . . and you seem to be getting along just fine."

She grinned a little, "It's different for me. I have my work. And I have to deal with people all the time. You know how many clients I have and you know how demanding they can be. I could socialize

with them more . . . I could be going out all the time.
I've chosen not to. I wanted to spend weekends with
you and Dad. And I want time to myself, too. I'm
also reasonably happy with my life now, I mean right
this minute, but I can change at any time. If I get
lonely, or decide I want more people around me, all
I have to do is make a few phone calls to start going
out again. You see, there's the difference between
you and me. You're not happy—you're lonely and
you don't know any people to call."

I felt so much love for her right then. I appreciated her trying to help me and her honesty about
her life. But was she really happy? I looked at her
face the same way I'd looked at Grandad's the night
before, wondering what was behind it, too. But then
Grandad yelled from outside, "Hey! Where is everyone? The Won-Ton's on!" His bad joke reminded me.

"Oh! I forgot! Grandad went for Chinese food."
I jumped to my feet.

"Great . . . I'm starved!" cried Mom, jumping up,
too. "Nothing like a Maturity Lecture to work up
an appetite." She smiled at her own joke, then looked
thoughtful. "There's just one other thing, Brina . . .
I do love you. My mother never told me she loved
me. I guess I knew she did. But she never said it. I
haven't said it to you for a while, and I always think
it's important to say you love someone when you do.
Think about everything I said and when you feel like
it we'll talk some more. I ain't goin' nowhere . . .
except to get some Chinese food," and she raced for
the door with me right behind.

After all the tension, it felt good to relax. Grandad entertained us with funny train stories during our
Chinese picnic. He acted out all the parts and Mom
and I both got hysterical.

After we ate, Grandad went back to his rose bushes, Mom went back to her workroom and I went back to the front porch—this time not to brood, but to think about things the way Grandad had told me. Sifting through the opinions and picking out what was important to me.

3

Monday was a hard day to get through, because I knew Paul was on his way to camp and a life without me. I'd never felt more alone or lonely in my life.

I tried to think up ways to meet people. I made up my mind to be absolutely surrounded by masses and masses of people by the time Paul came back. I'd show him! The trouble was I didn't know where to start. Summer was a bad time anyway . . . kids were away or working.

Ella always met people through her church groups, but we didn't really belong to a church. We went occasionally to the Mount Hope Methodist Church, for Christmas and Easter, but we weren't at all involved there.

I called a downtown art school and asked them to send me their summer schedule. That was a step in the right direction. The money I had to spend on camp could be used for a class. Maybe sculpture. Something different.

Tuesday was a little better than Monday, but not much. Time seemed to stand still while I decided what to do with my summer. Then Ella called to see if I wanted to go swimming at the Mount Hope pool. I would have gone anywhere!

After our first dip, we sat around the pool and talked. Mostly about Ella. She and her church choir were going to be in a recital at a hall in downtown Pittsburgh. She would have a solo and she was all excited. It would be sometime in August, but they had already started practicing. I could understand that this was a step up for her. But it meant that she would really be busy all summer long.

She was concerned about what to sing and I suggested one popular song and one spiritual. We bickered back and forth all afternoon about which ones to do. If she noticed there was anything wrong with me . . . she never said anything. But then Ella is one of those people who doesn't ask questions. She'll listen if you want to tell her, but she never pushes.

While we were at the pool, I looked at the other kids there. The pretty girls all stuck together, led by our class beauty, Ingrid. I had gone through grade school, junior high, and even shared classrooms with Ingrid, but I don't think I'd ever really talked to her.

She waved at us that day and we waved back, but I had no desire to go over and talk to her. I really didn't think we had anything in common. I didn't fit in with her group. I wasn't ugly, but I wasn't exactly beautiful either. Grandad said I would be extremely attractive one day. That day seemed pretty far off to me.

My best features are my eyes and my hair. My eyes are sky blue like Grandad's, and I'm lucky enough to have long thick lashes. I had long thick hair, too, all the way down to my rear end. I loved having long hair, even if it is just brown. I asked Mom if I could get it streaked, but she turned me down flat. Every once in a while she suggested getting it cut, too. She said with my skinny little shape, I looked like I was all hair and eyes. But then I would remind her that it was *my* hair and not hers. She usually accepted that, but sometimes when she caught me with it all down in front of my face, she'd pull it back sharply and accuse me of hiding behind it. I liked to peep out from under it while people were talking around me or at me. It made me feel safer when they couldn't see my whole face.

Not that there was anything wrong with my face—it just seemed like my features didn't all fit together. My eyes are real big, my nose real small and my mouth real wide. Anyway, I didn't fit in with Ingrid and her crowd.

Ella would have fit in just fine with the black beauties at the pool, but they stuck together, too, and she just wasn't interested in them. Ella is beautiful, though. Her hair always crackles in a fluffed-out Afro style. It's her own look. She has a great figure too—tall and rather stately. She always wears a lot of white and beige, a bikini at the pool, and, when she's dressed up to sing, flowing dresses. Her only jewelry on those occasions are huge pierced earrings. She's had pierced ears ever since she was a baby. I envied her a lot of things, but most of all the pierced ears. I had days when I thought everything would be all right with me if I could just get my ears pierced, but Mom said, "no," "not yet," and "maybe when you're older." It was the Big Issue before Paul, especially when Ella had another hole pierced above the original one in her right ear, so she could wear a single earring left over, after losing one of a pair.

The other groups at the pool were made up of an

assortment of people. The wild kids stuck together . . . and I didn't like them at all. They were always in trouble because of drugs, stealing, whatever. The girls would disappear periodically and either have babies or abortions. Then they would come back and get into some kind of trouble again. Definitely not my kind of people . . . I had no desire to see the inside of the Mount Hope jail.

And then there were the intellectuals. I wasn't stupid . . . I just wasn't that smart. Even as they sat at the pool, they were poring over college catalogs.

I didn't even want to go to college, at least not right after high school. I wanted to go to art school, which was only two years, and then get some sort of job, maybe as a fashion illustrator. Then I could study painting seriously. Mom hadn't objected to that, thank goodness. She was great about some things.

By Wednesday, I hadn't gotten any farther with my plans for meeting people and I was back on the front porch. It was a beautiful, sunshiny bright afternoon and I was trying to get interested in an Agatha Christie mystery—a Miss Marple. I have loved mysteries since I discovered Nancy Drew at the age of ten. At twelve I decided Nancy Drew was a snippy little snot and graduated to Miss Marple. I threw the book down. "What an old busybody!" I said aloud. I figured if Nancy Drew survived all her adventures, grew up and into an old lady, she would be just like Miss Marple—an old busybody instead of a young snot.

I sat there and pondered. Grandad said pondering was much more important than just thinking, and I'd been thinking too much. Time to ponder. I could go upstairs and get my watercolors and go paint something. I could go over to Ella's and see if she wanted to go swimming, but she would probably be practicing scales or something. I could go over and watch Grandad play chess in the park. What to do? I was bored and lonely.

I watched a car going slowly by. I wondered if the people inside were looking at the houses being built across Larchmont Lane. They weren't much to look at yet. The workmen dug holes, put up a few sticks, congratulated themselves, and went on strike.

I paid a little more attention to the car. I was curious about the people who might move in around us. There might be kids my age. We were set far enough away from the street that it was hard for me to see. There were three dogwood trees blocking my vision, too. I didn't want to call attention to myself, so I sort of hunched down on the glider and peeped over the side of the porch. The car stopped near the woods to the left of the house . . . my woods. It seemed strange that they parked on the wrong side of the street. I could see a man on the driver's side and what looked like a little girl on the passenger side. I tried to get a better look and saw the man opening his door and starting to get out. From that distance the little girl looked like Annie. Just what I needed—another Annie in the neighborhood. Instead of the kids my own age I wanted.

The phone interrupted my spying. I jumped guiltily and ran into the house. I caught the phone in the hall on the second ring.

"Brina, this is Mrs. Duvall," the voice on the other end said.

"Hi. How are you?" I answered politely. I figured she was calling about baby-sitting.

"I'm O.K., but I can't find Annie. She was supposed to be back from the library for lunch and she's almost an hour overdue. Is she with you?"

"Nope. I haven't seen her." Or had I? An alarm went off in my head. The library . . . a man! What if. . . . "Don't worry. . . ." I practically yelled, "I'll go look for her!" I hung up before Mrs. Duvall could say anything.

I was out the door in a flash. The car was still there. Empty now. I ran down the porch steps. Across the lawn. Around the rose bushes to the edge of the woods. I stopped there and listened. I heard a man's voice and then a muffled scream. It seemed to be coming from the clearing. I hesitated and thought about going back and calling the police. But what if I were right? I crept silently into the woods and heard another louder cry. If I were wrong—I'd look pretty silly. But if I were right? I didn't think it over for very long. Who cared if I looked silly anyway? I started yelling.

"Annie! Annie! Are you in there? I'm coming and Grandad's here, too!" I crashed through the woods. Yelling. Making noises like an army. I stopped long enough to pick up a rock and throw it against a tree. More rocks. Throwing them around. Crash—crash! Then I hung on to one to use as a weapon. I stopped just short of the clearing and listened. I heard footsteps thrashing through the woods, away from me, toward the street. A door slammed. The car started up. All was quiet. My heart was beating furiously.

I started into the clearing. I saw a patch of red to my right, near a fallen log. I ran over to find a body. My worst fears were realized. It was Annie.

"Annie . . . Annie!" She was unconscious. "Annie . . . Annie! Wake up!" I shook her, then stopped. Remembering you weren't supposed to shake someone who was unconscious. Or was it you weren't supposed to move someone with a broken limb? Couldn't remember.

"Annie . . . Annie. Please wake up." I knelt down beside her.

Her eyes opened up. She looked dazed. She had a bruise on her chin and when she tried to sit up, she winced. I felt the back of her head. There was a big lump. She must have hit her head on the rock underneath her when she fell.

"What happened?" I asked as I helped her to her feet. She started to cry then. Tears ran down her pink cheeks. I asked her again, "What happened?"

She opened her mouth to speak, but the words, when they finally came, were tripping all over themselves. I could only understand a few. It sounded like, "A man, same man. Candy—car. Daddy. Mommy. Bit him—hurt me."

She stumbled against me and I held her close. "I've got you now. C'mon, I've got to get you home to your mother. She's been looking for you. You can tell her what happened."

She looked at me through her tears. "No! No . . . I can't tell her, Brina. Don't make me," she wailed.

After a lot of struggling, I got Annie out of the woods. We groped along the street to her house. Her mother had been watching for her, because the door flew open and she ran out.

"What happened? Did she fall?" Mrs. Duvall asked, "Where has she been? Where have you been, Annie?"

Annie ran into her mother's arms. Mrs. Duvall struggled to hold her and open the door at the same time. I ran to help. Between the two of us we got Annie into the house and on the couch in the living room. Mrs. Duvall sat down beside her and I collapsed onto a chair nearby.

"Brina—what happened?" Mrs. Duvall asked me again. "Did she fall?"

I looked at Annie. She had stopped crying by then and was giving me her begging look, the same one she used for staying up late when I baby-sat. But I wasn't buying. I was sure, from what she'd told me before, that the man she had seen outside the library was the famous child molester and that he had gone back and grabbed her. I was also sure she didn't want to admit it. The police told us not to be ashamed if we were taken in by the man. They said a lot of kids were either ashamed or afraid to admit it or report him. They didn't even know for sure how many kids he had attacked. Annie's eyes were still begging me not to tell. But I knew, even if she had been stupid, her mother and the police would have to know about this.

All this ran through my head, while Mrs. Duvall waited for an answer. I started, "I'm afraid Annie got picked up by the man who's been molesting kids."

She stared at me, horrified. "Oh, no! My poor Annie!" She reached down and held Annie tight while I told her what I'd seen and what Annie had said. Then, with waves of guilt washing over me, I told her that Annie had mentioned seeing the man before, but that I hadn't taken her seriously.

Her mother said, "You should have told me, Brina!" Then she jumped up and ran to the phone. I listened while she called the police and then old Doc Warnick. When she came back over to the couch we both comforted Annie, who began crying hysterically again.

The police didn't take long to get there. And Doc Warnick wasn't far behind. The living room became total confusion. There were three cops in uniform and two who looked like plain-clothes detectives. They were all milling around asking each other what happened.

Doc Warnick pushed his way through the crowd. He's a big scruffy-looking man. All of the kids in Mount Hope, including me, really like him. He's what Grandad calls a dying breed, a real old-fashioned general practitioner.

"I'll just take this little lady upstairs, and we'll have a little chat," he said, looking down at Annie kindly. She was quieter now and I thought she was beginning to enjoy all the attention.

"Brina, bring my bag up," he said to me, "and Jean, you make these gentlemen some coffee. I'll be down soon." He picked Annie up.

I grabbed his old medical bag, and followed him up the stairs. When we got to Annie's pink-and-white room, he laid her on the ruffled bed. He took his bag from me and said, "O.K., Brina, you'd better leave us alone. Go and see if Mrs. Duvall needs any help."

I left rather reluctantly. I wanted to stay and help. To do anything but face Mrs. Duvall and try to explain why I hadn't told her about Annie's story. All the way down the stairs, I tried to explain it to myself.

By the time I reached bottom, the living room was empty. All the cops were out in the kitchen. I guess they figured the coffee and freshly baked chocolate cake wouldn't walk into the living room by themselves.

"Is everything all right upstairs, Brina?" I nodded and she told me to sit down. She automatically put a piece of cake and a glass of milk in front of me. As usual in times of trouble, I was starving.

The two plain-clothes cops sat down at the table with me. The other three just stood around. Mrs. Duvall leaned against the sink and gave me an accusing look. She started to say something, but the bigger cop held up his hand for her to be quiet. The other cop was a real skinny little guy. He looked a little like Don Knotts on a bad day.

"O.K., honey, what's your name?" The big cop smiled at me. I looked him over. I'd never been that close to a cop before. He wasn't bad looking. About six feet tall, with lots of light brown hair. Nice grey eyes. I noticed his nose had been broken and was sort of crooked. He had a small crescent-shaped scar on his right cheek. It was altogether a nice face—not your typical movie star cop—but certainly not bad looking either. I thought I might like to draw him sometime.

"Your name, honey?" he prodded gently.

"What's yours?" That came out suddenly, but I was on edge and wanted to know who I was talking to, too.

"I'm Detective Wallace—Pittsburgh police." He nodded to the scrawny one, "And this is Detective Perkins." He looked anything but perky to me.

"Pittsburgh police? Not Mount Hope?" I asked.

"No," he answered. "We're on temporary assignment to catch the creep, ah, I mean the man who's bothering children in this area."

I guess I started liking him then. I decided I'd better tell him everything, including having messed up. I felt so guilty. Whatever happened to Annie might not have happened if I wasn't so concerned about my problems, if I'd have told Mrs. Duvall what Annie told me. I took a bite of cake and washed it down with some milk to quiet my leaping stomach. I looked into his grey eyes and said, "My name is Sabrina Randall. I live over on the other side of Larchmont Lane."

"Sabrina? That's a pretty name."

"My Grandad said that Mom had a flight of fancy when I was born." Why'd I say that? "Anyway, everyone calls me Brina."

"O.K., Brina, how did you happen to find Annie? Where was she? What did she say to you? Tell me everything that happened." He was really shooting the questions at me, but in a quiet way. His whole manner was calm and relaxed. I trusted him. I told him my story quickly. After all, I didn't have much to tell. Then I took a deep breath and said, "This isn't the first time he went after Annie."

"Mrs. Duvall told us," he said.

She gave me a hard look and said, "Brina—it was totally irresponsible of you not to tell me. I don't see how you can excuse yourself." She was shaking all over.

I looked down at my cake and for the first nervous time in my life, I wasn't hungry. And I didn't have an answer for Mrs. Duvall. How could I explain how many other things were going through my mind when Annie told me her story. How could I tell Annie's mother that I thought Annie was making up the story anyway. This was not the time to say that I thought Annie was a bit of a liar. I said nothing.

The silence seemed to go on forever. Mrs. Duvall finally broke it by saying, "Well, Brina, I guess you don't have an explanation. I don't think I can have you baby-sitting for Annie anymore."

"Wait a minute, Mrs. Duvall. Don't be so hard on her," said Detective Wallace. "If it hadn't been for her being so alert, making all that noise, running into the woods like that, Annie would probably be a lot worse off. Believe me, I think Brina here is very brave."

Mrs. Duvall looked at him for a moment and then looked back at me. "I guess you're right. I am grateful. But Brina—you should have—. Oh—I can't think. What's taking Doc so long?" She looked like she was about to fall over. Detective Perkins stood up and guided her over to his chair. Then he took her place at the sink.

Detective Wallace smiled at me again. He was rapidly becoming a very good friend. "Let's get back to this afternoon. Did you get a look at the man?"

"Not really. I saw him in the car and just then the phone rang."

"His car . . . what kind of car was it?"

"I don't know, I'm no good at cars," I said, feeling kind of dumb. But it was true. Grandad had an old Buick, and he'd been letting me drive it on back roads. He said I was a good driver and he would take me for a license as soon as I turned sixteen. Mom had a Ford station wagon that she used in her business, so the sum total of cars I was familiar with was an old Buick and a Ford station wagon. Well, there are a million different kinds and new ones come out every year.

"Dark? Light? Medium? Think about it." There was that encouraging smile again.

I shut my eyes and ran the whole thing over in my mind, sort of like a rerun on television. "It was dark. Dark green and small. Like a compact, I guess." I opened up my eyes and looked into his again.

"You see? You remember more than you thought. Now, let's go back to the man. Think real hard and see if you can remember anything at all about him." Again a smile—I liked his smile, but I had the feeling I was being charmed. I hadn't run into much of that lately, so I let myself be charmed. I smiled back.

"I really couldn't see anything from where I was sitting. He had some sort of hat on. That's all I could tell."

Detective Wallace said, "Look, honey, if you remember anything else, anything at all, call me at the Mount Hope precinct."

The charm session ended then, because Doc Warnick came into the kitchen. "Jean, you can go up to Annie now. She's all right. The man didn't get very far before Brina started yelling. Annie heard her and had a chance to bite him. She's a scrapper—that one."

Mrs. Duvall jumped up and poured him a cup of coffee. Her hands were still shaking as she handed it to him. "Are you sure?" Her voice was almost a whisper.

"Yep," he answered. "But I gave her something real mild to quiet her down for a while. She'll be a little woozy. But except for the bruises and the lump on the back of her head, she's fine. I'll come over this evening, just to make sure. She'll be over the wooziness by then."

As he finished talking, Mrs. Duvall ran out of the kitchen and up the stairs.

Doc lowered his bulk into the chair vacated by Mrs. Duvall, and Detective Wallace asked gently, "What was Annie's story?"

Doc told it simply. "Annie came out of the library and she was already late for lunch. She'd lost track of time looking for a book, and she was hungry. She knew her mother would be worried, so she was in a hurry. The man in the car pulled up beside her. She'd seen him before. She said he called her Ann."

I nodded—a nervous reaction I guess.

"Annie said she told you, Brina?" His keen eyes probed into mine. "Why didn't you? . . ."

Detective Wallace interrupted him, "We've already been through that, Dr. Warnick. I think Brina feels badly enough."

I guess my feelings were showing all over the place, but it was nice to have someone stick up for me.

Doc Warnick sort of shrugged and went back to his story. "At first Annie ignored him, but then he told her he was a good friend of her parents and would give her a ride home. He knew where she lived. Then he gave her some candy and she fell for it. Well . . . she is only a little girl and he must have done some fast talking. Anyway, she got into the car. He drove close enough to her house to make her relax. But then he stopped by those woods. It's pretty deserted around there, except for the Randall's and their house is set far enough back from the street to make him feel safe. Where were you, Brina? On the porch?"

I nodded again.

"Well, I'm sure he couldn't see you. Was your grandad's car in the street or in the garage?" he asked.

"In the garage. He always puts it away at night and if he's not using it, it stays there," I answered. "He's over at the park playing chess, and he always walks there."

"I know—I know. I've been trying to find the time to join him in a game over there. But everytime I stop by—my pocket buzzer goes off and I—oh well," he sighed. "Anyway—your house would look empty. After he stopped the car by the woods, he grabbed Annie's arm and pulled her across the car seat, out of the car, and into the woods. He stopped after a while and told her to take off her clothes. She started fighting him and he hit her. That's when she heard Brina making all that noise and she bit him. He pushed her down. She hit the back of her head and passed out. He must have taken off then."

"Thank you, Dr. Warnick. I knew if she talked to someone she knew, we'd get the whole story. I didn't want to scare or upset her." Wallace smiled that charming smile again. This was a policeman? He seemed so understanding. "But I do have to talk to her . . . could you be there to sort of hold her hand?"

"Yes. Of course. And thanks for being so gentle with her," said Doc.

"No thanks necessary. She's only a baby and I've seen too many of these cases to jump in and start asking questions. It's always better to get a friend or doctor to ask the first questions. No sense upsetting the victim more."

Victim! Annie was a victim! I started getting a little sick to my stomach. My cake had stayed on my plate, but now I reached, a little wobbly, for my milk. They let me stay there and listen. Either they forgot I was there or, more likely, they were teaching me a lesson, because I hadn't told anyone what Annie had told me. Well—I was learning a lesson the hard way. I took a great gulp of milk and almost choked. Everyone looked at me. Doc patted my shoulder with his big paw.

He said to Wallace, "Let Annie rest this afternoon, and come over this evening. You can talk to her then." Wallace nodded and Doc turned back to me. "I know another young lady who needs some rest this afternoon. You've had enough excitement for one day, Brina. You'd better run along home. I'll just go upstairs and check on Annie. Then I'll go over to the park and get your grandad. It will be better if he's home with you." He stood up and lumbered out of the kitchen.

One of the uniformed cops yelled up the stairs to Mrs. Duvall that they would be patrolling the neighborhood. I was sort of glad to hear that myself.

Wallace said to me, "Doc had the right idea, honey. You've been very brave, but you'd better go home and get some rest. Don't worry about Mrs. Duvall.

I'm sure when she calms down, she'll forgive you. I'll talk to her tonight, when I see Annie, and remind her that now that you've made this mistake you'll be five times as careful as before."

I stood up and tried to smile, but his kindness had given me the old lump in the throat and I was afraid I was going to cry before I got out of there. I tried to say "thank you" . . . or even "it was nice meeting you," because it had been, but I couldn't get my throat working around the lump. I just bobbed my head up and down a few times and headed for the door.

The last words I heard from him that day were—"See you around, honey."

I hoped so.

4

I ran home. I wanted to get to the safety of my own house as soon as I could. I was amazed when I burst into the kitchen and saw the time. Only about ninety minutes had passed since I left the house.

Soon after I got there Grandad showed up. Doc must have raced to the park. I was sitting at our kitchen table, trying to get myself together, when he came storming in.

"Sabrina? Are you all right?" I knew he was really upset, because he only calls me Sabrina in unusual circumstances. "Doc filled me in on what happened."

I got up, ran over, and hugged him tight. Then the tears came, washing away the lump in my throat. What had happened to Annie really scared me. It could happen to anyone, anywhere. It could even happen to me. It wasn't just that part of it was my fault, it was that it had happened at all. It was real. It wasn't a TV show or in a newspaper article. It was Annie.

I cried and cried and Grandad held me close. He finally reached in his back pocket and pulled out the familiar bandana handkerchief. He mopped up my face and made me blow my nose.

"Listen to me, Brina. You've had a tough time today. Your feelings are all upset. Doc says you'd better stay quiet for the rest of the day. Maybe take a nap if you can. I'll be right here, so you don't have to be afraid. Later on we can go to the movies and get some pizza."

He knows I'm addicted to pizza and I think he caught the craving from me. But I still wasn't thinking about food. I gave one last sob into his jumpsuit and agreed with him. He pushed me toward the kitchen door. "Shoo. Go on upstairs and lie down."

I went up to my room and threw myself across the bed. I stared at a piece of lint on the rug below me. I thought about Annie. How could I not think about Annie? I guessed she'd eventually get over this, and she'd be more careful from now on. But the other girls the man had attacked . . . five in Mount Hope alone—now six, counting Annie. Annie was a statistic! And it was my fault.

There would be other kids attacked, but at least that wouldn't be my fault. I wondered if I could get hold of every little kid in the Pittsburgh area and warn each one. How could I do that? And even if I could, would they listen to me? Kids don't listen. I didn't listen when I was a kid, but nothing had happened to me. I remembered Mom telling me the facts of life when I was younger than Annie. I remembered her warning me about bad men.

I reached down and picked up the piece of lint and squashed it in my hand as if it were all the bad men in the world. Yes, Mom had explained to me about bad men and told me to tell her immediately if anything like that happened to me. But would I have? Or would I have been like Annie? Afraid or ashamed or whatever? No one should have to go through that. I felt like going out and hunting down the creep myself. Wallace had been right to call him a creep, even if it was a slip of the tongue. I wanted to fight him. I'd never thought about hating anyone before. I'd never had any reason to.

Now I felt hate, but it was hate mixed with guilt and fear. I lay there and hated with all my strength. Weird thoughts crossed my mind. Witch hunts and black masses. I couldn't get him that way. I had to be realistic. But—oh God—I wanted to do something.

I sat up on the bed and leaned against all my pillows. I looked around my room, as if I'd never seen it before. It was safe. No creeps would ever penetrate the security of my safe, lovely blue room. I checked it all out to make sure it was all the same as before, not realizing at that moment I had changed, not the room.

Mom and I had decorated it together for my fifteenth birthday. It helped to know someone in the business, because my room is perfect for me. The walls and rug are the shade of blue you can get lost in. The furniture is wicker, even the bedstead, except for an old drawing table and dresser. We had stripped them down and painted them cream. The accent colors are roses and lavenders.

The room itself is over the kitchen, and the two

small side windows look over the woods where I'd found Annie. The third window looks out over the backyard and when I lean out of it, I can see the kitchen steps and very often the top of Grandad's head. His favorite brooding place. I'd have to find a new one.

I know I'm lucky to have such a great room. Grandad and Mom have the two front rooms, facing the street. Mom has her own bathroom, and Grandad and I share the one at the top of the stairs next to my room. Beyond that there's a small guest room.

After I surveyed my room that day, an idea began to take shape in my mind. I was staring up at the ceiling and had a real idea! No witchcraft or anything. Then the idea became a plan! I had to talk to Detective Wallace again. He'd seemed like such a good person for a cop. Not that I had anything against cops. I'd never met one before, so they didn't seem like real people. But he was definitely a real person and the way he called the man a creep made him all the more human. He was super nice to stick up for me like that to Mrs. Duvall, too. At least I knew I could talk to him about my idea.

I hugged one of my rose-colored pillows and felt relieved. Having a plan of action was much better than just lying around hating the creep.

The next thing I knew, Mom was leaning over me. "C'mon, Brina. Get up. We're going out for pizza."

I woke up and sat up on the bed. She'd already changed clothes from work. She had jeans and a T-shirt on, just like me. That woman could make anything look good. But then I really woke up. There was something strange about her. She was as white as a ghost, and the blue veins in her temples stood out. There was a pinched look around her mouth as if she were clenching her teeth.

She reached out and took a strand of my hair and tugged it. "I know. That is, Dad told me about Annie. . . ." She couldn't finish the sentence because her teeth started chattering. She sat down on the bed, all in a lump. She let go of my hair and hugged herself. I put my arms around her. Suddenly I felt more like her mother than her child. She was so cold, and it was warm in my room.

"What is it, Mom?" I asked.

"N . . . nothing. I'll b-be O.K. in a min-minute." I rocked her back and forth, until her teeth stopped chattering and she felt warm again.

"I'm sorry, Brina," she said. "That all came over me so fast."

"What was it? You were so cold." I took my arms away, but held on to one of her hands. Her eyes looked like green glass, about to shatter. "Are you all right now?"

"Yeah." She tried to smile, "Dad told me about you scaring away the man—and it really upset me, but I didn't know how much until I actually saw you, and then I thought—it could have been you. Or he could have left Annie and come after you. Anything could have happened! He could have killed both of you. Brina, what a chance you took."

"I had to, Mom. I had to save Annie. I didn't think of anything else."

"I know that. Of course you did. But you'll be careful from now on, won't you? I just couldn't bear it if anything happened to you. You're on your own so much. He could come after you! I'd better stay home and work here for a while."

She looked so frightened, I rushed to reassure her. "Mom, I'm not a baby. Grandad is always here. Besides, that creep goes for younger kids."

"Brina, baby, I hate to say this, but you look like a younger kid, especially when your hair is down."

"I know I do, Mom, you don't have to remind me!" Looking younger fit right in with my plan, so I wasn't as upset as I pretended. "I'll put up my hair or tie it back. Don't worry, Mom."

"I can't help but worry. Look—if you still want to go to that camp, you can go. I'd rather see you safe and well, with your feelings hurt, than. . . ." She couldn't go on.

I thought that one over quickly. She put what I thought I wanted right there in my lap. And I couldn't take it. I wanted to do something about the creep, and during the past few days, I had realized she and Paul were right about me. It was time to get involved with others. If I could get Wallace to buy my idea, I would certainly be involved. If not, I would go door to door to every house in Pittsburgh, and tell every little kid personally to watch out for the creep. Either way—I'd be fighting back.

I looked at Mom. She was waiting for my answer. How to tell her? How much to tell her was more like it.

"Uh—it's O.K., Mom. I think I understand now what you were saying about Paul and me and I . . . uh . . ." An inspiration! "I don't want my feelings hurt either. I don't think Paul wants me there and I don't want to be where I'm not wanted."

"Well! I have to say I'm relieved to hear that! But there are other camps. Or you and Dad could go to Aunt Gertrude's farm. You've always liked it there."

She meant my Great Aunt Gertrude, Grandad's sister. She has a farm near Smicksburg, Pennsylvania. It's one of my favorite places, but I wasn't going anywhere. I had a crusade!

I was just trying to figure out how to get out of

that one, when Grandad called from downstairs, "Diana, Brina! Are you guys getting ready to go?" Saved!

Mom and I both got up and she gave me a quick hug. "We'll talk some more about this. I'd certainly feel better if you were away from here until that man is caught."

"Don't worry! I'll be careful. Let's go. I'm starving!" And I was. Now that I had an idea of something to do, I was back to normal. Ready to tackle a whole pizza by myself.

I ran downstairs, with Mom close behind. Grandad was standing at the bottom. He asked, "Is it pizza first, or movie first?"

"Pizza first—then movie—then ice cream!" I skipped the last few steps and leaped into his arms.

"Glutton!" he said as he caught me. "You must be feeling better."

"You bet!" I answered.

We got the pizza and then went to a drive-in, and stopped for ice cream on the way home. I knew Mom and Grandad were trying to keep my mind off Annie.

It was late when we got home, and we all went to bed without speaking of Annie again. But I couldn't get to sleep right away. I kept thinking about my plan and I decided to call Wallace first thing in the morning. I felt better about myself than I had for ages.

5

I slept late the next morning. When I finally woke up, it was around nine. I jumped out of bed and looked out the back window. It was a gorgeous day. I didn't remember about Annie until I was in the bathroom brushing my teeth. I stopped with a mouthful of toothpaste, remembering everything that happened. I also remembered my plan. I finished brushing my teeth in a hurry and ran back to my room. I ran a brush through my hair, got dressed in my cutoffs and a T-shirt, and thought about calling Wallace from Mom's room. I decided to have breakfast first. Hungry again!

I went down to the kitchen. Surprise! There he was! Detective Wallace himself! In the flesh, sitting at our kitchen table, drinking coffee with Mom. They were laughing when I walked in.

"Hi, honey. How are you today?" He looked at me.

I just stared at him. It was unreal, having him right there when I was just thinking about getting in touch with him.

Mom looked at me with a smile on her face. "Morning, Brina. Detective Wallace stopped by to see how you were feeling."

From where I was standing, it looked more like he'd stopped by to see how Mom was. Finally I asked, "You two met?"

I was being sarcastic, but Wallace answered me seriously, "Not before this morning, but we're getting acquainted."

"So I see," I said brightly. "You married?" That slipped out before I could stop it.

"Brina!" Mom warned. "Sit down and I'll get your breakfast." She was blushing! She started bustling around the kitchen as if my breakfast were the only thing on her mind. I hadn't seen her look like that since a few years before, when she'd dated that sappy lawyer. I was glad when that hadn't worked out. This looked much more promising. There had been other men around since the lawyer, but she hadn't blushed over a single one.

I sat down at the table, looked at Wallace, and answered his question, "I'm fine."

"I'm not married." He answered mine.

That was super! It fit right in with my plans. He was watching Mom while she fixed my breakfast. I interrupted him, "What's the latest on Annie?"

He tore himself away from Mom. "She's O.K., thank God. But she'll have to stay in bed for a few days. Listen, Brina . . . Annie has managed to completely forget what the man looked like. That's understandable—it was quite a shock. She remembers everything that happened, but when it comes to describing him, she draws a total blank. Maybe in time she will remember, but we're back to square one. Have you recalled anything at all about him? We could really use your help."

"I thought you came by to see how I was feeling."

"I did." He grinned. "But while I'm here. . . ."

"Yeah—you just want to pick my brains."

"Yeah—I do." A good imitation of my voice. "But, seriously, I did want to find out if you were O.K. You looked pretty shaky when you left the Duvalls' yesterday."

"I was. But I was O.K. after I got home." And thought up a plan to catch the creep, I wanted to say. But I figured I'd better wait until I could speak to him alone. I only had half his attention anyway. Mom definitely had the other half.

She set breakfast in front of me. "Wow! Thanks, Mom!" She'd fixed scrambled eggs, bacon, and a toasted English muffin. It was usually cold cereal when she was in the kitchen. Was she trying to impress Wallace?

"You're welcome." She sat down next to Wallace. "I told Jim . . . um . . . Detective Wallace that you draw really well." Jim. Already. This was looking better and better.

"Do you think you could draw anything about the man?" Wallace asked.

"I thought you had a composite sketch of him?"

"We do. But the drawing doesn't mean anything at all to Annie. And we've had different descriptions from the other girls, too. And he changes cars all the time. We're beginning to think there's more than one."

"Oh, no!" cried Mom. "It's bad enough that there's one! That's terrible!" She suddenly paled. Wallace looked at her with concern.

"Try not to worry, Diana. Brina seems to be able to take care of herself." At that moment I was taking care of the scrambled eggs, but I nodded. Neither of them noticed. Mom seemed comforted by him. I couldn't believe that two people could get so tied up in each other so quickly. But then Wallace was so comfortable . . . even I had forgotten to be shy with him.

I picked up my muffin, and then decided to bring

them back to the subject that interested me most. "How does he get different cars?" I asked with my mouth full.

"Who knows." Wallace looked back at me and shrugged his shoulders. "He's quick. He might steal them and return them before anyone knows they're gone. He might work in a garage. There are a lot of different ways. There could be two of them . . . one a copycat of the other."

"Who's a copycat?" Grandad walked into the kitchen. He looked slightly startled to see a stranger sitting at the table.

"Dad—this is Detective Wallace," Mom said. "Jim —this is my father—Harry Williams."

Wallace stood up and they shook hands. Grandad had on his denim jumpsuit and his hair stood up in the usual spikes. I wondered what Wallace thought about the jumpsuit. "We were just talking about the man who attacked Annie." He smiled his charming smile at Grandad. "I stopped by to see if Brina remembered anything."

"I thought you stopped by to see how I felt," I mumbled through the last of my muffin.

"Let's not go through that again." My turn for the smile. "And don't talk with your mouth full."

I swallowed, "I'm through now."

"O.K. You can talk."

"I don't have a thing to say." I smiled back at him as he sat down at the table again.

"Good." He laughed.

Grandad looked around the table for a minute, tried to figure out what was going on, gave up, and poured himself a cup of coffee. He sat down at the table, too.

It's a good thing we have a large kitchen and a table to match because just then Detective Perkins knocked at the kitchen door. He looked like he'd lost weight.

There were more introductions and more coffee poured and served. He sat down at the table, too. It would have been a regular party if it weren't for the reason we were all together—namely, the creep. Perky had made the rounds of all the houses around the Duvalls', asking questions, but no one had seen anything. They had gone through the woods the day before and not found a single clue.

I listened and planned how I would get Wallace alone. Mom finally decided she would go in to work after all, but she said she'd be home early. And would I please be careful? I said I would and she went up to change.

I started clearing the table and loading the dishwasher. Wallace and Perky sat and talked to Grandad for a few more minutes. They seemed to like him and his jumpsuit.

Mom was back downstairs quickly. She was really dressed up for work. I had the feeling she wanted Wallace to see her at her best. He really appreciated the effort, too. His eyes followed her all the way out the door.

After she was gone, Wallace and Perky picked themselves up, thanked us for the coffee, and went out the kitchen door. I waited a sec and then told Grandad that I'd forgotten to answer Wallace's question about drawing something on the creep.

I zipped through the dining room and the hall, and was out the front door in a flash. I was running down the front steps when they came around from the back of the house.

"Something wrong?" Wallace stopped when he saw me.

"I have to talk to you," I said.

"Shoot!" He looked down at me, puzzled.

"Not here. Not now. Could you come over later, while Grandad's at the park?"

"Couldn't you tell me now?" He was uncertain.

"No. This afternoon." I ran back up the stairs and into the house. I'd taken my best shot and I hoped he'd fall for it.

Grandad and I finished cleaning up. Then we went out to work in the garden for a while. I thought about my idea some more. I planned what I would say to Wallace and I was pretty quiet. Grandad was quiet, too, except for cussing out some Japanese beetles that had found a home in his precious roses.

I could tell Grandad was worried about something. It turned out to be me. He spoke, "Brina, I know you know a lot for a young whippersnapper, a lot more than I did at your age, or than your mother did, for that matter. You've seen a lot in the movies and on TV and you know about sex. Things aren't hidden from kids the way they used to be. But I wonder if you know how bad, how sick, this man who attacked Annie is. If he had cancer or a bum leg or something, we could feel sorry for him. But we can't afford any pity for him! He's like this weed here." He stopped to pull up a dandelion that was growing by the edge of the rose bed. "We have to get rid of it before it hurts the good plants. Now, if I couldn't get rid of this dandelion, I would move all the good plants away from it. Since I can't go out and catch the man, I'll have to make sure you're not around him. The only way I can do that is by sticking real close to you.

"I know you're not a baby, but you sort of look like one. And this guy wouldn't ask you how old you were if he . . . ah . . . took a fancy to you. So, from now on, until he's caught I don't want you to be alone. If you traveled in a group . . . I wouldn't be so worried about you. That's what we were talking about the other night. You don't—you're usually alone. From now until he's caught . . . you won't be alone. You can come with me to the park . . . or we'll go somewhere else. Stay home. Whatever. If you want to go somewhere with someone . . . that's O.K., too. Just as long as I know where you are and who you're with."

His blue eyes were full of concern by the time he finished. Just from the way he was speaking, I knew he had rehearsed the speech. I thought he was being a little overprotective. I didn't want to worry him, but I had to talk to Wallace about my idea. So I lied. I don't like lying and I was superstitious enough to cross my fingers behind my back, as I answered him. "I know you're afraid for me, Grandad, but believe me, I know how serious this is. I know what would have happened to Annie if I hadn't stopped it. I certainly don't want it to happen to me." I paused, then lied. "But I'm going swimming with Ella again this afternoon. And I'm sure her mother will take us there and bring us back."

"Well then, I'll call Ella's mother right after lunch . . . just to make sure. If she doesn't know about Annie yet, I'll tell her. She should know, for Ella's sake." He shook his head. "Everyone in the world should know about creeps like that!"

"You're sounding like Wallace now."

"I could think of worse things. He seemed like a real nice man. There seems to be a little something between himself and me darlin' daughter."

I laughed and put my hands on my hips. "Honestly, Grandad, sometimes you sound more Irish than Welsh. But your brogue needs a little practice."

"Don't you be callin' a good Welshman Irish!" Grandad tried to look stern but failed. He was proud of his

Welsh heritage, but the subject never came up until someone thought he was Irish.

"Well—you don't miss a trick! There's something there all right. Wallace said he wasn't married. . . ."

"Why'd he say that?"

"I asked him, before you came down to the kitchen."

"Talk about not missing a trick! At least you're not shy around him. It might be nice if those two got together. Yep . . . it might be real nice." He went back to pulling up weeds.

With him checking up on my story, I was kind of up a tree. But then I had another idea. I went into the house and made two quick calls—one to Ella to cover for me, and the other to the Mount Hope precinct. Wallace wasn't there, so I left a message for him to meet me outside the entrance to the pool, by the turnstile, at two-thirty. I hoped he'd get the message. Then I went back to the garden.

We had lunch around twelve-thirty. Sure enough, right afterward, Grandad called Mrs. James. I listened to him telling her about Annie, warning her to be careful about Ella and me. I still thought he was being overprotective. I looked like a little kid but Ella certainly didn't.

Ella must have covered my story well, because Mrs. James reassured him and said she would take us to the pool. He seemed relieved and told me he would go to his park after we left.

I was all ready when I saw the car outside. I yelled good-bye to Grandad, ran out, and hopped in the car. All the way to the pool, we talked about Annie. Mrs. James dropped us off and said she would pick us up at four-thirty. As she drove away she reminded us to be careful. The creep sure was causing a lot of anxiety. All the more reason to do something about him, I thought.

Ella and I went into the locker room. As we were changing, she asked me what was going on. I said I'd tell her later. She accepted that. Good old no-pry Ella.

When we got to the pool area, I spread my towel, sat down, and started putting on suntan lotion. Ella stood for a moment and then said, "Aren't you going in?" I told her I'd go in later. She shrugged her shoulders and took off. I saw her on the high dive a few minutes later. Her black skin glistened in the sun, as she did a perfect swan dive. I knew she'd be busy diving for a while.

The clock over the entrance to the locker rooms said two-ten. I had twenty minutes until I met Wallace in front—if Wallace showed. I sat in the hot sun for the next fifteen minutes, planning what to say.

At twenty-five after two, I went inside to my locker and put my shirt on over my bathing suit. Then I went out front through the turnstile and looked around. Great! Wallace was hurrying toward me.

"Brina, what's this all about?" he asked me gruffly as he took my arm and hurried me over to a nearby bench.

Now that I actually had him there—I wasn't all that sure of myself. I didn't feel shy around him before, but I sure did now. I tried smiling. He frowned. I cleared my throat. He frowned some more. I decided to jump in with both feet.

"I know how much you want to catch this creep." I had his complete attention. "And I know he usually goes for younger kids, but I could let my hair down— that makes me look younger. And I'm not really developed yet—." I didn't go into details. I didn't want to embarrass him or me. "Anyway—I thought maybe you could use me as a decoy. You know, I could hang out in public places and just sort of look to get picked up. You could follow me and watch from a distance. He might just try and you could catch him."

"Oh, honey, that's the craziest idea. You watch too much TV," he said softly. At least he wasn't mad. "It's too dangerous and my boss would never go for it."

"Couldn't we do it on our own?" I hadn't thought about his having a boss or any kind of red tape.

"That's too far out. Besides—what would your mom and grandad say? They'd go insane worrying about you. Whatever gave you this idea anyway?"

"Look, I've thought a lot about it. I didn't listen to Annie. I thought she was making up a story and I was concentrating on my own problems. If I had listened to her and told her parents—you police might have been watching her and caught the creep. That makes me involved already. Then I saw what he did to Annie. He hit her, and tried to do a lot more. That was nothing compared to what he did to the other girls. What he did to the other girls makes me mad, but what he did to Annie makes me feel guilty, and afraid. This creep does these things and he gets away with it. You've been looking for him for months. I don't want to hurt your feelings, but that's true, isn't it?"

"Longer than months." He sighed.

"Well—how many other kids are going to be hurt by him? How long is it going to go on? As for Mom and Grandad, they're already worried. So is every other parent in the Pittsburgh area. Wouldn't it be better to catch him once and for all? Kids aren't careful. They don't listen to anyone. As long as this creep's around, he'll always find some little kid to fall for his line. I look enough like a little kid that he might go for me sometime, with or without you. We might as well do it this way. How do you know? It might just work. C'mon Wallace—at least think about it. With you around, I'd be safe." End of speech. I was watching him closely, trying to guess his reaction.

He shook his head. "Are you sure you're only fifteen? You're not a forty-seven-year-old midget?"

"For what it's worth, I'll be sixteen in two weeks." I grinned at him.

"With plans like you got, kid—you might not make it." I couldn't think of a thing to say to that. I just looked at him. It was his turn to talk anyway. "You've got guts. And brains. I understand how you feel, but you mustn't beat yourself over the head with guilt. You made an honest mistake. I forgot to tell you this morning—even Mrs. Duvall doesn't really blame you. She admitted last night that Annie has been going through a storytelling phase. I imagine she'll call you herself, as soon as this has died down a little."

"I don't care that she doesn't blame me. I still feel guilty. I should have known and I want to do something about it."

"I'm not going to argue about it with you, Brina. But your whole plan has got to be the farthest-out thing I've ever heard of. I'll think about it, though. I may even talk to my boss—but I'm sure it's no sale." He paused and looked thoughtful. "When did you say you'll be sixteen?"

"Two weeks. Why?"

He got up from the bench. "Maybe I want to help you celebrate your birthday. Look—I know you want to help. But until I get back to you don't do anything. . . ."

"I'm not that stupid. I'd never go off on my own," I answered right away.

"You're not stupid at all, kid. And even if we don't use it—it's a hell of an idea."

He turned to walk away. I was proud he had complimented me, but I was also a little disappointed. Then he stopped dead in his tracks and turned around. "Brina, your mother . . . is she dating anyone or involved . . . ?"

"Not right now!" I practically cheered. "And if it means anything to you—you're all right with me."

"Like I said, Brina, you're a smart kid. Smart enough to know it means a lot. I'll be seeing you." This time I was sure he would. I watched him until he was out of sight.

Suddenly Ella was standing in front of me, blocking the sun. "I thought you wanted to go swimming," she said accusingly.

"I do!" I got up. "Let's go!" I ran back through the turnstile and into the locker room with Ella behind me. I was in the water and swimming merrily along before she could ask what I was doing in front of the pool. For some reason I didn't want anyone, even Ella, to know about my plan. By the time Mrs. James came to pick us up, she'd either forgotten or she was back to the old, don't-ask-questions Ella. In any case, she never said another word about it.

6

The next day was Friday, and it was another beautiful day. But I was too impatient to hear from Wallace to appreciate it.

Grandad wouldn't leave me alone for two seconds either. I couldn't think of anything I wanted to do, so I had to go to the park with him. I took my sketch pad along, and while he played chess with different people, I sketched them.

One odd old lady had a bottle in a brown paper bag in her big lumpy purse. While she played chess with Grandad, she kept taking it out and drinking from it. By the end of the game, she was really drunk, but she beat Grandad anyway. He was furious. He likes a good game of chess, but he sure is a sore loser. I made a neat sketch of her, with her bottle, with Grandad glaring at her. I showed it to him on the way home and it made him laugh. That made me feel better, too.

Mom was already there when we got home. She was early and seemed real excited. It turned out Wallace had called her at work and asked her out to dinner.

I got almost as excited as she. I sort of hoped he'd have some news for me. I knew it was too soon, but I still hoped.

She was running around like a crazy person, putting on makeup, taking off makeup, and changing her clothes every minute. By the time she decided on a simple wrap dress, in a shade of green that matched her eyes, beige sandals, and a straw clutch bag, Wallace was at the door.

I let him in, and Grandad gave him a drink. I wanted to ask him if he'd thought about my idea at all, but then Mom came down the stairs. The scent of her best perfume lingered around her, and she looked terrific. It was not the time to ask Wallace anything. He probably wouldn't know his own name.

After they left, Grandad and I went out to dinner. He didn't feel like cooking and we were both craving Chinese food again.

It was still light when we came out of the restaurant, so he asked me if I wanted to practice driving. I was all for it.

We drove down back roads to the old Polish cemetery. There are a lot of dirt roads running through and around it. We parked by one of the roads and Grandad worked the seat all the way up so my foot could reach the brake and the accelerator. I wondered if I would ever grow, because it was still a bit of a stretch. But then, the old Buick was a big car. I told Grandad that if I didn't grow by the time I was old enough to get my own car, then I'd have to get one of those tiny Japanese cars. He said, "How about a golf cart?" Ha ha.

I drove around and around the cemetery with Grandad giving me instructions, until some people came to light the candles set in ornate red glass lanterns stuck in the ground by each grave. It was beautiful to watch the flames being lit through the gathering dusk. Grandad said it was some sort of custom, and he would try to find out what it was.

We went home, popped some popcorn, and watched TV. I wanted to stay up until Mom got home, but I fell asleep on the couch. Grandad woke me up and sent me on upstairs to bed.

Waking up the next morning, I remembered immediately about Mom's date with Wallace. I was dying of curiosity. I got up quickly and ran downstairs in my nightgown. Since it was Saturday and a day off for Mom, I fixed her breakfast in bed—pancakes, bacon, orange juice, and coffee. I ran out to the garden and found an early, bright golden rose. The dew drops made it positively shine in the morning sun. I arranged the food on a wicker tray and added the final touch—the rose in a dark blue bud vase. It looked just like a photo from *Bon Appetit*, Grandad's favorite magazine.

I took the tray upstairs and knocked on Mom's door. I heard her say, "Come." As I walked through the door, she was just opening one eye. When she saw the tray, she opened the other. "Hooray! Breakfast in bed!" She sat up. "You may very well have saved my life. I'm a little hung over."

I set the tray on her lap. "How was last night? I'm dying of curiosity!" I admitted.

"Aha! So this is a bribe," she said, attacking the pancakes.

"Bribe? Me?" I asked innocently, as I sat down on the bed. She knew me entirely too well. "Tell me all about it. What'd you do? Where'd you go? What's Wallace really like? Are you in love? Tell me. Tell me."

She giggled happily. "Slow down, Brina. You really are something. O.K. We went to the Golden Coach for dinner and then downtown to one of those clubs to listen to some jazz. Jim is very, very nice. And the answer to your last question is none of your business."

"C'mon, Mom! Tell me all the details."

"That's all I'm going to tell you, except I had a really good time."

"When are you going to see him again?" I hoped he liked her well enough to continue dating her. As long as he was around, I could keep working on him.

"Tonight." She looked smug. "I invited him to dinner. I thought maybe we'd have a barbecue in the backyard and you could invite Ella and her parents."

"Good. I'll call her right away." I headed for the door.

"Brina—wait a minute." She swallowed a bite of pancake. "This will be our first barbecue in a long time without Paul here. Will you be all right?"

I turned around and looked at her. Her eyes were troubled. But I was surprised to realize I hadn't thought about Paul when she talked about the barbecue in the first place. I hadn't thought much about Paul at all, since Annie and my plan to catch the creep. Things had been happening so fast—but he was still someplace in the corner of my mind. I pulled out all the memories of past barbecues and gave them a quick going over, like going through a mental photograph album. It hurt a little—but not that much. Mom was still waiting for an answer.

"Oh, I'll miss him tonight, I suppose, but I can take it. I'm tough, y'know."

She was relieved. But she wasn't through. "Have you thought anymore about going away for a while? I know Dad would love to go up to the farm for a bit. He hasn't seen Aunt Gert since January. And now that Uncle Ronald is gone. . . ." Aunt Gert's husband, Ronald, had passed away in January and we had all gone to the funeral at the little church in Smicksburg that Ronald had helped to build. It had been a sad time, and I was sure that Aunt Gert would love to see Grandad, but I wanted to stay put until Wallace said yes or no.

Thinking fast, I said, "What? And leave you all alone to entertain Wallace? Besides, he's a cop and with him hanging around here—I'll be safe."

That distracted her, because then she said, "How come you call him Wallace?"

"I don't know. I can't seem to call him Detective Wallace. It's too formal. And I can't call him Mr. Wallace—I mean, he does have a title. And I can't call him Jim—I don't know him that well. Wallace just seems right."

"Humph." The last bite of pancakes disappeared. "Well, he doesn't seem to mind. And it's his name, so I guess it's O.K. He's awfully easy to get along with," she said thoughtfully, as she handed me her tray. "You can take this downstairs. It was good. Thanks a lot. At least I can make it out of bed now. We've got to go shopping for food for tonight."

"And I've got to call Ella." I grabbed the tray and went downstairs. I did call Ella and set it up with her. She said that Howard was going away anyway, and she was at loose ends.

I started Grandad's breakfast, planning to surprise him, too, but before I could get very far, he was in the kitchen. I told him about the barbecue and while we ate, we talked about what to have. He's very inventive about cooking, but when Mom came down, she squelched our plans for individual Cornish hens, stuffed with wild rice. She felt hamburgers would be easier. Grandad said that was fine, but he would stuff them with mushrooms. She said he must be in a stuffy mood. We both groaned over that.

The rest of the day sped by. We cleaned house and went to the store for food. I kept thinking about Wallace. Wondering this and wondering that. Daydreaming about being a famous creep-catcher.

Wallace came over early and helped Grandad and me set up in the backyard, while Mom fixed salad in the kitchen. Then he settled back in a redwood chair with a drink. Grandad fixed the hamburgers and I shucked the corn and wrapped each ear in foil. I kept waiting for Wallace to say something—anything—to me, but he seemed sort of distant. I couldn't speak to him about it with Grandad there. I tried not to think about my plan.

Ella and her parents got there at six and the barbecue began. Ella and I ate everything in sight. We had tons of corn on the cob, had two stuffed hamburgers apiece and topped it off with toasted marshmallows, on chocolate squares on graham crackers. Wallace had never had them before and everyone explained about their being called S'mores, because once you have one, you want some more. We all had some more, including Wallace.

We took turns playing badminton, and when I played Wallace I beat him. Ella and I told stale jokes and giggled together. Toward the end of the evening she and Grandad started singing softly together, harmonizing some old tunes. Grandad has a fine singing voice. He says he inherited it from his father, a Welsh coal miner. It was nice listening to them; their voices fit well together. It was just a nice evening altogether. I hardly missed Paul at all.

The Jameses left around twelve-thirty, and when I went up to bed, Wallace and Mom were holding hands on the front porch and Grandad was watching a western on TV. I fell asleep right away.

7

Someone was shaking me awake. I wanted to be left alone, to go back to sleep. I heard, "Sabrina! Sabrina! Wake up this instant!"

I opened my eyes and saw Mom leaning over me. She shook me again. Her face was all flushed with anger. She had turned on the overhead light and I could see the veins in her temples again. But this time they seemed about to burst.

"What time is it?" I asked. "Is the house on fire?"

"No! The house isn't on fire. And it's almost four-thirty in the morning. Get up this instant. I'm not going to wait any longer. I've been up all night and now you're getting up, too. You're going to listen to me— you little sneak!" She was almost screaming.

I struggled to wake up enough to find out what this was all about. Pretty soon I was sitting on the edge of the bed, and she was pacing up and down in front of me. She turned and glared at me.

"How dare you? How dare you offer yourself as some sort of sacrificial lamb? To the police. The *police!* What is the matter with you? Don't you think they know what they're doing? Do you really think they need a runt like you? Sabrina—I am furious with you! Furious." She stopped to catch her breath.

That bum Wallace had told her. I'd never expected that. I hadn't thought beyond telling him and having him think it over. Once the plan was accepted, I'd had a vague idea of handling Mom then.

"Look, Mom—" Wrong move. She had been winding down and that started her up again. She went on ranting and raving. Tears began to trickle down her cheeks. Pretty soon they were a flood. But she kept yelling, like some sort of hurt animal.

Grandad came to the door of my room. "Diana—what is this? What did Brina do?"

She gulped a few times and looked at him helplessly. I'd seen her upset before and I'd seen her angry plenty of times, but I'd never seen her like this. From the way Grandad looked—I doubted if he had either.

She finally calmed down enough to tell him, while he sat beside me on the bed.

She came to a halt when he said abruptly, "All right, Diana, that's enough. Calm down. So Brina had a stupid idea. It won't be the first or the last time. I'm sure she was just trying to help. There's no need to get this upset about it—especially in the middle of the night!"

"Oh yes, there is! You don't understand, Dad. The police are actually considering her idea. They're thinking of sending a little kid out on the street to catch a pervert. But they need my permission. Jim wants my permission tonight! They won't use her until she's sixteen, but they want to train her. Would you believe it, Dad? They want to train her as some sort of child cop! Of all the stupid perverse ideas. He didn't even know how to tell me. After I got over my first shock, I got furious at him. But not as furious as I am with you—Sabrina!" She was spitting the words out.

I looked up at her. "Ah, Mom."

"Don't you 'Ah, Mom' me! Dad—what are we going to do? Jim is still waiting for an answer."

"So—tell him no," said Grandad.

I got up from the bed and stood in front of them. I remembered the passage in the Bible about little children leading them. I wasn't a little child and I couldn't lead my way out of a paper bag, but I decided to give it a try.

"O.K., you guys. I know you don't want me to do it. And I can't do it without your permission anyway. But you can at least listen to me. I want to do it. Because what happened to Annie is my fault. And what happened to her could happen to any of the other kids we know. Or kids we don't know. It keeps happening. And the point is next time it could be worse. Next time he could kill someone. I'm not being brave or anything. Grandad is right—I just want to help catch him and see he gets put away."

"Oh, great! A one-girl vigilante. Off to keep the world safe for little children."

"Diana—you don't need to be sarcastic. It's not that bad an idea," Grandad said disapprovingly.

"Dad! I'm surprised at you! Surely you don't approve of it?" Mom's tears were gone and the redness in her face was ebbing away. She was turning pale again when Grandad answered.

"The idea itself is good and I can understand the police considering it. If I were in their shoes, I probably would, too. But I don't understand why they'd use Brina for it."

"If I don't do it—who else will?" I asked.

"No one in their right mind," said Mom. "You're both crazy." She stopped pacing up and down and perched on the edge of one of my wicker chairs. "I know why they're considering her. Jim and I went all over that. She's small and she looks very young, but she will be sixteen soon. They figure she'll be old enough to volunteer her services to the police. If they get my permission," she shuddered, "which they won't."

"If they're thinking about using me," I said firmly, "they must be pretty desperate. After all, Wallace wasn't too thrilled about it the first time he heard it."

"I'm getting pretty desperate, too. With you!" cried Mom. "Suppose you were hurt? Have you thought about that?"

"Wallace would look after me. I bet he wouldn't leave me alone for a second. He'd never let anything happen to me. He likes me."

"You're right, kid," came a voice from the door. Wallace was standing there. We'd all been making so much noise, we hadn't heard him come up the stairs. "I do like you. You can be a real brat at times—but I like you. And I'd make sure nothing would happen to you. But we still can't do it without your mother's permission."

"And I won't give it!" She leaped up from the chair and crossed over to him.

He put a hand on her shoulder. "If I'd known you'd get so upset about it, I wouldn't have talked to the sergeant at all. But I did and he's very interested. I can call him and tell him it's no dice, if that's what you want."

"That's exactly what I want. Get it over and done with. Brina and Dad are going to the farm as soon as I can pack them off." She sounded so final. Just as final as she sounded when she said I couldn't go to camp.

I figured my cause was lost. But then Grandad spoke up. "Wait a minute, Diana. Maybe Brina is right after all."

"Dad!" She whirled around and stared at him.

"I'm sorry, dear, but I've listened to you and I've listened to Brina, and I'm beginning to understand what she's saying. And she is right about the police being desperate—isn't she, Jim?"

"Yes. I'm afraid so, Harry. There was another little girl attacked the day after the attack on Annie. This one didn't get away. She's in the hospital and it looks pretty bad for her. As usual—he got away, leaving no clues behind. We have to catch him and we need all the help we can get." He looked at Mom. "But, Diana, I could never do anything to hurt you."

They stared at each other long enough for me to wonder how involved they were. They seemed to be talking to each other without saying anything. But I had to interrupt their silence. I had to know. "Wallace—when did it happen to the other girl?"

He turned to me. "Around twelve-thirty on Thursday, but she wasn't found until after one o'clock. It was pretty grim."

"Where? Where did it happen?"

"The woods behind the Mount Hope pool. I was there right before I saw you on Thursday."

"How I hate that creep!" I almost yelled. I felt disgusted and sick all over. He was everywhere. "You never said a word about it."

"I know, honey. That's part of being a policeman. You're not supposed to let the job get to you. But I'll tell you the truth, I'm sick to death of this. I want to catch this maniac. I have to. I have to put him away where he can't hurt anyone." He went over to one of the wicker chairs and sat down suddenly. "I keep thinking of a normal life. Normal hours. Oh, never mind." He ran his hands through his hair.

No one moved for what seemed like ages. Mom was frozen by the door and Grandad and I sat stiffly on the bed. I had the feeling that this was the first time Wallace had ever broken down like that.

Then we all started moving. Mom went over to Wallace and sat down on the floor beside his chair. She put a hand on his knee and looked up at him. Grandad got up and started pacing up and down. I got up, too, and went to the closet to put a robe on. I don't know why, but I was suddenly cold. I sat back down on the other chair.

Grandad stopped pacing in front of Mom and Wallace. "Well, now it really makes sense. Things are worse than before. I guess if it were up to me I'd give my permission to use Brina—as long as I could be there, too. What about it, Jim? If you take Brina—you take me, too."

Wallace managed a tight little smile. "As far as I'm concerned, you're on." His smile vanished when he saw that Mom was on the verge of tears again. "Diana, forget it. I'm sorry. We won't use Brina and we won't use Harry. Please don't cry."

She scrambled to her feet and pushed Grandad aside. When she got to the door of the room she turned and cried, "Can't you understand? She's too young. You're all against me. Well, let me tell you something . . . I've been there! I know what it's like to be a child and have someone attack you. I've lived with it since I was twelve years old. That's twenty-six years that I have lived with hatred and anger for one man. You think you hate this creep, Brina? Well, you don't know what hate is. I will not have you go through what I went through. What I still go through every time I think about it. His hands all over me, tearing my clothes, and me not even knowing what he was doing. All I knew was it wasn't right and I had to get away. He said that he would let me go, but if I ever told anyone he would kill me. I was constantly afraid of him."

She collapsed against the doorframe, slowly slid to

the floor, and hugged herself the same way she had when we first talked about Annie. Now I knew why she had had such a reaction. Her story was similar enough to Annie's to have brought it on.

I jumped up and got to her quickly. I sat down beside her and put my arms around her.

Wallace stepped over us and ran downstairs. He was back quickly with a bottle of brandy and a glass. He untangled us and propped Mom up against the doorframe. He gave her the glass to hold, while he poured some brandy in it. Then he forced it down her throat until she swallowed it.

Wallace didn't take his eyes off her, but he said, "She'll be better in a minute. I think this has been a long time coming."

"Twenty-six years is a long time," said Grandad. I don't even think Grandad realized that tears were wetting his whole face. He half sat, half fell back on the bed.

It was as though some sort of earthquake had struck, right there in my own room. We were all shaken to the very core.

I went over and sat next to Grandad, as close as I possibly could. He said softly, "Diana, why didn't you come to me? Why didn't you tell me?"

She looked at him and quickly looked away. "Because I was scared. After I was a little older, I think I realized he would never kill me. I wanted to tell you, but Mom was so sick and you were so worried about her."

"It must have been horrible for you," Wallace said, as he helped Mom to her feet. They went back to the wicker chairs and sat down.

"It was." She looked at us each in turn and said,

"Now you all understand why I can't let Brina go through anything like that." She was almost triumphant.

I reached out and held on to Grandad's hand for a minute, and thought it over. I came to a decision and started talking. "No, Mom, I don't understand. You think that I would go through the same feelings you did. I wouldn't. If the creep or anyone tried to do anything to me, I would know exactly what he was doing. I would have at twelve. Things are different now. Remember? You told me the facts of life when I was younger than Annie. You made good and sure I understood them. And you explained to me about bad men. You've always been honest with me. And if I had met anybody like the creep, I would have known immediately that it was wrong. And I would have fought. I would fight now. Don't you see, Mom—if I was used as a decoy, I would know what I was dealing with. If I caught him or he was caught because of me I might save some other little girl from what you've been going through for the past twenty-six years and from what happened to Annie."

Grandad didn't seem to be listening to me. He was still thinking about Mom. "I remember how you looked at twelve. You were already lovely and you had started filling out, promising to be the beautiful woman you are today. Yet there was something so innocent about you. I'm sick that I failed you."

"Dad . . . please. You didn't know." Mom looked like she wanted to end the discussion.

"That's the point. I'm like Brina—I should have known. Who was it?" Grandad demanded.

"That neighbor, Leonard Barstow . . . who lived up the street. I would never be afraid of someone like him now, but at the time he frightened me badly," answered Mom.

"Leonard Barstow? High and mighty, pillar of the community Barstow? Never would have thought it of *him!*" Grandad spat the words out. "I guess that's the problem here. The creep that Jim's trying to catch must be someone who's above suspicion."

"You're right," said Wallace. "Somehow we're missing some important facts about him. He is clever, a fast talker, and a charmer. He picks the most innocent kids, too. He must study human nature. Annie is smarter than most, but even she fell for him." Wallace paused. "We've even thought he might be a cop. I don't know what we're going to do. We'd step up patrols but there have been too many cutbacks lately. We just can't be everywhere."

"You can't be everywhere—that's my point," Mom said. "You can't guarantee anything. Even if you could —I can't stand the thought of it."

Wallace looked at me. "It was a good idea, Brina. I wasn't for it in the first place, but after I got used to it— it began to make sense. It was good of you to offer. I'm sorry it didn't work out."

I felt terribly sad then. For him, for Mom, and for all the little girls the creep would hurt before he was caught, if he was caught.

Mom was still huddling in the chair, hugging a pillow to her chest. She sat up violently and hurled the pillow at me. "You win!" She looked around at all of us. "You all win. I'll give my permission. I wanted to keep you safe, Brina. I wanted to keep you from being hurt. Not just physically, but in any way. I guess I can't. I told you to find new friends, to learn to reach out to other people, but this is not what I had in mind. I was hoping you would get involved with people . . . but this involved, I didn't mean."

Grandad laughed a tiny laugh. "You're going to get

through this just fine, Diana. Your sense of humor is coming back."

"I have a feeling I'm going to need a lot more than a sense of humor. Right now, I'm going to have another brandy." Grandad passed her the bottle and the glass.

"Help yourself," he said. "I'm going down to make us all some breakfast. Look outside. It's daylight. Come with me, Brina. I think they need some time to themselves."

He got up and pulled me along with him. I looked back over my shoulder and saw they were lost in each other again. I was happy they still liked each other after all we'd been through and I was positively gleeful that I would have my chance to catch the creep.

8

By the time Mom and Wallace came downstairs, Grandad had one of his special breakfasts ready—waffles with pecans. He fussed and fussed over Mom. He was trying to make up for all those years, and he wasn't making any bones about it.

She seemed relieved to have her deep dark secret out in the open at last. We were all honest about our feelings that morning. We had been through a crisis, been shaken up, but we were stronger and more united than ever. Wallace seemed glad to be with us, almost grateful. I started wondering about his life.

We finished our breakfast and he called his boss from

the phone in the hall. When he came back to the kitchen he said it was all set. He talked Mom into going up and taking a nap. I ran up after her to change my clothes. She still looked tense when I gave her a quick hug in the hall and told her to get a good rest. She sort of snorted.

I changed quickly and shoved away my guilt feelings about upsetting her. It was bad enough I was guilty about Annie. I could take on anymore.

On the way downstairs I passed Grandad going up to change, too. He said that Wallace was waiting for us on the porch. Eventually we were settled, me on the glider with Grandad next to me, and Wallace in a squeaky old rocker.

Wallace started explaining some of the things he thought we should know before we started our adventure. "First of all, let me explain about the section of the force I'm on. It's called the Sexual Assault Section." I sort of gulped. That was really laying it on the line. He went on. "It's made up of twenty detectives who are thoroughly trained in all the aspects of rape and child molestation. We are involved in the psychological makeup of both the perpetrator and the victim. We attend several seminars a year to further our basic training. The detectives in our section are all chosen because of our ability to listen, to be kind and sympathetic, and to not fly off the handle. We are all patient and genuinely concerned about the people who come to us for help. We are—" he grinned a little apologetically, "considered very fatherly."

"Yet, you've never had any children, have you?" asked Grandad.

"No, I never got married. For a while when I was a rookie, and then later on, I assumed I would get married someday . . ." his voice trailed off. "Time went by and I started college. The force is really good about that; they adjust your schedule to take courses. I took several psychology courses, and I became very interested in people—the victims of the crimes you see every day in the paper. You see, in any crime there are innocent people involved. Kids like Annie, adults, old people. When they are assaulted or even threatened their fears come out in the open. Their privacy and personal safety are taken away from them. It's hard to explain unless you've seen it firsthand and you've been close, Brina. Not just Annie, but you saw how your mother acted upstairs. The experience can be devastating. Some people can't live with what they've been through, so they retreat. I've seen it drive people totally insane.

"Anyway, that's what I have to deal with every day. And you both may come into contact with it on this job. And it is a job, Brina, not a hare-brained scheme. The training, both physical and mental, will be more difficult than you can imagine. If it should become too much of a strain, I want you to come to me and we'll call the whole thing off."

I looked him straight in the eyes. "I didn't expect it to be easy. Look, I'm not all that sure of myself. I just want to do something. I don't think the creep or anyone should get away with this stuff. I'd never thought about it before Annie, but there seem to be more rapes now. Are there?"

"We honestly don't know. More and more cases have been reported to us and to the news media. But there's no way of telling whether it's because people are being more honest about it or not. There was a time when the police were at fault because they blamed the women themselves. There was a myth around that there was no such thing as **rape**. Those types are long gone off our section and hopefully off the force by now. Oh—there are probably some left all around the country, but at least our men are trained and qualified to handle these crimes without upsetting the victims more. It makes me proud to be a policeman and proud to think that some-day police work will be known as a real profession."

"There are only men in your section?" I hadn't real-ized that. "Wouldn't women be more capable of han-dling rapes?"

"I don't know . . . who does? Women have only been allowed on the force for the past couple of years. They are still in training. They have to be in uniform for at least four years before they can qualify as detectives."

"You have the rank of detective?" I asked. He nodded. "Well, how does that work? I thought the po-lice department was something like the army with cap-tains, lieutenants, and sergeants."

"Some are like that. In Pittsburgh we have Detectives First Grade, which is what I am. Second Grade, which is Perkins and Third Grade which is the first step out of uniform. We all answer to the head of our section, a sergeant, and he answers to the assistant superinten-dent of all the various detective sections."

"Will I be meeting the assistant superintendent?"

"No, you'll be working with Sergeant Oskar Zolkal-ski. The super might look in on your training, but most of it will be up to Perkins, the Wizard, and me."

"The Wizard? Who's that?"

Wallace had a gleam in his eye when he answered, "That's our nickname for the sergeant, partly because of his name and partly because he's the most intelligent man we've ever met."

"Oh! I get it!" said Grandad. "The Wizard of Oz. Oskar Zolkalski."

"That's it. But don't call him that to his face. Don't either of you slip up." We promised not to.

Wallace rocked back and forth a bit. "And don't expect him to take to you two right away. He's a bit standoffish. He's not really sure of this idea yet, or how to handle it. By the way, Brina, have you been over to see Annie lately? It might be a good idea for you to talk to her; see if she remembers anything else. You're going to have to study her anyway. Remember, you'll have to act like her to attract the creep."

I felt myself blushing. "I've been afraid of Mrs. Duvall. I haven't worked my nerve up enough to face her."

"You can't let that stop you from seeing Annie," said Wallace. "It's important. Mrs. Duvall is just like most parents, she's become overprotective. She won't let us talk to Annie. She won't let her out of the house. You could really help us there. Go over and talk to her. Make your peace with Mrs. Duvall and then try to talk to Annie alone. Find out what you can."

That was easier said than done, but I said I'd try.

"Please don't tell anyone what you're doing though," stressed Wallace. "Not about the decoy business. Nothing. I can't caution you enough about that. We don't have any idea who the creep is—he could be anywhere. You never know who might be listening. Who might tell whom. Another thing—right now you are officially attached to the police department. You must keep in touch with me all the time. I want to know where you are and what you're doing. You have to learn to follow orders."

I respected the tone of his voice. I got up immediately and said, "I can take orders. I'll go right over and see Annie. Maybe I could take her to the movies or something. If she hasn't been out of the house, she must be getting antsy."

"Brina . . . here's some money." Grandad handed me a ten. "Shoot the works if it'll get Annie to talk."

"Wait a minute, Harry, this is on the department." Wallace handed me another ten. I was tempted to keep them both, but I handed one back to Grandad. Wallace said, "If you need a ride anywhere . . . call me and don't forget to keep in touch."

I said, "O.K.," and, "See you later," and took off.

By the time I got over to Annie's, I had my apology all ready. I figured if I was as humble as possible, Mrs. Duvall would let me talk to Annie. It turned out better than I'd thought. She'd been protecting Annie so carefully that Annie was not only antsy, she was positively nerve-racking. After I made my apology and told her I would be extra careful, Mrs. Duvall drove us up to the Mount Hope shopping center and I took Annie to the movies. Afterward, we stopped at a local soda shop and, over hamburgers, and then sundaes, I asked Annie about the creep. I kept making up different games to spark her memory.

She finally remembered that he was wearing a cap with a visor turned down low, and sunglasses. She thought he was about the same height as her father, about six feet. She thought maybe he had a mustache. That was it. She either couldn't or wouldn't remember any more.

I had called Wallace from the Duvalls' when we were leaving, and then from the movie, and again from the soda shop. I was feeling pretty silly as I headed for the phone again to let him know we would take the bus home. But he had been so firm about keeping in touch, and I wanted to prove I could take orders. I guess there was a bit of the secret agent in me, too.

Annie wanted to know who I was calling all the time. I told her I was checking up on a sick friend. She assumed it was Ella and I didn't bother to correct her. When I got Wallace on the phone, he said to sit tight, and he would come and get us. We split another sundae while we waited.

He picked us up about fifteen minutes later. Annie wanted to know how I knew him so well and on and on. I told her the truth . . . that he was dating my mother. She got so excited about that (who knows what excites a ten-year-old or why?) that she chattered about it all the way home.

Wallace stayed in the car while I took Annie to the door and said good-bye to her and Mrs. Duvall, who seemed a lot more relaxed. She thanked me gratefully and I felt much better.

"What did you find out?" Wallace asked when I got back in the car.

I told him all Annie had said while we drove slowly back to the house.

He listened carefully, and then said, "Well, that's more than we got from her. You've done well, Brina. I think this thing is off to a good start. At least you do take orders."

"So I passed your test—huh?"

"Yes—this one." He smiled when he said it.

He parked the car in the street and on the way into the house I asked how Mom was feeling.

"Better, now that she's had some rest. She was a bit shocked that I was using you to question Annie, but she'll get over it."

"You must be tired, too," I said as we climbed the porch stairs.

"After you called from the movies and I knew where you'd be for a while, I took a nap on the glider. I'm used to odd hours and catnaps to keep going."

Mom had circles under her eyes and a worried look on her face. She looked like she wanted to grab me, run off to a cave and hide me somewhere. "I hear you had a sort of assignment already. How did it go? Are you all right?"

"Sure. I'm fine. Annie's better, and please stop worrying, at least until there's something to worry about."

"I know I'm acting crazy. You'll have to bear with me." The worried look didn't go away. "Jim wants to take me out to dinner. Do you mind? I'll stay here if you want me to."

"No . . . I'm tired. You go on and get out of here. Try not to think about all this for a while." I hugged her.

She hugged back. "You're growing up. Maybe I'm not ready for it."

"You'll get used to it." I was feeling a lot older than she.

They finally left after Wallace told me to get some sleep. My training was to start the next morning and I was supposed to be bright-eyed and bushy-tailed for it. I promised I'd put drops in my eyes and comb out my tail. I asked him what kind of training it would be and he said, "Pint-sized. Because you're pint-sized." Ha ha.

I was very tired, but I headed for the kitchen to see what Grandad was up to. I found him sitting at the kitchen table, staring into space. "And how are you?" I asked, as I sat down at the table, too. I was beginning to feel like a social worker, tending to various cases.

He picked up the salt shaker and stared into it as if it were a crystal ball. "I can't help wondering what's going to happen." He looked at me. "And I can't help worrying. I know Jim will look after you, and Perkins and I'll be there. But I'm an old man. Maybe I won't be able to help you."

The tired feeling passed quickly and was replaced by anger.

"Grandad! You are not an old man. You see old

people every day in that park of yours. Some of them have been old since they were born. You're not like that! You've always been young and you help me every day. I don't know what I'd do without you. Oh, Grandad—don't cop out on me now."

He straightened himself up in the chair and looked a lot better. "I hope that wasn't a pun? Cop out—you want me to cop in?"

I groaned a hearty groan. "You and your bad jokes." But I laughed.

He put the salt shaker down with a thud. "I guess you're right. I was just feeling sorry for myself for letting Diana down. Afraid I would let you down."

"You're not going to let me down. It's not in you to let me down. And as for what happened to Mom, well, you just didn't expect it and you weren't watching for it. It's over now. That was a long time ago and this is a whole different thing."

"You're getting all grown up so fast! You've changed a lot just in the past few days." He gave me an admiring look.

"I guess so." I was feeling happy he had noticed. "But I don't understand something. I thought you and Mom were so close, and yet it took her so long to tell you about . . . what's his name?"

"Barstow. Leonard Barstow," he said bitterly. "You see . . . Diana and I weren't really close until she was all grown up, been married, had you, and been widowed. Your grandmother had been sick a long time and I was all tied up with her and the railroad. After your grandmother died, I sent Diana off to college. She was seventeen then and I buried myself in the railroad. I sold our house in McKeesport and took an apartment. But I wasn't there much. I worked all the time—took any and all shifts. I guess these days you'd say I was depressed and needed a shrink, but people weren't quite as aware then as they are now. Diana did her best to stay away from me those years she was in college. I wasn't much company. I cared deeply for Hattie—your grandmother." He smiled, and his blue eyes twinkled a little. "We were Hattie and Harry. We used to have a lot of fun with that. We used to have a lot of fun period—before she was so sick. But any illness is depressing and it went on for so long before she died."

The twinkle was gone, and he picked up the salt shaker and stared into it again. I waited. Eventually he shook himself. "Sorry, Brina. Anyway, all of a sudden Diana married your father, Peter. She was only nineteen, but a grown-up married woman with a life of her own. You came along four years later and the first time I held you in my arms—such a tiny baby you were and so full of life—I felt myself coming back to life. I wanted to be part of a family again. Diana and Peter were good to me then. They must have realized my great need. Peter was very possessive of you, but he shared you with me."

"Dad was possessive of me?" It seemed strange to talk of someone I could barely remember.

"As possessive as any father can be toward his most prized possession. You used to do all sorts of things together. I guess you don't remember any of that, do you?"

"No. I try every once in a while and some things do come back to me. But it's all kind of blurry. I seem to remember after he died though. At least I remember missing him. That was when you came to live with us, wasn't it?"

"Yep. You missed him so much, you became sort of withdrawn. I felt needed then. I'd needed you all, but no one had needed me for a long time. I had already been with the railroad for forty-four years and it only takes forty to retire, so I was ready for my pension and could take an early retirement."

"Forty-four years?" I exclaimed. "How old were you when you retired?"

He chuckled, "I was only fifty-eight. When I came over from Wales I wanted a job right away. So I lied about my age. I started working for the railroad when I was only fourteen, but everyone thought I was sixteen. I told them my birth record had been destroyed in a fire in Wales and no one bothered to check on it. So for the next forty-four years, I was two years older than I really am. When I retired—everyone thought I was sixty. They gave me this gold watch, you know." He took the watch out of his pocket proudly. I nodded. "I'm really rambling on here, Brina. I'm sorry."

"That's O.K. I'm really interested. So I withdrew after my father died?"

"Yep." His long fingers were still fondling the watch. "Diana started her business with the insurance from your dad's death. You were already in school, but someone had to be around when you came home. Diana couldn't be and she couldn't afford to pay someone. I volunteered. So there we were, two adults living in the same house, sharing the costs and looking after you. I learned to cook and clean. Diana built up her business and we both worked at keeping you happy. But you know, in some ways I don't think you ever got over your father's death. It must have seemed as if he deserted you. I think that's why you reacted so strongly when you thought Paul was deserting you and why you seem to be so shy about making friends. You might be afraid they'll leave you, too. But people have a way of leaving each other to go on to different things, and then coming back. You have to learn to let them go and welcome them back. That way you'll always have something to talk about."

Grandad didn't usually talk so much himself, but then I'd never listened as intently before. I'd just accepted his presence and never wondered about the whys and hows.

He smiled a little apologetically. "Sorry again . . . I seem to be analyzing you. I've been reading a lot of those self-help psychology books lately. Some of them aren't bad. At least they make you feel you're not alone—that others go through the same kind of feelings you do."

"Hmph . . . maybe I should borrow some of them and analyze you! We could have a group therapy session," I said. "Actually, we did have one this morning." And I was still curious. "So you and Mom weren't close until she was . . . until she lost . . . my dad." I was so unused to talking about him.

"Well—as I said, we were together in this house, and our main concern was you. So, we started talking to each other as adults and we became good friends. I thought we were real close, until now."

It was my turn to comfort him again. "I think there are always some things that people keep to themselves. This would never have come out if I hadn't had my idea. But don't you think it's better that it did?"

He shrugged his shoulders, sighed, crossed one leg over the other, and opened his watch to see what time it was. "Oh—I suppose so. Yes—I'm sure it is better."

"What would you have done if you'd known about it? Would you have believed Mom?"

He nodded his head up and down emphatically. "Yes. Don't have any doubts about that. Diana doesn't tell lies or make up stories. It's not in her. If she had told me at the time, I don't know what I would have done.

83

I don't think anyone ever knows how they'll react when they're threatened. I might even have killed him. I'm not very violent—but I do have a temper and I do fight back when someone gets my dander up. But then again—I might have just handed him over to the police and taken Diana as far away as possible. For sure, I would have acted like Mrs. Duvall and become overly protective. I would have hidden her away." He creased his forehead and looked at me lovingly. "I'm of two minds about this thing you want to do. In some ways, I'm all for it. We'll work together to catch the creep and get him put away. But on the other hand, I'd like to take you up to the farm and keep you safe until he's caught. Let someone else do the dirty work."

I answered, "As I said upstairs, if I don't do it— who will? Sure, he might slip up and get caught, but he hasn't so far." I got up from the table and went around to him. I took one of the spikes of white hair in my hand and tried to pull it into place.

He stared off into space again and said, "I just don't know what I'll do if anything happens to you."

"Don't think about it until it happens. You know me, Grandad . . . I'm small but tough. If I get ahold of the creep, I'll beat the stuffing out of him."

He looked up at me and smiled, gave me a hug and said, "You're tough, huh? I wonder if you haven't taken on more than you bargained for. I said before and I'll say again—you are growing up fast. If you can handle this, you'll be able to handle anything. Including making new friends."

"One problem at a time. Besides—I already made a new friend—Wallace."

I moved over to the refrigerator and opened the door to see if anything exciting was going on in there. I found some roast beef just begging to be made into a sandwich. "I don't know about you, Grandad, but all this talk has made me hungry."

He laughed an old Grandad-style laugh and said, "As usual! How many sundaes did you and Annie have?"

"Just one and then we split one. We had hamburgers before, but they were small and the sundaes were small," I said, taking out some rolls and stuff to make wonderful sandwiches.

"I hope you never have to worry about gaining weight." He got up and reached into a drawer for a knife to slice the beef.

"Like I said, Grandad, one problem at a time."

We had our supper at the table and talked about the training, wondering what it would be like. Then about Mom and Wallace, wondering if things would work out between them. I finally got so tired I could hardly keep my eyes open. That one day had seemed at least three or four days long, with no sleep for any of them. I hugged Grandad good night and went up to bed. I was asleep before my head even touched the pillow.

9

My subconscious attacked at the crack of dawn and reminded me that I was about to start my new career as a creep-catcher. I ran downstairs and found Grandad outside on the kitchen steps. He was still in his pj's, watching the sun come up over the woods. His hair was standing up in more spikes than usual and he looked tired. My conscience bothered me a little when I realized he probably hadn't slept well because of me.

I sat down next to him and he put his arm around me. We didn't talk—we'd said it all the day before. We watched the sun until it was a yellow ball in the sky, with little pink puffs all around it. It was going to be a hot day.

Mom came to the kitchen door. She still looked tired. They both looked like it was the end of a hard day instead of the beginning. I was the only well-slept one of the group.

"O.K., you police people—" she said, "you'd better come in for breakfast."

I got up and kissed her soft cheek good morning. She tugged at my hair and gave me a grim little smile. We all had breakfast and after we cleaned up, I went upstairs to figure out what to wear.

Wallace had mentioned that I would have to work out in the gym as part of my training. I put on about a million different things, and then decided to wear a blue-flowered skirt with a matching scarf. I put on a simple blue T-shirt and tied the scarf around my neck. I decided to leave my hair hanging down straight. I wanted to impress the sergeant with it. Then I took a canvas tote bag from the closet and put my dance leotards in it. I'd quit dance class after I discovered that I danced like a baby elephant. I hoped I'd have better luck with this training, but then I was always good in gym class. I put my sneakers in the bag and some rubber bands to keep my hair out of my face while working out and I was ready to go.

Grandad was already waiting downstairs. He had on a khaki jumpsuit, one of his best. His hair was carefully combed; all the spikes were temporarily under control. His precious watch was in one of the pockets. The long heavy chain draped across his middle and was attached to the pocket on the other side. He looked real spiffy and I told him so. He said he was going to work out with me, so he was bringing his tennis stuff and his sneakers. He said he was looking forward to a little physical activity because he hadn't been playing much tennis lately. I reminded him that he hadn't played tennis for at least two years. And that he had given up the game when he kept losing to the little old ladies in his senior citizens group.

While I was teasing him I took a good look at him. After our conversation the night before, the thought did cross my mind that he wasn't as young as he used to be, but I dismissed it after looking him over. Despite his lack of physical exercise lately, he was certainly healthy. There was an excited flush in his cheeks, and his blue eyes were brighter than ever. There was no longer any evidence of being tired.

We waited impatiently for Wallace. I was afraid there might be some last minute slip-up, but he was there at eight o'clock. He had time for a cup of coffee with Mom. I heard him murmuring to her back in the kitchen while Grandad and I sat on the front porch. I imagined he was reassuring her.

They finally came outside, and we said good-bye to Mom. The way she looked, you would have thought we were going off to the crusades and wouldn't be back for a decade or two. Wallace tore himself away from her, and we piled into his police car. It was different from his regular car—unmarked and a very nondescript dark blue color. It had a portable siren on the floor, just like I'd seen on TV programs. I knocked it over and it went off with a screeching wail. I was embarrassed, but he just laughed and said it happens all the time.

It only takes twenty minutes to get to downtown

Pittsburgh from Mount Hope. By the time we turned left on Grant Street and headed for the huge fortress-like building where the police have their headquarters, I was beginning to get extremely nervous about meeting the Wizard.

I was fairly familiar with the building because our class had toured it when I was in junior high. I thought it looked about three hundred years old, but Grandad said it was built in 1898. It's dark, dingy, dim, and forbidding from the outside. It sprawls over a whole city block and connects to the old jailhouse on the next block by an overhead ramp. All it needs is a moat to make it look like a medieval castle. I was very surprised, the first time I was in it, to find an inside courtyard garden, with flowers, benches, and a fountain. But somehow that little oasis made the rest of it even more like a castle. A Wizard would be right at home there.

We drove through the big iron gates to the dark underground garage. After being in the hot morning sunshine, it was positively creepy down there.

Wallace parked next to a huge police van and we all got out. When we got on the elevator, he pushed the second floor button. He said, "Don't forget—you're not to call the Wizard—I mean Sergeant Zolkalski—Wizard. Oh, you know what I mean. Don't call him the Wizard to his face." He looked like a kid who'd been caught talking behind the teacher's back.

I looked up at him innocently and said, "What?"

"Don't give Jim a hard time," laughed Grandad.

We all laughed then, but mine was a nervous one. I tried to concentrate on taking it one step at a time and to forget my feelings of nervousness and terminal shyness.

The elevator stopped on the second floor, the doors slid open, and the first thing I saw as we turned right was a huge desk with a uniformed cop behind it. It ran from one end of a wall to the next and was almost as high as I was. I wondered how the cop got behind it, but then I saw a door behind him and guessed the entrance was off the maze of hallways to our right. I guessed it was a sort of barrier, to stop any criminal from leaping over and strangling the cop behind it.

Wallace stopped at the desk and signed in. He said good morning to the officer, who was giving us the once-over. For some reason I felt guilty, as if I were a criminal or something. I tried to look as innocent as possible.

We wandered through endless hallways—past signs that said: "Homicide," "Narcotics," "Theft," "Organized Crime," and other such goodies.

It felt weird to be that close to so much crime.

When we got to "Sexual Assault," we walked into a big room with lots of desks and people, mostly men, sitting at them typing and talking on the phones. Others were running back and forth, and there was a lot of quiet confusion. No one paid any attention to us. But then they were used to seeing all sorts of types in the police station. The thought did occur to me that if anyone noticed us being escorted around by Wallace, they would ignore us, because they would assume I'd been raped or molested or something. I hoped they didn't think Grandad was the culprit and that made me feel even weirder.

When we got to the door on the far wall, Wallace knocked. A soft voice answered, "Come in." We went in.

Wallace introduced us to Sergeant Oskar Zolkalski. He was standing behind an uncluttered desk in the small uncluttered office. I don't know what I'd expected, but not this man. He didn't look at all like a Wizard. Everything about him was medium—medium height, medium build, medium brown eyes, and medium brown hair. There was nothing very interesting about his face. It was one of the few faces I had ever seen that didn't give me the itch to draw.

He told us to sit down and we sat ourselves as comfortably as we could in the straight-backed institutional chairs. The Wizard asked Grandad and Wallace if they wanted coffee and they both said yes.

Then he looked at me and said, "What about you, Sabrina? Would you like some soda pop or something?"

I surprised myself and the others by asking for coffee, too. I wanted to appear grown-up. Unfortunately my voice came out in a whisper. I cleared my throat and sat up straighter in my chair. After all, I was playing in the big leagues.

The Wizard looked at me as if I were crazy but he picked up the phone and ordered four coffees—one light with two sugars. I felt like telling him I would take it black—but the only coffee I ever had was a sip of Grandad's black coffee and it tasted like somebody's armpit.

Wallace muttered under his breath, "Next thing you know—she'll be smoking cigars."

They all talked politely about the weather and stuff, while we waited for the coffee. I looked around the office. Several citations for bravery were framed and hung on the soupy-green walls. There was a diploma from a Pittsburgh college and photos of the Wizard with various mayors, congressmen, and other Pittsburgh notables. I looked back at the Wizard and found him gazing at me. I had the feeling he was sizing me up and I tried not to fidget. The coffee came and I was sipping mine—it wasn't bad—with the sugar it tasted like warm coffee ice cream—when he cleared his throat and started talking.

"Well, Sabrina Randall, I'm sure you're wondering why we decided to go along with this idea of yours."

I hadn't lost any sleep over it. Wallace had already told me most of why they were using me. At least I thought he had. I didn't answer, but just put a questioning look on my face.

"Let me explain." He lit a cigarette and then went on. "The man we're looking for has been around even longer than we knew. After several cases were reported and the news media got hold of the story more girls admitted to their parents to being followed, accosted, or raped. Their parents came to us. All together there have been twenty-seven cases reported in the last two years." Twenty-seven! No wonder Wallace was so disgusted.

The Wizard let that sink in. "This man is very clever, and we are at our wits' end trying to catch him. He seems to be able to get his hands on different cars and he changes his appearance somewhat. He moves around a lot. He has hit several of the upper-class suburbs and rural communities where the houses are far apart. He favors public parks and libraries and has even used the museum twice. He works quickly and quietly, during the slow times of the day, when there aren't too many people around. Lunchtime and early afternoon have been his favorite times. Occasionally it's been morning—once he even took a little girl from a public park, while she was on a nature study hike. She was with a day-camp class and had strayed away from her friends.

"He knows the Pittsburgh area very well. We're sure he lives here. Sometimes he's known his victims' names and where they live—the way he knew Annie Duvall's name and other facts about her. We've tried to find something—anything—these girls have in common. You know—where they could have met him. But so far, it's no go. Other girls seem to be picked up quite by chance. He probably cruises quiet areas until he gets lucky."

He paused and gave me a medium brown look. I was taking it all in.

"All of the girls have a lot in common. They are between the ages of ten and thirteen, very well-mannered, nice looking, and feminine. They were from the suburbs or rural communities. He seems to be attracted to the sweet-looking, pretty types—not to tomboys.

"Now, Sabrina, I've given you some background and details about this man and how he operates. We are dealing with the worst possible criminal, very sick and very dangerous."

He paused and looked around at Grandad and Wallace. He seemed to be trying to find the right words and he began again. "There is something you have to know. He is getting worse. In the past two months, he's attacked eleven of the twenty-seven cases that we know about. In the first year it was seven girls, and up to two months ago it was nine. Now, all of a sudden, in the past two months—eleven sweet little girls." He shook his head sadly.

He looked me up and down before he went on. "In order to make this plan work, we're going to have to change your appearance somewhat. Your hair is good, very good. But maybe some hair ribbons. We'll get you some frilly dresses and perhaps some makeup. Some pink face color. You'll have to practice being a much younger girl than you are. Try to act as much like your friend Annie as you can."

He paused again, and I nodded. He was treating me like an adult and I appreciated it.

"As Detective Wallace has told you . . . you'll have to go through some training. We aren't sure how to go about this so you'll have to bear with us. After all, there is no police department in the world with a training program for kids your age." He sort of smiled and looked a little more human. "The first thing on the schedule is for you to take a little test. It's a psychological exam to show us your emotional stability and how you will react to stress. This is very important. It will tell us how much we can count on you when the chips are down. From what I've already heard about you— the way you rescued Annie and the information you got out of her yesterday—I would say you won't have any trouble with it."

He seemed to know a lot about me! I would have loved to have been there when he and Wallace talked about me. I couldn't help wondering what had been said. I wondered if he knew about my shyness. But at that point, I had almost forgotten it myself.

He lit another cigarette—a chain smoker. "Then, after you take the test, Detective Wallace will show you around the station, so you get used to it. Then it will be time for lunch. After lunch you will report to the gym, and start your physical training. We have limited facilities here in the station, and the gym is quite small. It's no more than a workout room really. Most of the training is done at the armory or outside at the police park in East Liberty. Our gym was constructed primarily for the policemen who are stuck here during the day, but who have to keep physically fit in case of change of status. Unfortunately, or maybe fortunately in this case —it isn't used much."

He stabbed his cigarette out and I wondered if he ever used the gym. I couldn't see him working up much of a sweat if he did.

"Anyway, every afternoon you'll work out in the gym with a teacher. She will show you some self-defense tricks—not karate or anything—but just how to use your arms, legs, and elbows to distract someone enough to get away from him and run. It's a little like judo or ju-jit-su. You'll practice running, too. We want as few people as possible to know about this, so the gym will be locked while you're in there. As I said, it's not used much anyway." He lit another cigarette.

Grandad spoke up, "Is it all right if I take the same training as Brina?"

"You'll have to get a doctor's O.K. and sign a release, sir."

"Dr. Warnick will vouch for me. I'm sixty-seven, and I'll take all the training. I'm pretty fit!" said Grandad, proudly.

"O.K., sir." The Wizard turned back to me. "Now, Sabrina, in the mornings you'll have classes in general police procedure, witness observation, code terms, radio communications, hand signals, and time signals. All of the things that might come in handy in this operation. You'll be taken to the different departments for a thorough tour. You'll see all of the things that go on in a police station.

"And, one last thing, Sabrina, you must not tell anyone what you are doing here. The fewer people who know about this the better off we'll be. Sometimes the news media gets ahold of something like this and blows the whole thing. It would make us all look like fools. We have to see if the plan works before we can let anyone know about it. For the time being, we'll tell anyone who asks that your grandfather is a writer, doing research for a book about the police department and that you, his granddaughter, are tagging along to write your own paper for school. It's weak enough. Everyone will believe it. If necessary, we'll pretend you're relatives of the mayor or something. No one would ever think the truth anyway, but no matter how friendly you get with anyone around here, don't ever volunteer any information. Policemen are not infallible, and we don't know who this man is—" He didn't finish the sentence, but I got the point. Wallace had said they thought he could be a cop. And he had to know a lot to get away with so much.

The Wizard lit still another cigarette and peered at us through the smoke. "Are there any questions? Sabrina? Mr. Williams?"

We both said no, so the Wizard said, "Well, that's enough for now. Each morning we'll have these meetings to go over what you're learning. Right now Detective Wallace will take you to a classroom on the fifth floor and you can take the test I mentioned."

"Shall I take it, too?" asked Grandad.

"Yes, sir, I think that's a good idea. Even though you won't be in the same position as Sabrina, at least you'll get some idea of what is expected of her. Sabrina, I'm sure you're going to do just fine—but if you have any problems, my door will always be open to you. And to you, sir."

He shook hands with Grandad. "I know you'll be supporting Sabrina and I'm glad to have you with us, too."

We were all standing by then and we left the Wizard's office, went back through the busy room, to the elevator, and up to a small classroom on the fifth floor.

We sat down at two wooden desks and Wallace gave us the test. He explained that it wasn't geared for us. It was meant for regular rookies and that that would be taken into consideration when the tests were scored. He also said for us to relax and not get up-tight if we didn't understand or couldn't answer a question. I should get that kind of understanding in school!

The first part of the test was multiple **choice** and had

questions about how you feel about other people, then how you feel about yourself and how you would handle different situations. Most of them were simple enough and I just picked out the most logical answer.

Then there was the true-false section. Really dumb questions: Most people are basically honest. True or false. If you weren't basically honest, you could answer true—and fool the test scorer. Hopefully, most people were basically honest and answered truthfully.

Then there was an essay question on why I wanted to be a police officer. I didn't want to be a police officer. I just wanted to catch a creep and I was basically honest enough to say so.

I was relieved when Wallace said we both scored O.K. Then he took us on a quick tour of the station. He explained that later on we would go back over each department and into more detail. He introduced us to a lot of police people. Most of the women were in uniform, and Wallace said the ones who weren't were clerk-typists.

Somewhere along the way Perky joined us. I haven't the foggiest idea where—all of a sudden he was there. He tagged along with us down to the basement, where there was a small cafeteria. We had lunch and the food was terrible, even worse than in the school cafeteria. My ham sandwich tasted like paper. Surprisingly, I wasn't that hungry, so I just had a glass of milk and another cup of coffee. Wallace said I was getting addicted.

He said we could go out to lunch during the training if we wanted to, but I thought the cafeteria was exciting. The police women interested me the most. I'd thought they would be a rough-tough bunch, but some of them were really feminine, even with the dark blue uniforms and all the stuff hanging off their belts—handcuffs, nightsticks, guns, and the like. I decided to bring lunch from home.

Then we went to the gym, which was on the top floor. Grandad and I went to separate locker rooms to change. When we got out on the gym floor, I saw what the Wizard meant when he said it wasn't a real gym. It was small and very compact.

Wallace introduced us to our teacher—Mrs. Fiona. She was very dark, of medium height, and stocky— certainly not the wonder woman type, but she wasn't a police officer. She was a physical education instructor.

Wallace left and locked the door behind him. Our training began.

10

Mrs. Fiona sat us down on the gym floor and explained what we would be doing—that every day she would be giving us a lecture of some sort or other, partly to let our lunch settle and partly because she believed in verbal communication with her students. It was an interesting approach. She, of course, was one of the few who knew why we were there. She was amused, slightly, when I called him the creep.

The most interesting thing she explained during the lecture was the dummy. It was a funny-looking stuffed man, about six feet long. It weighed about a hundred and eighty. She had studied the alleged physical proportions of the creep and this dummy was the same height and weight. She used it to explain the vulnerable parts of the body, which were all painted on in red. It was the ugliest thing I'd ever seen. She said we would throw it around—throw it around! I couldn't even move it— and tie it to one of the poles in the room to practice jabbing, kicking, and hitting.

Then she said she would be giving us some first-aid training. I remembered not knowing what to do for Annie and I was glad I'd be learning that. But Grandad had already had first-aid instruction at one of the senior citizens centers. Mrs. Fiona looked at him sternly and said that a refresher course never hurt anyone. I had to laugh—Grandad the student! I choked the laughter back quickly enough when she looked my way.

When we started the physical training it was unbelievable. We ran, jumped, and climbed the parallel bars. We learned to kick, bite, and gouge. Mrs. Fiona showed us how to use our knees and elbows as weapons. We made them as stiff as possible and jabbed short quick jabs at the dummy. She said that was better than trying to hit or punch because you can maintain your balance better. So we jabbed continuously at the dummy's stomach, groin, solar plexis, and whatever.

She said the groin was the easiest way to disarm a man. One good knee-up and the pain would destroy him for quite a while. She showed us how to use the palms of our hands as weapons, again making them as stiff as possible and pushing the palm upward into the nose of the dummy. She said this could knock a man out and perhaps even kill someone. I think I killed the dummy.

She showed me, specifically, how to use my head to butt into the dummy's stomach. She said this could knock the wind out of someone. We practiced all she said for about two hours.

Then we had a rest period. I needed it, but surprisingly, Grandad was still going strong. After the rest, she went on to explain about force. She told us how to use an attacker's force against him, by giving way in the same direction he was coming from. Grandad would take a swing at me and I would pull his arm toward me instead of trying to push it away. I'd grab, pull, and duck and he'd end up on the mat. Half of the time I'd end up there, too. Mrs. Fiona said that it was all a matter of balance and I would have to learn to maintain mine better, by distributing my weight evenly on both feet.

By the time five o'clock came, we were exhausted— even Grandad. It was as though we'd played every game in the Olympics. I don't know how those girl gymnasts do it. Mrs. Fiona was a real toughy. She pushed us to the limit—no nonsense. She finally dismissed us to go to the locker rooms. I was so grateful, I could have kissed her feet.

I stood in the hottest water of the shower for a long time. When I was toweling myself off, she came in for her shower. As she passed me, she mumbled something like, "You did well." At least I think that's what she said. I didn't ask her to repeat it. I was too afraid she would order me back to the gym for more practice.

Wallace drove us home and stayed for dinner. He was becoming a permanent fixture around our house. Things seemed to be better and better between Mom and him, and as long as he was around she put up a brave front. When he wasn't, I would catch her staring at me, her worries pinching her face up again.

That evening Ella called and for the first time in my life I lied to her. She'd been calling me all day. I told her I was taking a class at the art school downtown. I said it would go on for six weeks, hoping that would give us enough time to catch the creep. I felt rotten about lying to her. Someday I would explain it all.

For the rest of the week, we did everything the Wizard said. We'd watch a movie of someone holding up a bank or a store, or shoplifting. Then we would have to answer questions about what they looked like, what they wore, how they acted, and even what their voices sounded like. I started carrying a notebook around with me and writing everything down. When Grandad saw it, he slapped his head with the side of his hand and said, "Now look who's a dummy! I'm supposed to be a writer and I forgot to look like one!"

He brought a notebook with him the next day, and while we were meeting in the Wizard's office, we told him about it.

The Wizard said, "Good thinking, Sabrina. But that reminds me. When you do go out on stakeout, you're going to have to remember yourself at all times. When you're out on the job, you'll be dressed like a little girl. But again, we have no idea who our man is. A good cop is never really off duty. If you go somewhere with your mother or grandfather, you'll still have to be aware of the things around you. And I think it would be a good idea to look as different from the little-girl image as possible when off duty. When you're officially on duty, of course, you'll act as young as you can, but when you're off duty change the image and act older than you are. It could be difficult to remember which you are, but I'm counting on you. We don't want any slip-ups. Do you understand what I'm saying?"

I did. I didn't want the creep to figure out that I was a decoy either.

Our training went on and on. We were shown several photographs for thirty seconds each and then we would have to answer questions about them. We were shown

one film of a heist—I kept calling them heists and
Wallace would say, "They're crimes, Brina, crimes."—
and then we had to pick the perpetrator out of a line-
up. We did it, too.

Then Wallace and Perky would take us out on the
streets. We were driven around different areas and an
hour later we would answer questions about what we
saw. That was the toughest part, and I was amazed at
how observant Wallace and Perky were. Wallace said
it was all a matter of training yourself to be more
aware. I began to notice more and more things that
went on around me. I noticed details about people and
places that I had totally missed before. And I could do
it in a very short amount of time.

We learned that crimes are divided into two great
classes—felonies: punishable by death or imprisonment
for more than one year, and misdemeanors: punishable
by less than one year's imprisonment.

There was a lot more to it than that, but that's all I
really needed to know—that and that rape was a fel-
ony: perpetrating an act of sexual intercourse with a
female of unsound mind, or with a female against her
will, and by the use of force, or with a female under
the age of eighteen.

Wallace said that the wording of this particular law
was outmoded because there were attacks on young
boys, too.

I was given the reports of the cases the creep was
involved in, or suspected of being involved in. I studied
his M.O.—that's Latin for *modus operandi* . . . his
particular way of operating. Included in these was a
personality profile of the creep, put together by a
police psychiatrist. It wasn't very complete since there
were few known facts about him.

It said that a traumatic event must have taken place

in the man's life around the time of the first attack two years before. This had triggered a psychotic episode and the man had broken down and translated his feelings into action. There was more stuff about the age group he was attracted to. The shrink felt that the creep was probably sexually impotent with adult women and was acting out his anger toward them by picking on little girls and hurting them before they could hurt him.

The profile also said that he was probably a quiet, lovable, nice-guy type who kept his feelings under control most of the time. But either the sight of a sweet little girl or some thought about the past event would trigger another attack. I thought that was unusual but when I got around to studying other cases that paralleled the creep I found almost the same personality profile. Most of the men arrested in these cases were like that—nice and quiet, wouldn't-hurt-a-fly types. I began to get a little paranoid then, thinking of all the nice quiet types I had ever met, including teachers, ministers, and neighbors. It shook me up a little to think of them.

The morning I studied those cases the creep acted again. He picked up a little girl near her home in Dormont. He knew her name—just as he had known Annie's and some of the other girls. As soon as she saw how he was acting, she realized her mistake. When he stopped at a busy intersection, she jumped out of the car and ran. When I first heard the news, I cheered her. But then I got angry again. I really beat up the dummy in the gym that afternoon. I broke a seam and his stuffing came out. I'd told Grandad that I would knock the stuffing out of the creep, the night of our long talk in the kitchen, and there I was knocking the stuffing out of the dummy. He and Mrs. Fiona both congratulated me.

But by the time we headed home that evening, all I could think of were the words "nice," "quiet," and "lovable" in the psychiatrist's report. I found it hard to concentrate on dinner or anything that was going on around me. Wallace cornered me on the front porch after dinner.

"What's going on, Brina? You hardly touched your dinner and that's not like you at all. You're acting pretty quiet, too. Are you having second thoughts?"

"Not really," I answered. "But I feel a little strange about that profile I read today." I went on to explain to him what bothered me about the report—the bit about the creep being nice, and I ended up with, "Get that! Lovable!"

"Oh, Brina, every man you meet who is nice and quiet and lovable isn't a potential rapist." He smiled. "After all, I'm nice and quiet and lovable and I'm not a rapist. Your grandfather is nice and quiet and lovable and he's not a rapist. The psychiatrist meant that the creep has repressed all his feelings and uses a facade— a front of being nice and cheerful. You see, I'm nice and Harry is nice but we do get angry at times. We do cry. We have all the normal feelings of jealousy and pride, sadness and happiness. We're all balanced out. This creep will never show anyone his anger or despair and so he hides behind a niceness that doesn't really exist. For the rest of your life, Brina, be wary of the overly polite people. They may be hiding something. It may not be rape or murder or anything near that, but there just might be something else wrong with them. Go with your instincts about people. If someone is open about their feelings you can usually trust them."

"How many psychology courses did you take in college?" I asked.

"Quite a few." He smiled again. "I believe, to be a

good policeman, you have to be something of a psychologist. We have to know certain techniques in dealing with people, how to ask questions and size up the answers. Harry told me about telling you of his depression after his wife died?"

I nodded and he went on, "Well, there you see a normal reaction to a crisis. If he hadn't admitted to being depressed, and eventually worked out of it, he might be a very sick man today. He worked out his feelings and he is stronger now because of it. That's an oversimplification of the facts, but the point is, whatever crisis triggered off the creep, he must have smothered his anger, depression, hatred, or whatever feelings he had and just got sicker and sicker."

"Whew. I guess I understand," I said. "But I think I'll still be a little paranoid whenever I meet a Mr. Goodie Two-Shoes."

Maybe you should be until he proves you wrong. Always remember you're the most valuable property you have. Not just your body, but your mind, too. And the time to give either is when you're sure about the person you're giving it to and also that you'll get something in return.

"Brina, you're so young. Sometimes I think I'm talking over your head. So if there's anything you don't understand, about anything at all, promise you'll come to me and ask me about it. I'll do my best to help you understand."

Mom came to the screen door then. She looked as though she were curious about our discussion, but she didn't ask. Instead she said, "Hey, you two, there's a cop movie on television. Don't you want to watch it?"

Wallace groaned but he got to his feet. "Yeah. Sure. C'mon, Brina. Let's see how many mistakes they make."

They made quite a few.

The very next day Grandad and I talked to some of the other detectives working in the sexual assault department. They believed our cover stories about being writers. One of them, a very tall heavyset man, with grey hair and a moustache, was really kind. He warned me to be careful because of the rash of rapes in the Pittsburgh area. I sort of laughed to myself about that one, seeing as I was going out soon looking to get caught by a creep.

By Friday of that week we'd been to most of the departments of the police station. We saw mug books, labs, the lock-up downstairs in the station, and even had a short tour of the jail. I didn't enjoy seeing the people behind bars, but luckily we weren't there long. I had my fingerprints taken, and I got to keep a set. I thought that later I might have them blown up to poster size for my room, but when I told that to Wallace he gave me a peculiar look. He said, "This isn't a game."

11

We had a quiet weekend and it seemed especially quiet after all the activity of my first week of training. Mom and Wallace went out to dinner on Friday night and Grandad and I went to the Polish cemetery to practice driving. When the people came to light the candles in the holders, he said again that he would have to find out why.

On the way home we talked about going for my driver's license. First I had to apply for a learner's permit. Then I could take the driver's test and, if I passed, I would get a temporary license. It seemed like a lot of red tape since I had already been driving for a year. I was glad that my sixteenth birthday was coming soon. That meant I would get my license before the end of the summer.

My birthday was the following Thursday. I wondered if I would get the day off from my police studies to celebrate.

Saturday was a gloomy, overcast day and I didn't even feel like getting out of bed. My muscles, the ones I didn't know I had before Mrs. Fiona's workouts, were screaming terrible things at me. I dragged myself out of bed and into the shower. By the time I got downstairs I felt better, but Grandad was so peppy and cheerful that he exhausted me again. He said the workouts in the gym were doing him a lot of good. He even thought we should drag an old mattress from the attic down to the basement and work out some more. I pictured him, after training and after catching the creep, going back to the senior citizens' tennis group and whipping the gym shoes off those little old ladies.

I told him I wanted to go over and see how Annie was. He looked so disappointed that I said I would be back for lunch and we could work out then. I hoped something would happen and I'd get out of it.

I picked up one of the "Citizens' Watch" pamphlets I'd gotten at the station and went over to Annie's. When I got there I gave it to Mrs. Duvall, explaining that it had a lot of information on safety for children. Then I went up to Annie's room. She seemed just fine, a little more subdued perhaps, but otherwise her usual self. Since it was a lousy day, we sat around and painted for the rest of the morning. I'd wanted to talk to her about not being afraid. I wanted her to be careful, but according to the pamphlet, you weren't supposed to make children paranoid about sex. Since I had just been through a bout of paranoia myself, I thought I would try and explain it to her. It didn't work out that way. She started talking first. She said she knew there were bad men and good men and she was going to be careful from now on. I guess she's smarter than I thought or that she's growing up. Then I knew how Mom felt when I didn't look to her for every answer—useless.

I went back home to lunch, Grandad, and the old mattress. He had dragged it down to the basement by himself. Wallace came over in time to see me throw Grandad. He was pleased and took us all out to dinner and a movie.

On Sunday morning, Grandad had an attack of religion and got Mom and me out of bed to go to church. I sort of enjoyed the service, but I only prayed to catch the creep. Grandad told me later that he'd prayed for my safety.

Ella came over in the afternoon. She asked me how my art classes were going and I almost said, "What art classes?" But I remembered just in time. When Wallace came over we all got kind of secretive around her. She must have sensed something was afoot, but she didn't ask any questions. She said she had to pack for a trip her choir was taking to Philadelphia, and left early. She wished me a super happy birthday and hoped I wouldn't be disappointed about not getting my present until she got back.

During dinner I asked Wallace if I would take my birthday off. He said, "Sorry Brina—but we're on a tight schedule as it is. The last two days of this week we have to go over everything you've learned and evaluate you." I must have looked nervous, because he went on, "Don't worry. The Wizard's pleased so far. You'll be going over first-aid techniques with Mrs. Fiona that day, so you won't have to work out in the gym. How about going someplace special for lunch? All of us." He looked around the table.

Grandad said, "I'll skip lunch and I've had first-aid training. I'll come home and fix up a little birthday celebration. Do you want to ask Ella, Brina?"

"No, she's going out of town. I'd love to go to that famous seafood restaurant for lunch, though."

"You got it!" said Wallace.

"Maybe just a family celebration for dinner, but I'd like to ask Perky and the Wizard over for cake and ice cream afterwards," I said. "Do you think they'd come?"

"Sure they'll come. That would be nice. But by a family celebration for dinner . . . do you mean me, too?" Wallace looked serious, but he knew I meant him, too.

I balled up my napkin and threw it at him. "Of course I mean you, too, dummy. You're here so much these days, you might as well consider yourself an honorary member of the family."

He threw the napkin back at me and laughed. "Thanks kid, I accept."

After dinner Grandad and I shooed Mom and Wallace out of the house. Grandad said, "Go on. Go off and relax somewhere." I was glad to see them go. Mom was always so tense that sometimes it hurt to look at her.

We cleaned up the kitchen and I went upstairs with a book on police procedure. I fell asleep with it in my hands and dreamed of a creep chasing me all night long.

On Monday morning the sun was back up in the sky and I was up with it. My muscles weren't saying nasty things to me anymore and I was beginning to feel tough. When I asked the Wizard to my little birthday celebration he seemed pleased.

Back to work. Wallace showed us various forms of communications. I learned how to work a two-way radio, a car radio, and walkie-talkies. The most important device was the concealed microphone I would wear under my clothes. It was attached to a transmitter that I would have to tape to my side. If I were to have total communication, I would have to have a "bug" in my ear. That's a small microphone that picks up sound. They felt it wasn't necessary to use it and that I would have enough to handle with one microphone. Wallace said it was more important for them to hear me than it was for me to hear them. He assured me they would be around, whether or not I saw or heard them.

I would have been blind not to notice that Wallace, Perky, and the Wizard always wore their guns. Whenever Wallace was at our house, he would take off his jacket, unstrap his shoulder holster, and hang it over the door of the hall closet. If we were out in back of the house, he would bring it with him and hide it under the kitchen steps. I asked him about it once and he said it was one of the rules of being a policeman, to always know where your gun was. Even when he was off duty, and out with Mom, he had to wear it. But when he was at home or at our house he just made sure it was safely tucked away.

I was half-teasing him one day and asked if I should wear a gun. He answered me seriously. Sometimes I couldn't tease him at all. "Our creep doesn't carry a gun as far as we know, and if you had one you might hurt the wrong person or yourself. I guess you could learn a little about guns if you want to. We'll go down to the shooting range later."

We did go before lunch. Wallace introduced us to the uniformed officer in charge of the range. He showed me every kind of gun they had. He was an expert on firearms. He gave me so much information in such a short time that I immediately forgot most of it. He did let me shoot a rifle, though.

It was only a twenty-two and I had to shoot it lying down in what's called a prone position. He said because of my size it would be easier for me to handle the rifle. I didn't hit the target at all until the second round. By that time, I was feeling pretty silly lying on the floor.

It was a good thing the creep didn't carry a gun. I could just hear myself saying, "Hold on there a minute, mister. I have to get into a prone position." Then I'd shoot his foot.

By Thursday, my birthday, I was feeling pretty confident and I whipped right through the tests. The questions had to do with general police procedures and judgment on a stake-out. This time they were all multiple choice questions.

Mom and Wallace took me to the seafood restaurant for lunch and I had shrimp scampi for the first time. Terminal garlic breath. I hoped I wouldn't knock Mrs. Fiona out during our first-aid session. If I did, I hoped I wouldn't have to revive her with mouth-to-mouth resuscitation. It went fine and by the time we were headed home, the garlic was just a beautiful memory.

We got there just as Mom was pulling into the driveway and we all went up the kitchen steps together. We found Grandad up to his ears in chocolate cake batter, whipped cream, chocolate frosting, and cherries. He was just putting the finishing touches on the most beautiful cake I'd ever seen. The words—Happy 16 Brina— were written across it in white frosting.

"I just finished it," he said proudly, wiping more chocolate frosting in his hair.

"This kitchen's a mess!" said Mom.

"I tried out a new recipe and I miscalculated a little,

but the end justifies the means." He wiped more chocolate, some whipped cream, and a cherry on his jumpsuit. "It's a Black Forest cake."

"And you look just like an elf," laughed Mom, "a little big for an elf, but maybe you got kicked out of the Black Forest for making a mess?"

"I'll clean it up," he said.

"I'll help," I said.

"I'll help, Harry," said Wallace, as he popped a cherry into his mouth.

"That's right, Brina," Grandad said. "You shouldn't have to work on your own birthday. Why don't you go up and get dressed in something special."

"I'm getting out of here, too. This kitchen is a disaster area!" Mom said. "I'll set the table in the dining room." She bustled away.

I took Grandad's advice and went up to change into a long birthday-type skirt and a gypsy blouse. I remembered what the Wizard had said about trying to look older, and practiced a little. I put my hair in a French twist and put on some blue eyeshadow and a touch of light brown mascara. I almost looked my age, but not quite.

While I was practicing I heard Grandad come up. A little later I heard him in the shower washing off all the gook and singing, "Happy Birthday, Brina," as only he could sing it.

By the time I got back downstairs, the table looked absolutely smashing—a blue linen tablecloth, matching napkins, sparkling silverware, and a centerpiece of pink roses and baby's breath in a silver basket. Trust Mom to make things look great.

Mom and Wallace were in the kitchen kidding each other while they worked. Mom was making a salad and Wallace was peeling potatoes for French fries. I stood in the doorway for a moment before they noticed me, enjoying their happiness. When they did see me, Wallace said I looked great. Mom thought maybe I was growing a little, that I seemed taller. I thought she was just being nice, but I ran and looked into the hall mirror anyway. I couldn't tell if I had grown or just looked taller. I felt taller with all of the things I had been doing.

When I came back to the kitchen, Wallace reminded me not to grow, as the catching of the creep depended on my looking as young as possible.

Mom said, "Can't we forget about the creep—just for one night?" She turned her back to us and switched on the garbage disposal, drowning out the sounds of any replies we might make. By the time she switched it off, Wallace and I had agreed by eye contact to make it a creepless evening.

Grandad came back to the kitchen, all spiffy and shiny in his best denim jumpsuit. We all went into the dining room and sat down to a sumptuous feast of steak, French fries, salad, and stuffed mushrooms. Grandad started to say something about the creep, but Wallace and I signaled him and he quickly changed the subject.

After dinner, we moved to the living room. The Wizard and Perky arrived with a box of imported chocolates for me and some champagne. Since I was sixteen I was allowed to drink the champagne, too. Bubbles!

While we were celebrating, Wallace went out to his car and brought in a beautifully wrapped present for me. I was quite surprised when I opened it. He had gone to the trouble of locating a fine quality—and I was sure rather expensive—set of watercolors for me. There were tubes of beautiful colors instead of pans, and three brushes. I was so happy that I gave him a big hug. He said, "You're a special lady, Brina. You deserve a special present." I got kind of misty over that.

That tender little scene was broken up by Mom's handing me her present. It was a very small box and when I opened it I got the thrill of my life. In it was a little pair of gold earrings with a certificate from the Mount Hope jewelers saying I could get my ears pierced there any time in the next three months. She had given in on the Big Issue and I loved her for it.

Then it was time for Grandad's present to me. He was grinning ear to ear, so I knew right away that it was something special. I was right! A blue denim jumpsuit, just like his! A railroad cap, just like his! Then he told me to look in the pocket of the jumpsuit and there was a gold watch on a chain. Almost like his! It was smaller and the chain wasn't as thick, but it was close enough. A special clip was attached to the clasp so I could wear it around my neck or double it and wear it as a pocket watch. I ran upstairs and tried on the whole outfit. When I got back to the living room, Grandad and I did a little song-and-dance routine and some slapstick comedy. We made quite a pair.

After that came the cake cutting, more champagne, and some ice cream, as if that cake needed it! Such a celebration! The Wizard seemed more relaxed and more human than I thought possible and Perky was his usual quiet self-contained self.

Since the Wizard was Polish, Grandad asked about the candles in the cemetery. The Wizard said that friends and relatives of the dead lit candles on special days like birthdays and saints' days, or even when they were lonely and wanted to talk to the people there. I thought that was a really neat idea, and I wondered if I should get a candle for my dad.

All too soon the party came to an end. Perky and

the Wizard left and we all pitched in and cleaned up the house. Wallace and I were straightening up the living room when he said, "Brina . . . tomorrow is the last day of your training and you'll be going out on the streets soon. Are you sure you don't want to change your mind? I'd understand if you did."

"Nope. I'm in it now. When do you think it'll be?"

"Maybe Monday, if everyone is happy with you."

I grinned. "How could anyone not be happy with a great kid like me?"

"Don't get too cocky. We have to make sure you're prepared." He looked so stern I reassured him that I was only kidding. Mom walked in then and we both shut up.

I kissed everyone good night and thanked them all for my super party and went up to my room. I looked over all my presents before getting into bed and thought about Wallace getting me that paint set. He must have known I was ready to have a more sophisticated set than what I had before. I realized how great it was to have him around. I hoped he'd be around forever.

I was almost asleep when I remembered it was Paul's birthday, too. I hadn't given it one little thought. He hadn't sent me a birthday card, but I couldn't be very indignant about that. I hadn't sent him one, either. He hadn't seemed very important to me at all since the day I'd found Annie in the woods. It had been only fifteen days—just two weeks and one day since then. And my whole life had been turned upside down, inside out —been rearranged. As I turned over to go to sleep, I wondered if Paul would ever be important to me again.

12

Friday started out well. We had a meeting in the Wizard's office and went over the test results. He said he was pleased. He explained the right answers to the eleven questions I had wrong. Eleven out of a hundred and ten questions was not bad. We had a quieter lunch than usual since we all knew the training was ending and we would be creep hunting soon. I was kind of sad about it. I'd enjoyed the people I'd met and the physical training. Now I was to face God-only-knew-what. You get used to one thing and then it changes.

That afternoon we had a world war in the gym. I had to run an obstacle course that was unbelievable. I had to crawl through a tunnel, scale a wall, and then jump over a fence. In a gym that small it was even worse because the obstacles were so close together.

Then I had to throw Mrs. Fiona. It took two tries but I did it. She was pleased. She'd warmed up considerably during the course. She realized I wasn't kidding around. I felt like I could beat King Kong.

Afterward in the locker room, I thanked her for everything and gave her a little present. It was cologne and bath powder in one of those gift packages. She liked it and told me to call her if I had any questions or wanted a special workout. She even gave me her home phone number. That was unexpected and very sweet.

Wallace was waiting for us when we came out of the

gym. He looked upset and he blurted out, "He did it again. He attacked another girl early this afternoon. She's in Presbyterian Hospital. He really did a job on her. She'll be all right but it'll take a long time."

We went over to see her in the hospital. The Wizard, Perky, and Wallace had a meeting after the attack and decided it would be best for me to see how bad things could get. I wasn't too happy about the idea, but I followed orders.

There was a uniformed cop outside the little girl's room. Wallace showed the cop his badge and we all went in. She was lying there with a tube up her nose, and she was covered in bandages. We walked over to her and while I held her hand, Wallace asked her questions. She just stared up at him with a blank look on her face. She was so badly beaten up, I started to get sick to my stomach. I was sure I was going to throw up. Grandad took my free hand and pulled me out of the room. Wallace came right after us and as we walked down the corridor the sick feeling started going away. Raging anger took its place.

I turned to Wallace and demanded, "We will start on Monday, won't we? Or maybe we should start tomorrow?"

"You know his M.O. as well as I do. He's never attacked on weekends. There are too many people around to suit him. But we will start on Monday for sure."

I had to agree. "Yeah. I guess you're right. He'll stick to his old patterns. He's been successful that way."

"Besides," said Grandad, "he did a job on that child in there. He'll be lying low for a while."

"That's right, Harry. You and Brina are to rest up over the weekend while Perkins and I shop for your new clothes."

"You and Perky? I don't believe it. Why can't I pick out the clothes?"

By this time we were on the elevator. A middle-aged lady was staring at us all, so we shut up until we got outside and in the car.

As Wallace started up the engine he said, "Brina, if you went to pick out the clothes you would pick the ones you like, not the ones you need for the job. Write down your sizes for me and we'll do our best. There's a certain image you have to project."

I supposed he was right, but the thought of those two shopping for frilly dresses made me laugh. I almost forgot about the girl in the hospital. Almost.

On Saturday Wallace stayed away from the house. I missed him, but we were busy all day. By nine o'clock we were already at the Mount Hope shopping center. We stopped at McDonald's for breakfast and then went to the jewelry store to get my ears pierced. I thought it might hurt, but it didn't at all. It took two seconds, one for each ear.

We got to the state police by eleven to fill out the application for my learner's permit and since we were on the right road anyway, we continued to an old trolley museum outside of Little Washington. We had lunch in a real neat restaurant, inside an old railroad dining car. Grandad really enjoyed that. He'd been so busy driving trains, he'd never had time to eat in one.

We went on to a huge flea market in the parking lot of a drive-in movie. I found a kewpie-doll I loved and Grandad bought it for me, for luck. Mom bought some Art Deco lamps and various knick-knacks.

We got home in time for dinner, but still no Wallace. I finally asked Mom where he was and she said he thought we needed some time to ourselves. She looked like she was about to say something else, but then she apparently changed her mind. I wondered if they had had a fight. If they had, I hoped it wasn't about my being a decoy. I went to bed early for a Saturday night. I'd had a really good time that day, but I was tired. Unconsciously I was preparing myself for the stake-out.

Sunday morning seemed to drag on and on. Wallace finally showed up in the afternoon, with a package under his arm. Grandad and I sat on the front porch in the same places we'd sat two short weeks before. Wallace explained the plan of action. I was as ready as I'd ever be, and he and the Wizard had decided I was to start the next day.

The plan was to pick a different place everyday— either a suburb or a public park, where there weren't too many people around. The target areas would be places where the creep hadn't either been before or hadn't been to for a while. I would go there on a bus or streetcar so it would appear that I was alone. Wallace, Perky, and Grandad would follow me in either Wallace's or Perky's own car. They couldn't use Grandad's car because it wasn't fast enough and it didn't have a radio. Wallace said they very often used their own cars on stakeouts, so they had had radios installed.

There would be an undercover back-up cop around me somewhere, too. I was to ignore the car and not try to figure out where the back-up cop was. Wallace said he would be keeping far enough away from me not to be conspicuous.

We went over and over the plan and training until I thought I'd scream. Then Wallace opened the package. I'd been curious to see how he and Perky would pick out my clothes. I found out. Yech! There were three dresses, one frillier than the next. Then there were the shoes. I think they're called Mary Janes. If not, they should be. And socks. Dainty little socks.

There was even a patent leather purse in red. I wouldn't have worn those clothes to a worm rassle, but then, I wasn't going to a worm rassle.

I'm afraid I showed Wallace exactly what I thought of them, but he laughed and said, "Just go and try them on. See if they fit. Perky and I worked real hard to find them."

I got up, holding the clothes in front of me as if they would bite and said, "Good old Perky. Even you're calling him that now. He's married, isn't he?" Wallace nodded yes.

"Well, I hope his wife doesn't dress like this." Wallace shooed me toward the door.

"I'm going. I'm going."

Unfortunately, the clothes fit.

After dinner Wallace asked me to take a walk with him. I thought he was going to warn me about being careful or ask me again if I'd changed my mind. I was wrong.

We left Mom and Grandad to clean up the dishes and walked outside. It was still daylight and it smelled the way only summer air can smell. We went up the street, walking alongside the houses that were being built faster now that the workmen were back on the job. I thought again about the people that might move in, about whether there would be kids my age.

Wallace didn't say anything for a while. Then he stopped and looked down at me. He reached out and took my hand. He looked so serious I didn't say anything.

"Look, Brina," he began, "we've had some long conversations about all sorts of things, and we've become pretty good friends, pretty fast. We've been thrown together in an odd situation, so I guess that's not unusual. But I don't really know you. I mean I don't know what goes on in that head of yours. I don't know what kind of experiences you've had, but I'm sure you know the differences between sex and love. Kids your age know all about sex, but maybe you haven't experienced the love that should go with it. I'm not trying to give you a lecture on the difference between love and lust. What I'm trying to say is—to put it bluntly—I'm moving in with your mother.

"I'd be staying in the house anyway, while this chase is on, as added protection. But I would be staying in the guest room. As it is, we've decided we want to live together for the time being. I could lie to you and go sneaking from the guest room to Diana's room after you fall asleep, but that's not my style. I think you appreciate honesty anyway."

I agreed. I did appreciate his honesty. I was shocked, but I would have been more shocked to catch him sneaking around in the middle of the night.

He went on. "It used to be that a man and a woman had to be married to sleep together. That's not the way it is now. People are pretty casual about that sort of thing. I want you to know that this isn't casual. I really care about Diana and she cares about me. I don't know if we'll ever get married, but this is one way to find out if we're suited to each other."

He stopped and I just waited. I was sure there was more coming.

"I'm not trying to take your father's place. But I want very much to become part of the family. You know, I think, that I've made my job my life and I think you also know what I've been going through lately. When I met Diana, right away I wanted to be with her all the time. And I wanted to be one of the family. I've been with you all a lot lately, but I want more than that. Do you understand?"

He was gripping my hand so tightly by now that it started to hurt. I took it away and looked up at him. I rubbed the sore hand with my other one. He had such a worried look on his face that I took hold of his hand again. He smiled gratefully.

We stood there staring at each other, the silence lengthening between us. I was at a complete loss for words.

I thought over what he'd said. I knew about sex, of course. I mean, wasn't I about to go out and hunt for a sex maniac? But somehow . . . I had never really thought of Mom that way. Does anybody ever really think about their parents that way? Even though I had wondered about Mom and whether she was happy once or twice, I guess I'd never thought about her sex drive. What kind of dummy was I? I should have known for some time that when they went out, they didn't go to a movie and hold hands. They were both much too healthy for that.

Wallace said again, "Do you understand?"

What would he say if I said I didn't? Would he leave and never darken our door again? Hardly. Funny, I'd been hoping he would stick around, until he said he was going to. Now I had all kinds of confused feelings —that I was losing Mom, that I was jealous. She had Wallace and I didn't have anyone. She was safe and I was going out to risk my life. And he was still waiting for my answer.

I said the first thing I could think of. "Does Grandad know about this?"

"Diana told him about it and we decided that I should be the one to tell you. You see, it's important for you to know that I care about you, too. And Harry is one of the finest men I've ever known."

He sure cared about all the right people—my mother and grandfather. And me. But I still didn't know what to say to this man, staring down at me, grey eyes anxious, the scar on his cheek turning white with the tension caused by his clenched jaw. Besides who was I to approve or disapprove? Mom wasn't my property. She had a life to live just as I did. She'd let me have my way about hunting the creep. I had set something in motion and if I could go back in time and change it, would I?

I shook myself and hung on tighter to his hand . . . I could think it all over sometime later. Right now some answer was important. I nodded my head, "O.K. Wallace . . . I got it."

He unclenched his jaw and bent down and kissed the top of my head. "Thanks, Brina."

On the way back to the house, we didn't talk at all. My thoughts were still too jumbled. In front of the house he stopped at his car and took out a suitcase. I thought to myself, "Well, I'm not losing a mother . . . I'm gaining a live-in cop." My own dumb joke almost made me cry.

When we got inside, everyone looked at everyone else and then looked away. Mom looked tense, Grandad was flushed, and I'd had enough. I wanted to be left alone. I said good night and went on up to my room. I took out my new watercolors and started painting some roses I'd picked earlier. It was late when I finally went to bed, but no one intruded on my privacy. I half expected Mom to knock on my door but she must have decided I needed to be alone with my thoughts for a while. I was glad. I knew that sooner or later we'd have to talk about it, but I wasn't ready and I didn't think she was either.

13

I slept poorly and woke up with the sun again. It was becoming a habit. I lay in bed and went over everything that had happened since I had found Annie in the woods. Again. I did it this time because if I hadn't been on the porch that day, Mom would never have met Wallace. And I wouldn't be going on a creep hunt.

My feelings of confusion and resentment had lessened, slightly. At least I was sure that Wallace would never hurt Mom. Even in his work, or maybe because of it, he seemed in control and kind of gentle in a rough way. I remembered his concern for her that morning, the morning of what I now refer to as our Group Therapy session. It would be strange to have him living in the house, though. Things would be different.

I rolled around and around on the bed for a while thinking about Mom, Wallace, and then the creep. I thought about the job I had ahead of me. A sudden feeling of fear gripped me. Then I remembered Wallace telling me I could back out any time I wanted to. I pushed away the fear and got out of bed. I wasn't going to back out. I'd started it and I was going to finish it.

I got dressed in my jeans, because I was shy of having Wallace see me in my nightgown. He had seen it that other morning, but he hadn't lived in the house then. I made my bed and laid out the frilliest of the dresses to put on later. Then I went downstairs.

Grandad was on the kitchen stairs again. He was already dressed in a blue-and-white seersucker jumpsuit. I sat down beside him.

"What do you think, Brina?" He put his arm around me.

"I don't know. What do you think?" We both knew we were talking about Wallace.

"I think maybe he'll be good for Diana. She must get pretty lonely sometimes. She has her clients, and you and me, but she hasn't had anyone special in her life for a long time. No romance. No love. No sex."

"It's hard for me to think of her as a person. I mean she's my mother."

He sighed. "You have to accept the fact that she needs Jim. And he needs her. In many ways they're a lot alike. They've worked hard at their jobs, they've excluded other people and sacrificed a lot, and they're both changing. They happened to meet at a time when they most needed each other. You have to understand that. And you . . . you're growing up, faster than I thought possible a few weeks ago. You'll be leaving here someday to make your own life. You wouldn't want to leave her all alone, would you?"

"No. But you're not going anywhere, are you?"

I waited anxiously for his answer, suddenly scared that he might want to leave. To change his life, too. Maybe he would even find a woman he cared about. It was over twenty years since my grandmother had died. I knew before he'd married her, he'd been quite a ladies' man. I'd seen an old photograph album in his room. He seemed to have a different girl in every picture.

He thought my question over. When he answered it was a surprise. "Not right this second. But I might someday. And I'm not the answer for Diana. I'm her father and I can't take the place of a husband or lover.

I can give her company, but that's not what she needs. And I've always thought, when you grew up, I might take a trip on a tramp steamer. I might like to take a trip back to Wales to see how it's changed, before I get too old to enjoy it. And I'd like to see the Orient. You know me and Chinese food." He laughed.

"A tramp steamer? Wales? The Orient? Heavens . . . you've been thinking about that for a long time?" He nodded. "You know, the more I think about these past weeks—I realize I've learned more about you and Mom than I ever knew before."

"Brina, darlin', I don't think you ever paid attention before. I'm not putting you down . . . but you're finally coming out of that little narrow world you used to live in. And you're coming out just fine! About Wallace . . ." he paused, "things have a way of working out for the best. Let's go in and make a special breakfast to welcome him to the family and get this creep-catching off to a good start." He got up. "Yes, sir. I feel like a good breakfast. Waffles again." As he opened the kitchen door, he mumbled, "I wonder what they have for breakfast in China."

Grandad had the batter all ready and I was frying ham when Mom and Wallace came into the kitchen. We made them sit down and made a big fuss over them. Wallace seemed nervous when they came in. I was, too. I wondered if I should start calling him Jim, but I seemed to have Wallace engraved in my brain.

We were all digging into the waffles when Perky arrived. We made him some waffles and poured him coffee. He had my mike and transmitter with him. Since I'd been thinking about first names, I asked him what his was. I wished I hadn't. It was Percy. Percival Perkins. I rolled that one around on my tongue a few times. Up to that time I'd avoided calling him anything to his face. I finally asked if he would mind my calling him Perky. He smiled. At least I think he smiled, but his face didn't change much. Anyway, he said it was fine with him.

I finished my breakfast before anyone else and went up to change my clothes. I took a shower, toweled myself off, and reached for my underwear. I paused and looked at my one-size-fits-all-even-a-midget bra. It broke me up to think I'd finally found something good about being flat-chested. I could never have been a decoy if I were built like Ella, or Ingrid, or practically anyone else in my class.

I hung the mike around my neck and taped the transmitter to my side. Then I put on the frilly dress. It had a strawberry print on it: red and pink strawberries on a white background, with ruffles around the neck. I hated the ruffles. As a matter of fact, I hated the whole dress, but the ruffles covered up the mike nicely. I put on the dumb socks, then the dumb shoes. I combed my hair straight down, and perched a red bow over my right ear. The final touch was some light pink blusher and a little light pink lip gloss.

I looked in the mirror hanging behind the bathroom door. There I was . . . a rather over-dressed, sweet looking twelve-year-old. All I needed was a prayer book and I'd be on my way to Sunday school. I stuck my tongue out at the image in the mirror.

I ran down and paraded for my audience. There was a standing ovation until everyone noticed the expression on Mom's face. We all sobered up fast.

Wallace went over the plan again. I was to go to the bus stop and take the bus to the Mount Hope shopping center. There I was to change buses for Briarwood, get off at the Briarwood library, go into the library for an hour or so, and then go to the park nearby. There I'd stay for a while, then go to the shopping district, and then back to the park. Simple. Even a twelve-year-old could do it.

With a slight tremor in her hand, Mom handed me the lunch she'd packed. I would have to find a place to eat it, because I had to be alone as much as possible. She hugged me tightly and whispered, "Be careful."

It was beginning to get hot when I left the house. I started itching in that dress and the Mary Janes were pinching my feet. I figured I'd better get used to it—I would probably be itching and pinching all day.

All the way to the bus stop, about a block and a half away from our house, I fought the temptation to turn around and look for Wallace, Perky, and Grandad. Even when the bus came and I got on, I felt like running to the back and waving. I knew it wasn't a game, but there was a desire in me to be sure I wasn't alone.

I changed buses at the shopping center and then got off at the Briarwood library, according to schedule. Once inside, I killed my nervousness by reading a book on the bloodiest crimes in history. The librarian probably thought I was nuts—a nice, sweet little girl, reading a weirdo book and casing the joint with a wild expression on her face.

At ten-thirty I left the library and went to the park. I sat on a bench. There weren't many people around, and I tried not to think about which one was my back-up cop. He was supposed to be there and that was all I was supposed to know. I wondered how many pairs of eyes were on me.

I kept saying something into the mike every five minutes or so, so they'd know it was working. I sang songs, told jokes, and chattered on and on. If anyone heard me, I'm sure I sounded like I was getting an early start on being a street-crazy. But it helped to pass the time.

I had my lunch at about twelve-thirty, on the bench. Mom must have been really distracted. It was worse than her usual. She forgot the mayo on the bologna and there was only one of those packaged cakes. Hardly enough to keep an active twelve-year-old going.

After lunch, I walked over to the shopping center. I walked in and out of the stores, bought a coke, was seen around, and then went back to the park.

It got pretty boring and I decided to bring a sketch pad and a book with me the next day. It was too bad I had to leave the book on the bloodiest crimes in history at the library. Some of the stories in it made the creep look like Alice in Wonderland.

At five I got on the bus to go home, hoping I wouldn't see anyone I knew. Wallace told me that if I did see anyone who knew me to be polite, act distracted and perhaps a little strange, and to get away from them quickly. So much for my preferred image of a smart, artist-type sixteen-year-old.

My first day was a real wash-out. Wallace told me not to be discouraged. We probably had a long haul ahead of us.

Tuesday, we went to South Park. At least I wasn't so bored, because I packed a tote bag with a book, my sketch pad, and lots more to eat. I wasn't as nervous and I was beginning to concentrate on my surroundings the way I'd been taught. I noticed everything and everybody. I roamed around the park, looked at the people playing golf, examined the Civil War monument, and settled myself on a bench in a rather secluded area. I sketched, which gave me the opportunity to study the people who came my way, and occasionally pretended to read.

On Wednesday, it was Fox Chapel, a very upper-class suburb. It was really deserted—the houses far apart and lots of woods. I kept imagining someone jumping out from behind every bush, and so I jumped at every sound. I had to eat my lunch on an old log by the road. I couldn't understand where my back-up cop was hiding but I found out later. He was going from tree to tree. He must have been part Indian. I hoped the mosquitoes got him like they got me. I kept walking around most of the day, just stopping once in a while to sketch something. I could always see Wallace's car, but when it wasn't moving, they all scrunched down and it looked empty.

On Thursday, we went to Greentree. I roamed a cemetery, an old church and a public garden. Yes, sir, I was really seeing the sights.

On Friday, it was North Park. I walked all around the outside of the park and looked at the houses in the neighborhood. Most of them were stately old mansions. I tried to imagine what it would be like to live in one of them, with a butler and maids to pick up after me. I gave up on that one and found a bench in the park, by the lake. There were a few people out in rowboats and I started sketching them. I had a very vague memory of having been there before, in a rowboat with my father. Since my memories of him were so few and far between I tried to hang on to it. It seemed to me that he'd let me row the boat, but it was so hazy. I thought I'd ask Mom about it sometime.

I left the lake and went over to a picnic site. I sat at a picnic table and got my lunch out. The decoy business certainly gave me a hearty appetite. Maybe it was all the fresh air. I was bringing half the refrigerator with me. If I could just bring a portable toilet, I'd be O.K.

I was still sitting at the table finishing my lunch when I noticed a group of old people having a picnic. One of the old ladies came tottering over and I thought she looked familiar. When she got closer I realized it was Grandad's drunken lady friend—the one who had beaten him at chess. I just had time to explain over the mike who she was, before she pounced on me like a long lost friend. I kept trying to get away from her, but she had to tell me her life's story and all about her friends. It seemed they had a picnic every Friday in different parks and she told me about every single park in Pittsburgh. She kept offering me a drink out of her brown paper bag, and I wondered what Wallace would say if I took her up on it. I was really tempted to, just for sheer devilment. But the stuff smelled so bad and I remembered my sick reaction to drinking with Paul. That had been good stuff and this was definitely Brand X. I left when she put her head on the picnic table and away as soon as she came over. I'd made a mistake by fell asleep. Wallace told me later, I should have gotten talking to her at all. I promised not to do it again.

That was the end of my first week as a decoy ... not very exciting, and I didn't know whether to be relieved or not. But I'd found out that creep-catching can be a tedious, boring yet nerve-wracking, scary job.

Since the creep was never active on weekends, and I had to stay close to the house and family, we just lazed around all weekend.

I asked Mom on Sunday evening about the memory of my Dad taking me boating in North Park. We were alone, sitting on the front porch while Grandad and Wallace played chess inside. We'd been rather avoiding each other since Wallace moved in and the creep-hunt had begun. It had only been a week, but it seemed longer. I thought asking about my father might help to start a conversation. It did. She told me that he had taken me over to North Park once and rented a row-boat.

She said, "I'm amazed you remember that, you were only four years old. When you came home, he was so proud that you rowed the boat." She chortled a little, remembering what must have been a happy time. "At least he said you rowed the boat. I didn't really believe it. But he was like that. He could kid you along and make you believe it. Then when you were truly hooked on his line of tales you'd catch a wild little gleam in his eye, and believe it or not, his hair would sort of rise up and stand on end. Then you'd know you'd been had again. He was a lot of fun. Everything was funny to him." The laughter gone, she sighed, "Sometimes that's good. Sometimes I resented it though and sometimes it drove me crazy. He would have made light of his own death, found something funny in it. I've thought about that all these years. Wondering what he could have found funny about a car crash." She brooded a moment. "He loved you so much. Anyway, he said you rowed him all over the lake that day."

"We must have had a good time. I wish I could remember more of it."

"You always had a good time. He spent so much time with you that after he died, you became very withdrawn."

"Grandad told me that. He thinks I've been afraid to make friends because I'm afraid they'll leave me, the way Dad did."

"Hmph. I suppose that could be." She ran her hands through her hair, scratched her head. "Well—Dad's been reading a lot of those books on being your own best friend and telling people who you are. I'll always be glad he was around when Peter died. When he came to live with us, you started coming out of it. I wonder what's left of those memories for you, for me." She shook herself a little, as if shedding old memories. "Brina—I have to ask you—what do you think of Jim? Do you like him?"

"Of course I like him." I swung back and forth on the glider. I was telling the truth. I did like Wallace, even more so after the past week, but every once in a while I had the same feelings of confusion I'd felt before. I didn't want to talk about them to Mom though. "Do you think you'll get married?" I asked nonchalantly. But I was really curious.

"Oh . . . I don't know." She sat up nervously in the rocker. "I'm happy the way we are now. I don't know if I'm ready for that kind of commitment. I was so heavily committed to your father, and then he died and I had to make my own way. I must admit I like being independent. I'm not sure Peter would have accepted that. He liked having me as a hausfrau. Jim does admire the way I handle myself and yet he lets me lean on him when I need to. He's steady and realistic. I think Peter lived in his own fantasy world and I don't know what would have happened if he'd lived. Brina, I have to be honest with you about him. If he had lived, I'm not sure we would still be married. He wanted to possess me the way he possessed you. At the time, I went along with it—I loved him, I let him possess me. And I never realized that I resented the commitment he demanded.

"But Jim is a different story. This is a different time. Oh! I can't compare the two—that's silly. To answer your question . . . I just don't know!" She threw up her hands and then laughed. "Listen to me. I sound like an idiot. I don't want you to think badly of your father— I loved him dearly—but I'm awfully glad you like Jim. I can imagine that this is difficult for you. I didn't even know how to tell you, but Jim volunteered. You're very important to him. I don't know how I'd feel in your place. . . ."

I didn't have an answer for her. She had opened up so much to me and yet I wasn't ready to tell her how confused I felt about Wallace and her. I avoided the issue by bringing up another.

"Well, besides liking him, I am glad he's around. He makes me feel safe."

"Then you are afraid? You've been acting so sure of yourself!"

"Sure I'm afraid." I was admitting to her that all the running around those parks and suburbs the last week had put me on edge. "The creep could be anyone, anywhere."

"You can stop, you know," she said hopefully.

"Sure I can. And a whole lot more little girls can get attacked. If you could have seen that girl in the hospital, you'd know what I mean."

She shuddered. "No thanks. I don't have the stomach for it. In many ways you have a lot more courage than I do."

"That's real funny, Mom—you're the one who taught me to be independent."

"Independent yes, but there's nothing wrong with a little healthy fear. Especially with all that's going on these days."

"Oh, I'm healthy all right and I'm afraid. But it ain't gonna stop me."

"O.K., Brina, you're not me and I'm not you, and I just have to accept it." She got up then and said, "Well, I'm sleepy. I think we've talked long enough, but if you want to know anything else about your father, let me know. I've all sorts of photos and scrapbooks you can look at. You've never showed much curiosity before and I'm glad to finally talk to you about him." She kissed me. "I think I'll go up and take a long hot bath with bubbles and find something to read—something light and happy to get my mind off creeps and ghoulies and things that go bump in the night."

"Try *Winnie the Pooh*," I said.

"Even Winnie had his fears," she said profoundly. And she went into the house to leave me to mine.

14

Bright and early the next morning I began my second week of decoy work. I set out for West Park. I needed a compass to keep my parks straight. At least this was more interesting. West Park had the Buhl Planetarium and the aviary. I walked inside the planetarium and looked at all the displays; I wished I could go to the sky show. I planned to come back after all this was over.

I walked out into the hot sunshine and over to the aviary. I watched the exotic birds until they began to get on my nerves. I did have a nice conversation with one of the myna birds, though. He kept saying, "Hello, hello hell. How are you. Hell, how-hello-hell. Hello. Helloo-helllooo hell." I told my audience over the mike that it was a bird and not me. I was still talking into the mike every five minutes or so, but I'd given up on the jokes after the first day. I only knew so many and I'd used them all up. Wallace said I'd never make it as a stand-up comedienne anyway.

For the rest of the day I walked in and out of the aviary and in and out of the planetarium. I felt dizzy by the end of the day.

I took the bus home as usual. I was beginning to know the entire Pittsburgh bus system, which is hard to say the least. Grandad says that Pittsburgh just grew. It was never planned so everything is a mish-mash.

When I got home, Mom was already there, frantically cleaning house. "What's up?" I asked as soon as I saw what she was doing.

"We all forgot. With all that's going on, we forgot. Tomorrow's the Fourth of July. Uncle Emory and Aunt Ethel are coming over from Johnstown. They're stopping at the farm tonight and then bringing Aunt Gertrude over here with them in the morning. We made the plans ages ago. Good Lord! You don't think they'll make you go out on the job tomorrow, do you?"

Emory is Grandad's brother and Ethel is Emory's wife. Every year since I could remember, we'd all converged on the farm for a sort of family reunion on the Fourth. But when Uncle Ronald died, everyone decided to do something different for Aunt Gertrude's sake. I vaguely remembered planning a to-do at our house.

Wallace and Grandad walked in then. Perky was right behind them. "What's going on?" asked Grandad.

Mom told them hurriedly and ended up with, "So they're going to get here around eleven tomorrow morning. They'll stop over at Alice's first and drop their bags. Then everyone is coming over here."

Everyone meant my mom's cousin Alice, her husband, and two kids, Aunt Gertrude, Aunt Ethel, and Uncle Emory. I counted heads mentally. "Cripes! That's eleven people!"

"That's not all. I invited Ella and her parents. I'm going crazy. How could I have forgotten?" She turned to Wallace. "Jim, does Brina have to go out tomorrow?"

"No, it's a holiday and the creep doesn't operate on holidays. I'm sorry. I knew the Fourth was coming up, but I just assumed you'd know that Brina doesn't have to work."

We all stood in the hall and looked at each other for a moment, trying to remember other, more normal times. Then Grandad yelled, "Food! We have to feed thirteen-fourteen people. How many people?"

"I don't know," said Mom, "but what the heck! Perky, would you and your wife like to come over tomorrow? We'll just hang around here and eat whatever and whenever and then later go over to the Mount Hope fireworks. I haven't seen them in years, but they were always fabulous."

"Sure. If I can bring my boys. I have two sons, you know." I didn't know that and I doubt if Mom did either, but she nodded.

"That's swell, Perky. The more the merrier. I don't know what we'll put together to eat, but we'll find something."

Perky said, "My wife makes the best potato salad ever. I'll get going now and pick up some supplies to make it. And some beer—so at least we'll be bringing something!" And he charged out the door looking more animated than I had ever seen him.

"Potato salad. That's one down. Now for the rest of the menu." Mom looked to Grandad a bit helplessly.

He spoke quickly, "There's a turkey downstairs in the freezer. We'll do that indoors. Jim, you and Brina go to the store and get hotdogs, buns, potato chips, you know—picnic stuff. I'll go bake a cake. Two cakes. Diana, keep cleaning." And we all raced to different doors, with Mom yelling, "I hate cleaning!"

We were in the car and halfway to the store when I remembered I still had my little girl clothes on. When I told Wallace, he slammed on the brakes and took me right back to the house to change. He reminded me to look older, as the Wizard had said. We couldn't be too careful, you know.

By the time everyone showed up the next day, you would think we'd been planning the party for months. We had cold cuts, hot dogs, and hamburgers for the barbecue outside, the turkey in the oven inside, potato chips, corn chips, and big fat pretzels, various salads, plus cut-up carrots, celery, and other relishes, and lots of different kinds of rolls. Grandad had baked the two cakes—one chocolate and one yellow.

Ella and her parents came over with beer and soda pop. Aunt Ethel brought home-baked cookies and Uncle Emory brought cigars, "for the menfolk. Heh heh." Aunt Gertrude brought pies—one apple and one lemon meringue.

It was so good to see them. Both Emory and Gertrude have the same sky-blue eyes as Grandad and me. It was like looking into a four-way mirror. We all have what Grandad calls the "Williams Look" about us. Alice looks like her mother, Aunt Ethel—dark and thin. She and her husband brought wine made from their own grapes; they live on a tiny farm in Library.

By the time Perky and his wife and sons got there, it was a real mob scene. I went out to help them carry in all the stuff they'd brought. When I met his sons, I could have died. One of them was absolutely gorgeous . . . not at all like Perky. I found out later he was sixteen, too. Blond hair and blue-green eyes—his name was Charlie. About five feet eight and a very muscular build. The other one was younger—around twelve—

and he disappeared right away with Alice's boy and girl. Probably off to terrorize the neighborhood.

The final member of our group showed up a little later—Ella's boyfriend Howard, his guitar slung over his shoulder.

Ella and he were still excited about the tour of the Philly churches. They had just gotten back the night before. Ella handed me my late birthday present. Guess what! A pair of gold hoop earrings! Mom and she had conspired together and that's why my birthday present was late instead of early. Mom didn't want me to know about her present before my birthday. I put the hoops right in.

Everyone ran around and ate and talked. The men were out on the front porch smoking Uncle Emory's cigars. And for some reason the women ended up in the kitchen. Perky and his wife Elinor seemed to enjoy themselves, and I liked their son Charlie. I was, of course, shy around him; he was so good-looking and self-assured. It was hard to believe he was Perky's son.

At one point in the afternoon, we found ourselves alone at the picnic table, gobbling up goodies. He said, "I really shouldn't be eating like this. I have to keep my weight down for wrestling."

I thought to myself, "Oh great. A jock." I was being sarcastic, but I was glad a minute later that I wasn't sarcastic aloud, because then he said, "I know what you've been doing—my father told me. He wasn't supposed to. But he was worried about you and he wanted my advice on how a kid our age would handle the situation you're in."

I sort of choked on one of Aunt Ethel's cookies. Surprised that Perky was worried. Doubly surprised that he would tell Charlie. And triply surprised that Charlie would tell me. "He did? He was? What did you say?" I honestly didn't know what I was saying, but I was suddenly relieved that someone outside of my own little group knew what I was doing. Someone my own age. Someone I might be able to talk to.

He smiled and I noticed a chipped front tooth. A flaw in his perfect beauty. Praise the Lord! He said, "I think it's great! It's about time someone did something about that guy. He hit our suburb, too, over in Briarwood. It was the first one he hit."

"I was just over there the other day!" I exclaimed. "I didn't know that's where Perky, er uh, your father—you all live!"

He laughed, "I know you call Pop, Perky. I love it, I really love it. It doesn't fit him so well—it actually fits him. We call him Pop-the-Cop."

We both laughed hysterically. "It wasn't that funny," Charlie finally said, still laughing.

"I know," I said, "but it's just that things have been so serious around me for what seems like so long. Even funny things haven't been funny, you know what I mean? Everything has been happening so fast and I didn't realize . . . I've been so tense . . . waiting and waiting for the big thing to happen . . . for the creep to get me. . . ." I felt tears welling up in my eyes. "And I haven't told anyone . . . I didn't know myself how scared I could get . . . I'm sorry. I don't want to dump on you . . . I don't even know you." And I got up and ran over to the woods.

He caught up with me at the edge of the woods and grabbed my hand. "Look . . . you're not dumping on me. I'm interested. And forget you don't know me. I've been hearing about you everyday for three weeks now. Every night Pop comes home and gives me a progress report. When he came home last night and said I'd finally meet you I got so excited I asked him if it was

O.K. if I talked to you about it. He said it was up to me, but not to let anyone else know that I knew. Then he said it would probably be good for you to talk about it. So you see you're not dumping. Don't worry. I knew you were over in Briarwood last week . . . after your first day on stakeout. I didn't know before and it's a good thing I didn't. I probably would have gone over to the park, just to see what you looked like in the dress they picked out for you. Just to see what you looked like period."

"Oh, no!" My hair had fallen down over my eyes. I stopped crying and looked through it, still hiding behind it. "It's bad enough to go parading around like a little girl, without having someone see me."

"Don't worry. I can't imagine you ever looking bad. You're great looking to me."

My heart started fluttering away, especially since I was still holding his hand. I let go of it . . . suddenly terribly embarrassed. I didn't know how to handle the whole thing.

He peered into the woods. "Is this the woods where Annie was attacked?"

"Yes . . . the creep brought her here. You do know everything, don't you?"

"Where did it happen? Where did you find her?"

I pushed my hair out of my eyes and took a good look at him. He *was* being sincere. I led him into the woods and over to the clearing. I sat down on the tree stump quickly, because my legs were too weak to hold me. He made himself comfortable under a tree nearby. I couldn't help comparing him to Paul, since we were in the same place that Paul and I had spent so much time. But I got over that. Fast. There was no comparison. Paul was Paul and Charlie was definitely

Charlie. And Charlie was treating me like a girl he was really interested in, not like a kid sister.

We sat there and talked about everything—my life, his life, my training as a decoy, his desire to be a cop. He told me he was working as a mechanic for the summer, in a garage over in Briarwood.

Then he said what seemed like magic words to me. "I know you're busy with all of this and I know you're not supposed to go out much now. But when it's all over, will you go out with me? I got my license in April and I have an old car that I'm working on, and Briarwood isn't very far away."

He really meant it! I nodded, not being able to think of anything to say.

"Good. Great!" He grinned, showing the chipped tooth again. "In the meantime I'll call and we can talk on the phone. If you get upset or anything, will you call me?"

I nodded again, this time gratefully. "Thanks, Charlie. . . ." And slowly I found the words, "It's helped to talk to you about this, and I will call. If I need to."

"Don't wait until you need to. Call me anytime! Call me every night! That way I'll get two sides to the story, your's and Pop's. Pop says every cop has to be something of a psychologist."

"So does Wallace!" I stood up. "That's it. That's the only reason you're interested in me. One fellow cop to another." I was only half kidding.

"Don't you believe it." He got up, too, and looked down at me. "I really like you, Brina. I liked everything I heard about you and now that I've met you. . . ." He was going to kiss me then, but we heard Ella and Howard yelling our names so we slowly went back to the house.

Everyone was in the backyard eating again, when we

got there. Later on, Howard played the guitar and Ella sang. Then Grandad sang. Uncle Emory did magic tricks.

At seven-thirty we all piled into our respective cars and hurried over to the Mount Hope park to watch the fireworks. Charlie and I rode with Mom and Wallace. I felt like I was on a double date with my own mother.

As Mom had said, the fireworks were fabulous. Since we had always gone up to the farm on the Fourth, this was the first time I'd seen them. I decided never to miss them again. It wasn't just the ones that shot up in the sky, but the ground works, too. They had a waterfall, battleships fighting, and the American flag. Charlie explained how they worked, but I was so fascinated watching the reflection of them in his eyes, that I didn't pay much attention to what he was saying.

As we were leaving the park, we ran smack into Ingrid the Beautiful. She said, "Hi, Brina, how are you?" as she looked Charlie up and down speculatively; I felt a twinge of jealousy. I mean Ingrid was just as gorgeous as Charlie. Both of them blond and Nordic looking. I answered the usual, "Fine, how are you?" And since I couldn't get out of it, I introduced her to Charlie.

But then she seemed to dismiss him and turned to me. "You look different Brina. Prettier." Funny, I never would have thought Ingrid would notice my looks, but I sure felt prettier with Charlie standing next to me.

"Oh, thanks, Ingrid." I smiled.

"Why don't we get together sometime soon and go to a movie or something? I got my driver's license. Did you?"

"Just my learner's, Saturday before last."

"Good. If you need lessons or anything, give me a call. See ya." I stood there looking after her, amazed.

Charlie poked me in the ribs. "What's the matter?"

I shook myself and looked up at him. "Well, Ingrid and I have never been the best of friends."

"So, she's trying. What's wrong with that?"

"Nothing," I laughed a little, "nothing at all." We left the park and caught up to everyone else.

The party broke up about an hour after we got home. While everyone was running around and picking up their various belongings, Charlie and I took a walk. We got as far as the dark side of the garage and he kissed me. It was wonderful. I was so happy when I went up to bed I couldn't get to sleep. I thought about Charlie a lot. I thought about Wallace, too, and how well he fit in with the relatives, how well he fit into our lives—period. I was accepting the relationship between Mom and him. It didn't seem to be bothering me anymore. But I wasn't a little girl anymore, at least not when I was my real self, and I didn't need Mom the way I once did. Grandad had been so right when he said I would be leaving her one day and that I didn't want to leave her alone. I even hoped she and Wallace would get married and I daydreamed about the wedding. What a beautiful bride she would be!

Right before I fell asleep, I thought about Ingrid and decided that after the creep business was over I would call her. I would see if we couldn't be friends after all.

15

I woke up with a start the next morning. It was later than my usual time and the sun was already streaming in my window. And it was time to forget about being sixteen years old, time to forget how I had felt last night, and time to forget Charlie—well, not forget him, but put him somewhere in the back of my mind. I had to go back to being twelve years old.

I went to the area around Allegheny cemetery that day. I visited some landmark houses that were open to the public. Since they were left over from the American Revolution, they had real low ceilings and tiny rickety stairways. I felt right at home for a while; they were the first houses I'd ever been in that were small enough to suit me to a tee.

When I went up the stairs of one of them, I had a bad scare. The house was deserted except for a little old lady with blue hair, at the souvenir desk in the hall downstairs. She had grudgingly accepted my fifty cents for admission when I came in, and with a nod of her blue head, permitted me to roam around.

As I rounded the corner of the stairwell a man lurched out of one of the rooms above me and stumbled down the steps toward me. I held my breath, forgetting the microphone around my neck, forgetting my training, forgetting everything. I was literally scared stiff. When he got to the step above me, he stopped and looked me up and down. He stepped down the step, smiled, and said, "Enjoy your tour, little girl." Then he went on past me. I sat right down on the steps and waited until I could get myself together.

I gave up on the house then and practically ran outside. I sat on a bench. I was shaking like the proverbial leaf, but I managed to speak into the mike and say, "I am O.K. and now outside."

I headed across the street to the cemetery and for the rest of the day I was extremely careful. I pledged to the graves to be extremely careful for the rest of my life.

That night Wallace and Perky said the Wizard was coming by. Perky stayed for dinner and I wanted to ask him all sorts of questions about Charlie, but I was too shy. I was nervous about the Wizard coming over, too . . . wondering why and all that.

He arrived after dinner and I found out why. We all, including Mom, plunked ourselves down in the living room. It was a totally different scene from my party and even the day before seemed a long time ago.

The Wizard began sternly. "I hear you had a scare today, Sabrina."

"How did you find out so fast?" I was stunned.

"You're forgetting the car radio. And the microphone around your neck picked up the sounds of your breathing and the man speaking to you. Even though you tried to make light of it when you did re-establish communications, Detectives Wallace and Perkins here would have to be awful fools if they didn't realize you were scared to death."

I was guilty and I admitted it. I told them all about it. I had been stupid not to tell them in the first place—false pride and all that.

The Wizard leaned forward in his chair. "After Detective Wallace called me on the car radio . . . we checked out the man at the house. He works there cleaning up part time and he is slightly retarded. Definitely not our man. But Sabrina, you didn't follow your training today. You're to report everything. The main thing you should have done was to say over the mike, 'There's a man on the stairs.' You left the rest of your team hanging, not knowing whether to leave the car and come after you or to wait. You were lucky it wasn't our man."

He lit a cigarette, blew out the smoke, but his eyes never left my face. "I know you were frightened and fear is a natural thing for you to have under the circumstances. It's natural, but it's a luxury you can't afford." He looked around the room then. Talk about fear— there was Mom, white-faced and pinch-lipped again. He smiled reassuringly; I wondered if he knew her secret.

He turned back to me. "Sabrina, I am going to tell you something I have never told anyone before. About fear—my own. When I first started on the force . . . I was scared all the time. The only reason I became a policeman was because it offered security. I came from a very poor family and it seemed the only way out for me. As the years went by, I really settled in and I've become a damn good policeman. I wouldn't be anything else. But to get back to my original fear . . . I handled it the only way I knew how. I'd divorce myself from it. I would pretend I was anyone else, other than myself. One day I would be Dick Tracy, another day the Lone Ranger. Another time it would be Clark Kent, waiting for a crime to happen so that I could step into a phone booth and become Superman. Those were our heroes then."

He sat back in the chair and put his cigarette out. He looked glad that his secret was out. "Everyday it was someone else and it worked. One day, during a bank robbery, I stayed calm and cool. And I wasn't pretending to be someone else. I was myself. I think that's the day I decided to stay on the force." He gazed at me. "I'm not saying you should never be afraid, but while you're on this job, you're going to have to stay calm during a crisis. Then after it's over, you can break down."

That made a lot of sense to me. I didn't know if I could do it, but it sure made a lot of sense. The Wizard stayed awhile and everybody told stories about the times in their lives they were most afraid, and how they handled it. It was another group therapy session, and I felt much better afterward.

The Wizard reminded me again to be careful and to report everything over the mike. It had been almost two weeks since the creep had acted and he was due.

Perky left right after the Wizard, but on his way out he winked at me and said, "Charlie wants you to call him as soon as you can."

I practically ran to the phone. Charlie answered right away and we talked for about a half an hour. I told him about the man on the stairs and the Wizard and everything. He said, "Wow! I wish I could have been there. I would like to have heard that! Who are you going to pretend to be?"

"I haven't decided yet," I answered. "There aren't too many invincible women characters around. There's Wonder Woman . . . but she must be at least six feet tall. Same for the Bionic Woman. Maybe I could make up a character . . . you know . . . another side of me that's strong, mighty, and able to make cheesecake out of any creep that crosses my path."

"Aha! Bionic Brina! Sounds good," he said, naming my new character.

We finally said good-bye after we decided to get

together sometime over the weekend, even if it was just to sit around my house. He had to work at the garage on Saturday and said he would call when he got home.

Friday morning I went over to Shadyside. It was spitting rain half the day and I got soaked; the other half I dried out. Being on a stake-out was no fun. It wasn't a good day at all. Besides getting wet, there were too many people around. I was glad when I got home and found out the creep hadn't acted anywhere else.

At breakfast on Saturday I told everyone that Charlie wanted to come over that night. Was it O.K.?

Wallace said, "Perky—I have to stop calling him Perky—told me he told Charlie about you." I said yes.

"Well . . . Charlie's a good kid and I guess it's all right for you to be with him . . . but I don't think you should go anywhere. And please, Brina . . . never, ever tell the Wizard that Charlie knows about this." I said no, never.

Then Wallace said, "I mean it's all right with me if he comes over. But I guess you'd better ask your mother."

He looked at Mom. Grandad looked at Mom. I looked at Mom. "Stop looking at me, all of you." She laughed, "Of course, it's fine with me. What do you want to do?"

"I'll call Ella and see if she and Howard want to come over. That way we won't discuss the creep at all and I won't be too far away from you." I looked at Wallace and he nodded. Everyone looked at everyone else and we all nodded.

Charlie came over at about eight. Ella and Howard were already walking up the front walk. We all decided to play badminton in the backyard. I was so glad Charlie knew about the decoy business because when Ella and Howard wanted to go for pizza, Charlie gave

Howard the keys to his car and told him to get it and bring it back.

After they left, Charlie said, "I know you're not supposed to be seen around too much as your regular self and you're to stick close to Wallace."

"Yeah, and it's a bit of a downer."

He shrugged, "Rules always are. But I think it's a good idea. After all, nobody knows who the creep is. Maybe he makes pizza."

"Somebody would have spotted the tomato sauce on his jacket, flour on his nose, and mozzarella cheese hanging from his ear."

Charlie dropped the subject and kissed me.

After everyone left and I was headed for bed, Mom stopped me by saying, "You really like Charlie, don't you?"

"Are you kidding? He's great!"

"What about Paul?"

"He's great, too, as an older brother."

She put her arms around me and kissed the top of my head. "I am so glad to hear you say that! Now if we could give up this creep business, we could all have a pretty good life." She looked hopeful again.

I looked at her and said, "Uh huh." She knew I wasn't agreeing. I was sorry to disappoint her, but I was tired of being sorry.

Sunday was just another quiet day, but I did talk to Charlie on the phone. He wanted to know where I would be decoying—his words, not mine—the next day. I told him truthfully that I didn't know. The Wizard always did the planning and I never knew until the last minute where I was going.

It turned out to be Highland Park and I spent most of the day wandering around the reservoir. We only had a few places left before we started recycling places.

I told Charlie that night on the phone that I might go
buggy soon. It had been two and a half weeks since the
creep had acted and he was out there somewhere, looking for some little girl. I hoped it would be me. I was
getting over my fears by pretending to be Bionic Brina.
But now the suspense was making me edgy.

16

The next day, Tuesday, was my eleventh day on the
job, since the Fourth didn't count. I left the house
around the usual time, nine o'clock. I was getting so
used to the routine, and was beginning to believe that
nothing would ever happen, that maybe the creep had
gone to some other place, had died, or had all of a
sudden become a normal man and given up raping de-
fenseless little girls. Wallace reminded me at breakfast
not to let my guard down. As I walked to the bus stop,
I reminded myself to stay on my Mary-Jane-covered
toes, that I was now Bionic Brina and if there were any
creeps around I would catch them.

I took the bus downtown and changed to the old
Eighty-one streetcar. Pittsburgh is one of the few places
in the world that still has streetcars. Some smart cookie
even came up with the idea of decorating them. Stripes
are painted on them in bright colors going in all direc-
tions, with the word "Streetcar" lettered on the sides.
As if anyone could ever confuse them with a bus! It was
fun to ride on one again—almost as much fun as the

inclines that run up and down the steep side of Mount Washington, across the river from Pittsburgh proper.

I sat on the streetcar, swaying back and forth, and thought about riding on the incline again. Grandad and I used to go a lot when I was little, but we hadn't ridden them for years. The inclines are a big tourist attraction, and the view of Pittsburgh from the top of Mount Washington its terrific. But when you live somewhere you take those things for granted. I wondered if I would get the same feeling, sitting in the front of the car as it whooshed 400 feet down the tracks. It gave one a sense of falling, and I'd always been afraid it might, but even at that I'd loved it. I had so many things to do after I caught the creep. Everything in my life was now planned around catching the creep. But I put the incline on my list, wondering if Charlie would like to go.

I got off the streetcar in Oakland and crossed the street to Schenley Park. Our target for the day was Phipps Conservatory and the park surrounding it. I walked up the hill, toward the conservatory. It was another one of my favorite spots around Pittsburgh, but I had been there recently, for the spring flower show. It had been crowded then, as it was every spring and fall during the special shows. But as I walked inside to the Palm Room, I saw it was deserted except for a few gardeners and one guard.

All together there are twenty-two rooms, all glass enclosed. Thirteen are display rooms and the rest are growing rooms. I've never been to any other conservatory, but I'm sure there can't be another as magnificent as Phipps is.

I started touring the rooms. The conservatory's always hosed down in the mornings and it was dripping wet. I felt the steamy dampness all through me, from

the tip of my Mary Janes to the top of the wilting
ruffles on that dumb strawberry-print dress. I threw a
few pennies into the wishing pond as I passed. I wished
to catch the creep and get this thing I'd started over with.
I passed through the Orchid Room, the Cactus Room,
and ended up in my favorite, the Cabin Garden Room.
It looks like a country garden with an old house at the
end and a working waterwheel. The garden in front of
the house was a wild mass of daisies, yarrow, mari-
golds, zinnias, and phlox.

I knew I shouldn't stay long. Being seen around and
then isolating myself was still the plan. I decided to
make a quick sketch of the house and sat down on the
curved bench in the front of the room.

There were more people around by that time. There
was a group of strange-looking women, who sort of
skipped through. Their leader, a stocky, tough-looking
woman kept saying, "Come along, ladies, don't daw-
dle." I couldn't figure it out until one of the women
stopped to talk to me. She was dressed completely in
green—shoes, stockings, dress, hat, gloves—the works
—and on such a hot day. I thought she looked a bit
bonkers and then she told me she lived in a wonderful
place called Eastern Psychiatric. The Looney Bin!

Her nurse soon came to get her and that's when I
spotted my back-up cop for the first time. It dawned on
me that I had seen him around before, but most of the
time I'd forgotten about him. He blended into the wood-
work so well. But at a flower show it was impossible for
him to hide anywhere. The guards would have shooed
him out from behind any of the trees he was so fond of
hiding behind. He was standing out like a sore thumb
because he was trying to use a newspaper for cover and
who reads a newspaper at a flower show? The dummy
was supposed to be looking at the flowers. It was even

funnier the way he would rattle the paper, glance furtively around, and then pretend to read. But he never turned the page. I suppose I was the only one who noticed how strange he looked, after all, I had to notice everything around me.

I finished my sketch quickly, walked back through all the rooms, and went outside. The sun was playing games with the clouds as I walked down the path to the Nature Study Museum. It was getting overcast. I hoped it wouldn't rain, and popped into the museum to see what was happening in there. Absolutely nothing. There was nothing to see either. They had a notice over the squirrel and rabbit cages that they had to let the live animals go because of lack of funds. It was too bad they didn't have any money, but a few minutes later, back on the grounds, I saw a squirrel running around and another climbing up a tree. I was so glad they weren't in cages.

I stood there for a moment deciding which way to go and the stifling thought occurred to me that I was in a cage, and that the creep was my keeper. I tried not to think about it. After all, the cage was of my own making.

I headed along a path away from the Nature Study Museum, crossed a road, and continued on behind the conservatory. I'd spotted Wallace's car in front of the conservatory when I went in and now I saw it through the trees on the road to my left. I kept walking until I came to a park bench near some thick woods. I decided, or rather my stomach decided, that it must be time for lunch. I sat down on the bench and told everyone over the mike where I was. The bench faced the road and when I craned my neck, I could just see enough through the trees to watch Wallace ease the car to a stop and scrunch down. The stake-out had to be hard on them, too—perhaps even harder on them than me. At least I was free to roam; they were confined to the car. They had a different cage than I did. Mine was in my mind.

I looked back toward the Nature Study Museum and saw my back-up cop again. He was waiting for a hot dog vendor to open up his cart. I wasn't the only one getting ready for lunch.

I looked around to get my bearings and saw the cutest stone hut in the trees to my left. It was probably built around the 1890s, the same time as the conservatory. It looked as though it wasn't used much. Maybe it stored the outdoor gardener's tools. I thought I'd sketch it after I ate and stay there for the rest of the afternoon. There was a tiny window on the side of the hut facing me. I thought maybe my back-up cop could hide inside it and watch me through the window. Probably not. He liked trees too much.

Off to my right the path became dirt instead of concrete and went through some very dense woods. I really was isolated, but tried not to let it bother me. I tried to get rid of the brooding feelings of being caged and watched and creeped up on that had been worrying me. It was getting gloomier and gloomier, looking more like rain, while I sat and convinced myself that I was Bionic Brina and that no harm could come to me after all.

I made myself as comfortable as I could on the bench. It was a pretty rickety old thing and it creaked dangerously as I reached into my tote bag for an apple.

Suddenly three boys came out of the woods on my right. They were about fourteen and real rough looking. They stopped and stared at me. I said over the mike, "Three boys coming my way. It's O.K." Famous last words. They whispered and nudged each other. They ran over to me. One grabbed my purse, the second my tote bag, and the third pushed me and the bench over! They were headed back the way they came in a flash.

I was trying to pick myself up when the door of the hut opened. A big man came charging over to me. He was dressed like a gardener, with baggy clothes and big gardening gloves covered his hands. He picked me up off the bench and said, "Those nasty boys! They hurt you. I'll take you into the hut and fix you up." He was holding me tight! Too tight! I pushed against his chest and managed to look up and into his eyes. They were wild and crazy. His whole face was distorted. He was breathing heavily. He started carrying me back to the hut. Toward the hut! And then I realized. I had found the creep.

I screamed. "The creep's got me!! The creep's got—" His strong hand covered my open mouth.

"Be quiet now, little girl," he said, in a soft whiney voice that sent fear down my back. I kicked out at him and made contact with his kneecap. Mary Janes are not the strongest shoes in the world and I hurt my foot.

Where was everybody? Why didn't they come? They must have heard me. They must have heard the creep. He kept murmuring, "Sweet little girl—so pretty."

He had me inside the hut with the door shut in two seconds. He dumped me on the floor. I tried to get up again, but he pushed me down. There was a dim, single light bulb hanging from the ceiling. It shed enough light for me to see the creep. He must have turned it on when we came in so he could see me. That was the gruesomest thought I'd ever had. I felt the bile rising in my throat. Where was Wallace? Grandad? Perky?

I opened my mouth to yell and he was on top of me, pinning both my hands behind me with one hand and covering my mouth again with the other.

I heard footsteps and shouts outside. I thought, "Oh, thank God. Now they'll find me." The shouts grew louder, they sounded like they were right outside. I kept thinking, "Hurry, Wallace. Oh hurry!" Then the noise outside faded away. The footsteps ran on by. I don't think the creep heard anything. He was too busy concentrating on me.

I tried to relax. Remember my training. Catch him off guard so I could knee him. But he was so big. It seemed like there was a truck on top of me.

He loosened his hold on my mouth and was reaching downward, sort of caressing my neck . . . I could feel the roughness of his gloves. I screamed, "Wallace. . . ." He hit me. I was stunned for a moment.

He grabbed at the ruffles around my neck. He ripped them right off my dress. Then the craziness started leaving his eyes. Surprise took its place. He had seen the mike.

"What the hell?" He was staring at it.

"I'm a cop!" I screamed as loud as I could.

It took him a second. He stared at me. Then he realized what I'd said and he was up and running for the door. I scrambled and caught his foot—not sick any longer, but fighting mad. He kicked me aside easily and went out the door, slamming it behind him.

He was gone. I struggled to my feet and tripped over a rake. I'd been right about it being a gardener's hut, but what a way to find out. Another precious minute to get up again. Then I yelled and screamed while I limped over to the door. "Wallace! Wallace!" I tried to open the door. It was stuck! He must have really slammed it. I heard a noise outside. I yelled again, "Wallace!" I pounded on the door. My throat hurt from screaming, my hands from pounding, and my leg from the rake.

"Wallace . . . I'm in the hut!" The door gave way and Wallace was on the other side. I rushed into his arms.

He dragged me over to the bench and propped me up with one arm while he righted the bench with the other. Then we both sat and I rubbed my leg when Perky, Grandad, and the back-up cop came along the path from the direction the boys had gone in.

"They got away," said Perky breathing heavily and clutching my red purse and tote bag to his chest. "They dropped these."

"What were you doing in the hut?" Wallace demanded of me.

"What do you mean, what was I doing in the hut?" I asked angrily. "Why didn't you go after the creep?"

"The creep? Where?" Wallace jumped up. "Where was he?"

"He was hiding in the hut. He must have seen me earlier and he ducked into the hut when he saw me coming this way."

"Oh, no! We really blew it." Wallace looked terrible. "When the mike went dead, we thought the boys had done something to you."

"The mike was dead? For how long? Didn't you hear anything?"

"Nothing. We heard you say the boys were coming toward you and that was it."

"They pushed me over. . . ."

"That's it. The mike must have come loose from the transmitter. We came up from the car and saw the boys running through the trees. We thought they were taking you off somewhere so we followed them. They split up and when I saw you weren't with them I came back to find you."

"Those damn kids. I'll kill them!" I was yelling again, "Will you get going? Get after him."

Wallace looked down at me. "We'll take a look, but I'm sorry, Brina. He's got to be long gone. Harry, take Brina down to the car. We'll be back soon." He signaled the other two. Perky went one way and the back-up cop went the other. Wallace headed back to the conservatory and Grandad helped me down to the car. We got in the back seat and I looked down at my leg. It was hurting more now and it was bleeding a little. My face still hurt, too, where the creep had hit me. Everything hurt. But the biggest hurt of all was loosing the creep.

Grandad took out his bandana and wrapped it around my leg. He put his arm around me and I snuffled into his jumpsuit. He said, "Don't feel badly, Brina. You did the best you could."

I raised my head and wiped the tears away with the back of my hand. "I can't help feeling awful. All that work I put into this and those damn kids come along and it's over. I had him and he gets away. I had him! Damn it, I had him!"

"Now, now, Brina. All sorts of unexpected things happen. You can never predict these things."

"But it's not fair!"

"I know it's not fair. Sometimes life just isn't fair. But you tried . . . oh, I don't know what to say to you. Where are all those wise sayings when you need them?"

I didn't even pay attention to Grandad's attempt at humor—I was too mad and I still hurt all over. "Those turkeys! I hope they get run over by a streetcar. I hope they die!" I babbled on and on. Grandad tried to comfort me and was still trying when Wallace came back to the car.

"Well, he got away for sure," he said as he got in. "The hot dog vendor saw someone run past the Nature Study Museum and then he heard a car start up. He thinks it went down Panther Hollow Road. The creep probably knows this area, too. That's only a service road and it goes all the way out the back of the park. He's probably in Squirrel Hill by now. The vendor didn't see what kind of car . . . didn't even see the creep really. We lost him. Damn it! Are you all right, Brina?" He looked worse than I felt. I knew this wasn't the time to complain to him. I just keep hanging on to Grandad, and nodded.

When Wallace radioed in to headquarters, the Wizard told him to take me to Magee Hospital, the nearest one, and have them check me over. All the way to the hospital I concentrated on every detail about the creep I could remember. I ran it over and over again in my mind, shutting out the anger and frustration. I barely noticed picking up Perky outside the park. It didn't register until later that he was still holding the tote bag and that stupid red purse. That was the only funny part of the whole thing.

My leg was bandaged at the hospital and they gave me an aspirin for my now throbbing head. Back in the car I took my sketch pad out of the tote bag and set to work on a description of the creep. I made notes and sketches. My notes were jumbled and my sketches were worse; it's hard to write in a car, let alone draw. This is what I wrote: About 5′ 11″ or 6′ tall, big boned and heavy set. Brown eyes, dark brown or black hair. Ruddy complexion. Heavy dark eyebrows. Small but bushy dark moustache. Old cap with a visor, pulled low. Khaki work pants and shirt. Could be passing as a gardener. No marks or scars that I could see. Wearing gardener's gloves. Forty-five to fifty. Slight cleft in chin. Ears average size as far as I can remember. Nose straight, slightly bulbous on the tip. Some heaviness in the chin which was slightly jowly, but no adam's apple.

Upper lip thin, lower lip full. Voice at first whiney, but changed to a lower range when he saw the mike. That was probably his normal voice. Didn't hear much of it, but might be able to recognize it again. Would be able to recognize him, though.

The difference between the way he acted before and after he realized it was a trap was strange. Before he seemed really crazy and after he was like an intelligent, sort of crafty person. Almost two different people.

I made some real quick sketches that I felt confident I could go over later and improve. I concentrated on shapes of his features—his face—more than on little details, and by that time we were at headquarters. I was whisked up to the Wizard's office where he was waiting impatiently. I walked in and the first thing I said was, "I'm sorry, Sergeant Zolkalski."

"I'm sure you couldn't help it, Sabrina, you've been a good police, uh, girl." That was the first time I'd ever seen him at a loss for words. But we were all at a loss for words.

We eventually began to get on with normal procedures. Grandad called Mom and told her what had happened and that I was alright. She was worried; I could tell by the way he was acting. He told her to come over and see for herself and to bring me a change of clothes, since the police would want mine.

That was true. The police lab would go over my clothes with microscopes and scanners. I'd seen the labs when I was in training. They would look for a hair, a thread, anything. They would go over the hut, too, for fingerprints, but he'd been wearing gloves.

A girl from the lab came up and looked at my fingernails and skin. She brought a lab gown and a funny striped robe for me and everyone waited outside while I changed. She took all my clothes with her, even the

Mary Janes. I found out later that even though the Mary Janes were ineffective in kicking the creep, there was a thread from his pants attached to one of them. They found no other clues, but still and all, a thread was a thread.

After she left, we all sat in the Wizard's office. I felt kind of dumb in that striped robe, but I forgot about it after we started looking at my notes and sketches. We all pored over them and I kept adding little details to this eye and that mouth. The Wizard said I would have to work with the police artist later.

He tried to reassure me and said that at least it was more than they had before. But I couldn't help thinking—if only—. And I should have—. I could have—. And I wish—. A whole lot of good that did me.

The Wizard found out I'd missed lunch and sent out for a sandwich and coffee—light with two sugars. I drank the coffee but the sandwich stayed in its wrapper. I felt like I'd swallowed a bunch of balloons filled with water and they were rolling around in my stomach.

The door flew open, and Mom stood there like an avenging angel. She was holding a shopping bag from a local department store and she ignored everyone in the room but me. She stomped over to me, threw the bag on the floor, and knelt down in front of me.

"Are you all right?" she asked, peering closely at me.

My tears of frustration started again. "Oh Mom!" I cried and cried.

She turned and glanced up at the group in the office, looking dumbly at each other. She said, through clenched teeth, "Get out! Leave my daughter and me alone!"

She didn't have to tell them twice. They all bumped into each other on their way out. Even Grandad had sense enough to leave.

When we were alone, with the door closed, she wiped my tears away and said, "How far did he get? Where are your clothes? Why do you have that robe on? What's that bandage?"

I answered her fast, "I was only alone with him for a few minutes. All he did was tear my dress." I told her about the boys, the creep seeing the mike, my clothes going to the lab, and everything.

While I was talking, she stood up and then sat on the Wizard's desk. I was glad he wasn't there to see it. She crossed her arms in front of her and listened.

"Are you sure that's it. He didn't do anything to you?"

I assured her that I was intact, except for my leg.

"Well! I'm so relieved it's over. This thing has been making me buggy," she said fervently. "I stopped by Gimbel's and bought you some jeans and a T-shirt. I got those dumb clogs you've been wanting, too. I'm sorry I didn't buy them before. All I could think of while I was buying them was you could have been killed."

Clogs! I'd been wanting them for ages. That distracted me for a minute, but then she started crying. Seeing her cry started me off again, too. We almost drowned the Wizard's office.

"We'd better get ourselves together," she said finally. "We can't stay here forever."

"Yeah. The Wizard must be lost without his office. I'll change my clothes."

Mom giggled nervously. "He'll have to mop up in here before he can use it. Picture him with a mop."

We both giggled at that. While I was changing into my new clothes she said, "I hope this is the end of all this—this terror!"

I hadn't thought about that, about what would happen next. Was it over? Should I try again? Could I even bring myself to try again? I decided—as long as the creep was out there—I'd try again. If I got the chance.

"Mom—if they want me to try again, I will."

"Haven't you had enough? It's bad enough that I can't take anymore of this. But you shouldn't have to. Have I raised some sort of masochist? Brina, please drop it now." She got up from the desk and stood in front of me. "It's over! Accept it. Become a normal sixteen-year-old! For God's sake—you're only sixteen!"

"But I've had the training."

"Yes! You had the training and you lost him! And now he knows what you look like. Have you thought about that? What goes on in that head of yours?"

I didn't know what was going on in my head. But I didn't want to let the creep get away. She took a deep breath and said again, "He knows what you look like! And that scares me! It would scare you if you weren't half-witted."

"I could always wear a disguise. A blonde wig or something."

"Very funny!" She grimaced. "C'mon, hurry up! I want to get you out of here, to get you home. We'll have to have Doc Warnick look at that leg, in case the hospital missed something." The mother instinct was going strong in her.

I was all dressed so she opened the door. Wallace and Grandad almost fell in. Perky and the Wizard weren't far behind.

Before I was given permission to leave, I worked with a police artist for about an hour. It was a sort of therapy for me, because it eased the frustration. His name was Wayne and he was short and very sweet. He was impressed with my sketches and said I made his job a lot easier. He asked if I had given any thought to becoming a police artist. I hadn't, but I said I would.

The drawing, when it was done to our satisfaction, not only looked like the creep, but had more life to it than most of the composite drawings I'd seen. He told me to call him if I remembered anything else.

The Wizard gave us a little speech about not telling anyone what had happened and I was allowed to leave. Wallace and Grandad started home in Wallace's car and Mom and me in hers. We didn't say much on the way home. I could see she was still upset and I wasn't exactly calm myself.

Doc Warnick came over soon after we got home. He believed the story Mom made up about my tripping over a rake in a friend's garage and then being taken to a hospital nearby. He said the doctor in the hospital had done everything that was necessary.

By the time he left the balloons were gone from my stomach and I was starving. Wallace sat Mom and Grandad down with drinks and he cooked dinner. I'd had no idea he could cook so well. He fried chicken, mashed potatoes, and made gravy. He said he had had to learn or he would have been fast-fooded to death. If the police artist was a sort of therapy for me, cooking apparently was therapy for him. He banged pots and pans around, picked things up and threw them down and cussed heartily at that poor chicken. When dinner was ready he was back to his normal self.

After dinner Perky called to see how I was. I got on the phone with him and he said, "You did a fine job, Brina. It's too bad we didn't think about someone else taking advantage of you being alone like that. But we all make mistakes, and this certainly wasn't your fault." That was the longest speech I'd ever heard from him. Then he sort of coughed, went back to being quiet

Perky, and mumbled that Charlie was waiting to talk to me.

I had to tell the whole story to Charlie—the kids, the transmitter, the creep, every single detail. He suggested suing the company that made the mike and transmitter. I suggested we go find the kids and string them up on the nearest tree. Before he hung up, he did say there was a consolation prize. He reminded me that there would be no more restrictions on me and we could really start going out and doing things. He said he'd come over the next night and we'd have a real date!

After that cheering conversation, I went out to the front porch and thought about it. No more fear. Maybe Mom was right after all. I could be a normal sixteen-year-old, with a boyfriend and everything.

I was just thinking along those lines when Wallace came out. He asked if I was O.K. and I told him what I was thinking. He looked very uncomfortable, sighed, looked out to the street, turned back to me, plopped himself down on the squeaky rocker and said, "Honey, I am so sorry about today. But it isn't quite over yet. The creep knows what you look like and he knows he was set up. More importantly he knows you know what he looks like—that you may be able to identify him. The drawing that you and the artist put together today is more than we've had to go on before, a lot more. It will be released to the news media the day after tomorrow. His face will be splashed all over the papers and on TV. He'll know that you helped the artist put it together. If he should see you around, he might want revenge or just want to get you out of the way."

I felt trapped again. "Then I can't go out with Charlie? For how long?" I stared at him.

"Give it a couple of weeks anyway." He got up from the rocker and came over to the glider. He sat beside me and took the hand that I had been unconsciously pounding on the cushion of the glider. "Then when you do go out, you'll have to remember what the Wizard said about changing your appearance and looking older. You'll still have to be extremely careful and you'll still have to let me know where you're going."

"I didn't think this would happen! It's bad enough I lost him, but now you're telling me I might still be in danger. Why don't you just put me back on the streets again? Let me catch him. I won't live my life being threatened all the time."

"We can't take any more chances with you. He wouldn't be stupid enough to pick you up as a little girl again. But if he saw you as your real self and realized who you were. . . ." He didn't have the chance to finish. I tore my hand away from his, jumped up, ran into the house, and up to my safe, lovely blue room.

By the time I got there, I was sobbing uncontrollably. Mom came up a few minutes later and held me until I was quiet. She talked about nonsensical things until I fell asleep. Neither one of us discussed the creep.

17

The next morning I was up and running around before I remembered there was nothing to do. At the age of sixteen, I was a retired police person without a pension. I remembered my outburst of crying the night before and felt a little ashamed of myself. I went downstairs and roamed around the house. Nobody was up. I made myself some coffee; I *was* becoming addicted to the stuff. I went out to the front porch and sat on the glider where it had all begun. I felt awful.

That's where Grandad found me. He came out in his pj's and sat down quietly beside me. "Brina," he said, "it strikes me that you and I need a small vacation. Let's go up to the farm for a week or so."

"You're trying to get me out of the creep's way, aren't you?" That came out spitefully and I was immediately ashamed again.

"Can't pull the wool over your eyes . . . can I?" He looked at me. "O.K. You're right. But after all you've been through lately, it would be good for you to get away. You had a terrible shock yesterday and last night was your reaction to it."

"Oh. So that was it. I wondered why I couldn't stop."

"Yep. It's only natural to react to stress that way and you're probably depressed now. So let's get away and forget the creep. Let's have some fun. At least you scared him off and I, for one, have had a lot more activity lately than I'm used to. I'd like to have a rest and enjoy myself for a change. And I can't think of a better place than the farm."

I really didn't want to go. I wanted to stick around and see more of Charlie but I couldn't go anywhere anyway. To go away and forget everything for a while might be good. The thing that finally decided me was Grandad. He looked worn out. He had supported me all the way through and it was my turn to support him.

"O.K. When do you want to go?"

"Tomorrow. I'll call Gertrude tonight and tell her we're coming. That way you can see Charlie before we leave."

"You got a deal!" We shook hands on it.

The next morning we loaded up the Buick and took off for the farm. I felt free for the first time in what seemed like five hundred years. Charlie had come over the night before and I had dumped on him a bit. He'd said he didn't mind. In a way, I guess he was like Perky, kind of steady and faithful. He said he'd be there when I got back. That was a nice thought.

It was a cloudy, rather damp day and as we traveled toward the farm I hoped it wouldn't rain. Rain always makes Grandad sleepy and sort of grumpy. I asked him how he ever managed to drive one of those big trains when it rained and he said he always sang to keep awake. We sang silly songs all the way over the new freeway toward Kittanning, Rural Valley, and Smicksburg.

When we made the turnoff to the farm we passed some Amish people driving their buggies on the bumpy old road. Grandad said they were buying up a lot of land around Smicksburg. Their original settling place at Lancaster, Pennsylvania, was getting overcrowded. They looked so interesting, I wished we could stop and talk to them, but Grandad said they kept pretty much to themselves. We passed one Amish girl on the road who turned and glanced at us with a fearful look on her face. I asked Grandad why she would be afraid of us. He told me they'd been hassled by some of the people around there who didn't understand their religion and picked on them because they were different. I had an impulse to get out of the car and reassure her, but I didn't. She reminded me too much of my own fear.

At the end of the road we came to Aunt Gertrude's farm. It's perched on top of a hill, overlooking Smicksburg. The town looks like a toy village under a Christmas tree from up there. It's so peaceful. It was hard to imagine anyone being afraid around there.

The door to the farmhouse opened and Aunt Gertrude came hurrying to meet us. "How good to see you both so soon!" she fluttered, her whole tiny self aglow. She looks a lot like both of us, but especially me. Same height, same blue eyes, short grey hair rather than long brown hair, but with a whole lot more energy. It seems to vibrate the very air around her. She buzzed and buzzed around us. Telling us over and over how glad she was we were there. Grandad had to stop her from carrying all our suitcases into the house by herself.

Inside the farmhouse I looked at all the super things there. Before Uncle Ronald had died, he had had a hobby of repairing old toys and games. Amidst the clutter of the large living room was an old bowling machine, a pinball machine, and an old jukebox. I wished Charlie could see it. There were wind-up toys, old battery-operated toys, and music boxes. All sorts of good stuff.

I took my suitcase up to the room I always stayed in and I was happy to see nothing had changed it. It still had the old-fashioned commode in the corner and the funny old bed with a rope net supporting the mattress instead of box springs. It was more like a hammock than a bed.

I unpacked my suitcase, then ran down to the big old-fashioned kitchen. It always has a good smell about it, whether anything's cooking or not. This time something was cooking. Aunt Gertrude is one of those people who cook enough food for an army even when there are only three people. She always says, "Well, you never know who might drop in." We had ham, home fries, and freshly baked apple pie—her specialty—for dessert. And that was only lunch.

After we ate, I left Grandad and Aunt Gertrude talking at the kitchen table and took my groaning stomach outside to check out the livestock, such as it was. Aunt

Gertrude had sold a lot of the land to the Amish people and only kept some chickens, a few pigs, one hog, and a gentle old mare. It isn't much of a farm by a real farmer's standards, but who cares? To a city-suburb kid like me, it's great!

I wished I could ride the mare, but I'd never learned to ride, so I contented myself by sitting on the fence and telling her what I had had for lunch. She was having grass for hers.

It never did get around to raining that day, so Grandad stayed awake and we went down to Smicksburg to say hello to his cousin George. He's the local postmaster and he collects antique toys and games just like Uncle Ronald. Visiting around there is like going to my own private flea market. He even had an old Charlie McCarthy ventriloquist doll, which he propped on his knee and did a whole act with. He tried to show me how to throw my voice, but I couldn't quite get the hang of it. Or the throw of it.

For the rest of the time I ate—oh, did I eat—sketched and painted and took long walks in the woods. Grandad taught me to ride the old mare. I fell off three times, but she was patient with me. I finally managed to ride her around the meadow.

We'd decided to stay for at least a week and a half and I was having such a good time, I almost forgot all my fears and tensions. But one day, when I was painting a picture of the barn, a new thought occurred to me. I had come to grips with the fact that I hadn't caught the creep, and I had faced the idea that I would have to be careful for awhile. But I still wanted to do something.

I had thought, so long ago, of ringing every doorbell in Pittsburgh and warning every little kid personally. I knew that wouldn't work, but an advertising campaign against the creep might. The sketch the artist and I worked on was in the paper the morning of the day we left for the farm. It looked good to me, but would it mean anything to anyone else? Would anyone else study those features the way I had? Would they be able to recognize the shape of the head, the eye, the mouth? Another artist might, but what about your ordinary everyday kid? Not unless they were warned to look out for the creep. And I could do that. I could warn people. An advertising campaign against him would work; I'd make it work. Then everyone would be looking out for him and he'd get caught. I wouldn't have to be afraid anymore.

After I thought up my new idea, I was anxious to get home and plan my strategy. I wanted to talk to Charlie. I was sure he'd help me.

I enjoyed the rest of the time at the farm, though. I gave my painting of the barn to Aunt Gertrude when we left. The other paintings and sketches I kept. I thought Wallace would like to have the one of Grandad sitting on the porch of the farmhouse, taking an afternoon nap, his railroad cap hanging off one side of his face.

We left on Saturday afternoon and all the way back to Pittsburgh I was excited, not only about seeing Charlie but about starting my new anti-creep campaign.

About twenty minutes from the house the old Buick gave a cough, a snort, and a wheeze. We just managed to limp into a gas station. We had to leave it there for repairs and Mom came down to pick us up.

When we did get home, it was to good news and medium bad news. The good news was that the creep hadn't attacked any more little girls and the medium bad news was that I still had to be careful. I would be allowed more freedom, but I still wouldn't be allowed to go anywhere without being with someone. That put a damper on my anti-creep campaign, but I figured I'd find a way. Undaunted—that was me.

Wallace got dinner ready while we all caught up on each other. I guessed that he had gotten used to cooking all the meals since Grandad and I had been gone, Mom not being much of a wonder in the kitchen. Mom looked wonderful—happy and much more relaxed. No more fearful looks in my direction. She said that Charlie had called twice to see when I was coming home. When he found out I'd be home for sure that evening, he said he would pop by. That was even better news.

Grandad said maybe Charlie could fix the old Buick. Wallace said to forget it, retire it and buy a new car. Mom seconded the motion, but Grandad got a little stubborn and said he'd give it awhile before he put it out to pasture.

Charlie did come over after dinner. We asked Wallace if we could go to a drive-in movie and he said that was fine. It was also fun! After the movie, we stopped at a drive-in ice cream place and I told Charlie about my new idea. He thought it over for a minute and then said, "Not bad. How are you going to go about it?"

I showed him one of the "Citizens' Watch" pamphlets I'd picked up during my training, and we looked over the hints for children's safety. I told him I thought if we took those hints and sort of condensed them, we could have leaflets printed up and then pass them out in shopping centers. The leaflets would be directed against creeps in general, not just my specific creep.

He thought it over. "It's sort of a drop in the bucket . . . I mean, how many could you afford to get? And where would you have them printed?"

I guessed I could go to one of those fast printers. I

had the money I'd been saving before all this happened. And even if it was a drop in the bucket . . . at least it was something I felt would be worth it, to reach one little kid or one parent of one little kid.

"You know, you might be right. It's kind of a far-out idea." He thought again, and again I could almost see his resemblance to Perky. "I've got it! Besides the leaflets—how about some posters for the kids. If we could get posters put up in libraries warning kids in simple language they would understand, then we'd be hitting your creep's and all the creeps' source."

"Yes! Yes. I can see that. Not just libraries, but stores where the kids hang out, places like that. But I don't know how many posters I could afford."

"I think my mother knows a printer. She's into a lot of community affairs. Maybe we could get a special price. Yeah . . . I like this idea. Let's rewrite these safety hints." Charlie took out a pen and we started rewriting and simplifying the hints in the pamphlet.

By the time Charlie took me home, we had a pretty good idea of what the leaflets and posters should say. I felt strongly that it was a good thing to do. The last thing Charlie said before he kissed me good night was, "I really admire you. Your first idea didn't work out so you get another. That's super!"

With such positive thinking, admiration, and kissing and stuff, I positively floated up the stairs.

I worked on the leaflets and posters all the next day and when Charlie came over that night I had them ready. I geared the leaflets for parents and used the same things the "Citizens' Watch" pamphlet said, but simpler, and I hand-lettered the whole thing in block letters. I drew an eyeball over the word eye. It was corny, but as Charlie said, "Eye-catching." It said:

KEEP AN EYE ON YOUR CHILDREN

YOUR CHILDREN ARE PRECIOUS. UNFORTUNATELY THERE ARE PEOPLE AROUND WHO MAY INTEND TO HARM YOUR CHILDREN. THESE DAYS THE NEWS MEDIA IS MAKING US MORE AWARE OF THE DANGER YOUR CHILD MAY BE IN. IF YOU ARE AWARE OF THE DANGER . . . YOU MAY BE ABLE TO HELP YOUR CHILD BE MORE AWARE AND EITHER STOP THE DANGER FROM HAPPENING OR POSSIBLY CONTRIBUTE TO THE ARREST OR CONVICTION OF A CRIMINAL.

FOURTEEN SAFETY HINTS
TO HELP YOUR CHILDREN:

1. TELL YOUR CHILDREN THAT A CRIMINAL RARELY LOOKS LIKE ONE. HE COULD BE ANYONE'S FRIENDLY FATHER OR UNCLE. REMIND THEM THAT SOME CRIMINALS ARE FEMALE.

2. TEACH YOUR CHILD TO BE AWARE. PREPARE HIM OR HER FOR DANGER IF IT SHOULD OCCUR. DON'T TEACH HIM OR HER TO BE CONSTANTLY AFRAID . . . JUST TO BE CAREFUL.

3. TEACH YOUR CHILD NEVER TO ACCEPT RIDES, CANDY, OR GIFTS FROM STRANGERS.

4. GIVE YOUR CHILDREN A SENSE OF INDEPENDENCE BY LETTING THEM PROTECT THEMSELVES AND OTHERS.

5. TEACH YOUR CHILD TO DIAL 911 OR 0 FOR OPERATOR IN AN EMERGENCY.

6. POST A LIST OF PHONE NUMBERS ABOVE YOUR PHONE. THESE NUMBERS SHOULD INCLUDE YOUR LOCAL POLICE PRECINCT AND AT LEAST THREE OF YOUR NEAREST FRIENDS AND NEIGHBORS.

7. YOUR CHILD SHOULD HAVE A KEY TO YOUR HOUSE OR APARTMENT . . . BUT THE KEY SHOULD NOT HAVE A NAME OR ADDRESS ON IT.

8. TEACH YOUR CHILDREN NOT TO ANSWER THE DOOR TO STRANGERS . . . EVEN IF THEY SAY MOMMY AND DADDY SENT THEM.

9. TEACH YOUR CHILDREN NOT TO GIVE OUT ANY INFORMATION ON THE PHONE. TELL THEM IT IS ALWAYS BEST TO GIVE THE IMPRESSION THAT SOMEONE ELSE IS AT HOME WITH THEM.

10. TELL YOUR BABY-SITTER THE SAME BASIC RULES—SUCH AS NOT OPENING THE DOOR TO STRANGERS AND NOT GIVING ANY INFORMATION OVER THE PHONE. CALL HER ATTENTION TO THE LIST OF PHONE NUMBERS POSTED OVER THE PHONE. ALWAYS GIVE HER A PHONE NUMBER WHERE YOU CAN BE REACHED.

11. ORGANIZE A GROUP IN YOUR NEIGHBORHOOD TO WATCH OVER ALL THE CHILDREN NEARBY DURING PEAK HOURS SUCH AS AFTER SCHOOL. IF YOU ARE NEW TO THE NEIGHBORHOOD, INTRODUCE YOURSELF AND YOUR CHILDREN TO YOUR NEIGHBORS.

12. INSTRUCT YOUR CHILD TO REPORT ANY STRANGERS IN THE AREA . . . EVEN IF THEY LOOK INNOCENT.

13. TEACH YOUR CHILDREN TO DISTINGUISH ONE CAR FROM ANOTHER, SO THAT THEY MAY BE ABLE TO REPORT THE ACTUAL COLOR OR MAKE OF A CRIMINAL'S CAR.

14. TEACH YOUR CHILD TO RUN AT THE FIRST SIGN OF DANGER.

BE CAREFUL NOT CARELESS.

I showed Charlie the poster next. I had drawn four pictures on it . . . one of a man in a car talking to a little kid, one of a man trying to give a kid some candy, one of a man following a kid, and the last of a man putting his hand on a kid's shoulder. Over each of the pictures I had drawn a big red X. Beside the pictures I hand-lettered the words:

ATTENTION CHILDREN:

DO NOT GET INTO A CAR WITH A STRANGER.

DO NOT ACCEPT ANYTHING FROM A STRANGER.

IF YOU ARE BEING FOLLOWED, GO HOME OR TO THE NEAREST HOUSE OR STORE AND CALL THE POLICE.

DON'T EVER TALK TO A STRANGER . . . EVEN IF HE SAYS HE KNOWS YOU.

"You don't think that's a little strong, do you?" asked Charlie.

"I don't know," I answered truthfully. "It's just that kids don't pay much attention to anything and I figured the stronger I made it the more they'd notice it."

He sighed, "Oh, I suppose you're right about that. People always think that things won't happen to them, but they do."

We both sat and thought that one over. Charlie was just saying, "I'll call up my Mom's printer friend tomorrow and see if we can talk to him tomorrow night," when Wallace came out on the porch.

We showed him the leaflet and poster and explained the idea to him. He looked a bit perplexed at first and then said, "But Brina, you're not supposed to be seen around too much. At least not for a while. How are you going to pass these things out and not be seen?"

"Oh, I'll just do like the Wizard said and really dress

older. My clogs make me look taller and I'll wear sunglasses. I'll look different enough." I said it with more emphasis than I felt.

Wallace still looked skeptical, but Charlie said, "Listen! I've got the answer to that! We'll get some other kids to do the actual passing out of the leaflets and then Brina and I will get the libraries and stores to put up the posters."

He looked pleased with himself. "Don't you see—that way Brina will always be with me and most of the time we'll be in the car. If we get enough kids together it will probably just take one day. After all, Brina wants to do this and she's paying for it so we can't get that many leaflets or posters. See, Jim, it will just be one day of anti-creep campaigning, and then we'll see how it goes before we do anything else."

Wallace listened to Charlie's speech, looked him up and down, and said, "A little publicity against the creep couldn't hurt . . . I could even get more of those "Citizens' Watch" pamphlets for you to hand out. We try to cover community groups with those, but we've never had anyone to hand them out before."

"Great," said Charlie. "Brina, how many kids do you think you could line up for this?"

I gulped. I paused. I shuffled my feet on the porch floor, "Well . . ." I said slowly, "there's Ella . . . and Howard . . . and don't worry . . . I'll get some other kids." I'd never told Charlie about my lack of friends and this was not the time.

My new philosophy: When you don't have the answer to a question . . . ask the asker a question right back. "How many can you get, Charlie?"

"I've got two close friends from my school . . . they're the only ones from my group at home this summer. They have jobs, but I know they'll help. You

177

see. . . ." He stopped and looked suddenly doubtful. "Oh no . . . I forgot. One of them . . . Dick . . . it was his cousin . . . she was the first little girl the creep attacked." But then he brightened, "But he was so angry over it . . . I'm sure he'll help."

Mom came out on the porch then and wanted to know what was going on. We told her about the anti-creep campaign. She looked upset again and said to me, "Honestly, Brina . . . you have a one-track mind. You get fixed on an idea and you won't let go." What could I say to that? Nothing. "I thought we were through with this creep business."

Wallace put his arm around her and said. "It won't be over until the creep is caught."

She shrugged off his arm and gave us all a dirty look. She snorted a little and went back into the house. Wallace gave me a sympathetic look and said, "Don't worry, Brina, I'll talk to her. You know she never stays angry long."

Then, of course, Grandad came out to see what all the fuss was about. We showed him everything and explained. Good old Grandad. He was all for it!

18

Early the next evening, Charlie picked me up and we went over to his mother's printer friend. I dressed a little older—longish full denim skirt with big pockets on the sides, and a square neck T-shirt with blue flowers embroidered on it. I put my hair up in a knot. With lip gloss, the clogs, my chain watch, and last but not least, my gold hoop earrings, Charlie said I didn't look at all like a little girl. When he stopped in front of the printers he kissed me and I didn't feel at all like a little girl either.

The name of the print shop was Harvey's Speedo-Printing. And of course the name of the printer was Harvey. I liked him immediately. He was all covered with ink when we arrived because one of his machines had broken down and he was fixing it. He had a full plump face, a big nose, and kind of muddy grey eyes. That was topped off by the worst toupee I'd ever seen. It was like a small thick rug, perched on the back of a turtle. It was constantly sliding around on his head. I was fascinated by it.

He was fascinated by the leaflet and poster idea. He wanted to know why and how and everything. I told him about Annie's being attacked and that I just wanted to do something. Nothing about already having done something.

Harvey leaned over the poster and peered closely at it. The toupee slid so far forward I almost yelled, "Whoops! There she goes!" Stopped just in time. He grabbed at it and slid it all the way back on his head so that I could see the bumps on his upper forehead. I tried to tear my eyes away from it and listen to what he was saying.

He said he would give me a special price on the leaflets if he could put his shop's name, address, and phone number on the bottom. Sounded like a good deal to me.

He went on to the poster. He said it was another problem because it had two colors. But if I would order fifty or more and let him put his name on the bottom of them, too, he would do them for seventy-five cents apiece.

I ordered fifty of the posters and five hundred of the leaflets. He added the whole thing up and it came to $47.50. Grandad had slipped me a ten on my way out of the house so I didn't mind spending that much money. I knew it wouldn't be cheap.

I paid Harvey right away and he said they would be ready by Friday morning. It was Monday evening, so that only gave me three days to find some kids to help. I had to get busy!

Charlie had to take me right home from Harvey's. He'd promised his mother to take his kid brother clothes-shopping. It was only seven o'clock when I got back. Mom and Wallace were out. After I told Grandad all about Harvey and hugged him extra hard for the ten, I went up to Mom's room and stared at the phone.

I was trying to work up my nerve to call Ingrid. I was almost overcome by that terrible, terminal shyness, but then I recalled what the Wizard had said about fear. If pretending you were someone else would combat fear, maybe it would combat shyness, too. At least make it not so fatal. It was worth a try.

When I picked up the phone to call Ingrid, I was pretending to be my own social and charming mother! I needn't have bothered. All I had to do was identify myself and Ingrid said, "Oh, Brina! I've been meaning to call you. I have to talk to you about something. I have a favor to ask you. Do you think you could meet me for lunch downtown tomorrow? I'll explain then. I'm modeling at Goodhugh's, on the fifth floor, and I get a lunch break at twelve-thirty."

"Oh," I answered, "I didn't know you were modeling this summer." How was that for a scintillating answer?

"I've been modeling at Goodhugh's since I was twelve

years old." She sort of laughed. "But I hate it, so I don't talk about it much. They're all such snobs there." It wouldn't have made any difference if she had talked about it—I'd never talked about anything much with her.

I made some mental calculations. Grandad could escort me to the store and pick me up someplace after lunch. This bodyguard business was almost as bad as the decoy business! I told Ingrid to hang on and ran down to ask Grandad if he would mind. He said it was fine and he would check out Goodhugh's jumpsuits while he waited.

I ran back upstairs and Ingrid and I made arrangements to meet. Ingrid put the right name to it, Goodhugh's is a very snobby place. It's exclusive and to use Grandad's word—hotsy-totsy. I'd only been in the store once in my life and that was when Mom needed a dress for a country club dance with that lawyer she dated. It's one of those places where the sales ladies make you feel they're doing you a favor to wait on you.

When Grandad and I got to the store the next day, I was still pretending to be Mom, so I wasn't too intimidated by the aura of snobbishness. Grandad took me all the way up to the fifth floor, patted me on the head, and kindly disappeared.

I walked into the Teen Shoppe and there was Ingrid, modeling the most fantastic wool pants suit. She looked fresh and cool, but it must have been ninety in the shade that day. Even with the store's air conditioning, I started to sweat just watching her.

She motioned me over and took me into another, smaller, stuffy room with racks and racks of clothes. There were other models and women fitting them running around in front of a full length mirror. I caught a glimpse of Janie Andrews, one of the black beauties of our class, sweeping out the door to the showroom, in a full-length formal.

Ingrid changed into a cool summer skirt and matching top and we escaped all the confusion.

We went to Goodhugh's Tea Shoppe. I swear everything in that store is one Shoppe or another Shoppe. As we settled ourselves at a tiny table with tiny chairs, Ingrid said, "This place has the worst atmosphere. I've never seen so many fat women trying to fit themselves into such thin chairs. But the food is great! And the desserts positively sinful. Unfortunately, all I can have is a dumb salad. I'm on a perpetual diet. I guess you're not, you're so little." She sighed, looked up at the waitress hovering above our table, and ordered a spinach salad. I looked quickly at the menu and ordered a club sandwich.

She positively groaned. "I remember what a club sandwich is. I had one about a hundred years ago."

"You've been modeling since you were twelve?" That seemed an early age to start, but Ingrid got better looking every year. I looked at her wheat blonde hair in a blunt cut to her shoulders, her strange, but wondrous hazel eyes, and her slim but mature figure. I wondered how much better looking she could get.

"Yeah, my mother pushed me into it. The money is good, at least more than I could make anywhere else. I've been able to save a lot, since I get a real good discount. By the way, don't buy any clothes until you check out what we have here. If I buy something for you, I can get the discount and you can pay me later."

"Thanks," I said, not being able to figure out why she was being so nice to me, "but even with the discount these clothes have got to be too expensive for me."

"Yeah, I know. But if you should want something

special, for a special occasion—check with me first. Speaking of a special occasion, the reason why I wanted to talk to you . . ."—She paused and I waited. I couldn't imagine what was coming—"is I'd like to have a party. But to be honest, I can't have it at my house."

"Why?"

"Because my mother is an absolute—well, she's just not a very nice person. She wants me to concentrate on being a big-time model and nothing else. She doesn't understand that I need friends—other friends than the ones she picks. See—for years now I've admired you."

"Me? Why?" I still didn't know why she was talking to me.

"Do you remember that drawing of me you did in junior high school?"

I nodded. I also remembered that I hadn't been very happy with it.

"I still have it. I had it framed. Anyway, I wanted to thank you, but you were always so stand-offish."

"Stand-offish? Me?"

"Yeah. You and Ella are both so talented and are such good friends that you exclude everyone else."

"Exclude everyone else?" I was beginning to sound like an echo.

"Well, that's what I thought, but then I realized I had never tried all that hard to be friends with you, so maybe it was my fault. That's what I wanted to talk to you about. The other thing is the party. . . ." The waitress brought over our order then and we were quiet until she left. Ingrid speared a forkful of salad, eyed my club sandwich enviously, and went on. "Like I said, I can't have it at my house. My mother would take charge and make me invite only the kids she approves of. She's such a pain sometimes. I mean I'd love to invite Ella and Janie Andrews. You know Janie?"

"Yes. I saw her downstairs just now."

"Un huh." She swallowed some salad. "Well, she's been modeling here for the past two years. Anyway, my mother is so prejudiced, she would never let me invite them. I'd like to tell her to stick it in her ear, and I probably will as soon as I'm eighteen. But for right now, I have to live with it." Another bite of salad and another look at my club sandwich. "So . . . you have a great place to have a party and I thought if we got together and invited people we really admire and want to get to know . . . and I'd pay for the party. Then maybe that way I'd get to know them or even meet new people. Do you know what I mean?"

All that came out in a sudden spurt and then she faltered. I never thought I'd see the day when Ingrid would falter. I realized in a hurry that it was up to me to say the right thing to put her at ease.

"That's a great idea, Ingrid," I said, patting myself on the back when I saw her relax. "I've been wanting to meet new people, too. And my Grandad is great at putting food together and I know Mom would be for it. She's been trying to get me to meet new people. And Wallace is a good cook, too. . . ."

"Who's Wallace?"

"Wallace—well, he and my Mom live together."

"They do? That's something!" Her hazel eyes were enormous. I decided to ask her how she did her make-up; it looked so natural, but now I could see she was wearing some.

"What does he do?" She lay down her fork and stared at me.

"He's a cop."

"I never knew a cop." Quieter this time, "How long have they been living together? Your mother and . . . what's his name?"

"Uh . . . I think it's only . . ." For the life of me I couldn't remember how long it had been. About a month? Only a month? I was so used to him being around. "His name is Jim Wallace, but I call him Wallace."

"Who's that boy you were with at the fireworks?"

"His name is Charlie Perkins. His father and Wallace work together."

"He's good-looking. Will you invite him to the party?" I nodded. "Will he bring his friends? If he has friends that look like him, it will be some party. I figured the last weekend before Labor Day. Sort of an end-of-the-summer party. What do you think?"

"That's O.K. with me. I have to clear it with Mom and everyone, but they'll probably say yes." I stopped and then faltered myself. It was my turn to ask a favor. "Ingrid . . . I wanted to talk to you, too."

I began with the attack on Annie, but of course didn't mention anything about my police work. I described my feelings of anger and guilt. Ingrid was very easy to open up to. She asked all the right questions in all the right places. I wound up with a description of the leaflets and posters. Then, "So . . . I need your help, too. In passing out the leaflets. . . ."

"I'll do it. Trade off for the party. But not just for that—I've got a kid sister, too. She's really cute and I've been afraid for her." She thought for a moment, "And I can get Janie and Lois Good. Do you know her?"

Lois Good was on the intellectual side of our class. Short and round, with little round glasses. And I didn't know her. "I thought she was kind of, uh, serious," I said.

"I'm beginning to realize no one is ever what anyone thinks they are. Lois came down here last Christmas to write an article about modeling for the school paper and I got to know her." Ingrid started to laugh. "You'd really be surprised. She's very quiet at first and then she lets loose with a real mad kind of humor. A total nonsense type. I really like her."

"What's Janie really like? Ella doesn't seem to like her that much."

Ingrid looked sober. "Well, Janie is real sweet. But she's had a hard life and it's not that easy for her to let her guard down. She lives with an aunt and uncle and they've treated her badly. They have a little grocery store over on Broadway Road and they started her working in the store when she was eight years old. Can you imagine that? She started here two years ago and at first I thought she was really stuck on herself until this summer. But this summer she asked me to help her. She's been hiding her money from her aunt and uncle, afraid they would take it from her. She finally had to open a bank account, but she asked me to keep her bankbook. She pays them board money now to keep from working in the store."

"What a rotten thing. Maybe you're right about no one really being what you think they are." I finished the last of my club sandwich.

"Exactly. I'm sure I'm different from what you thought I was." I stared at her. She smiled, "That's one thing about me—I'm honest. And I really want to be friends with you, Brina. Listen . . . do you want dessert? I can't have any, but I'll watch you."

I decided not to have any. She'd watched every bite of the club sandwich and I couldn't stand to put her through any more pain. After all, I really wanted to be friends with her, too. And she wasn't at all like I thought she was.

She grabbed the check before I even knew it was on

the table. When we parted at the entrance to the Tea Shoppe she thanked me for coming and said she would speak to Janie that afternoon and call Lois that night and then give me a call. I thanked her for the lunch and walked away feeling great about what we'd accomplished in such a short time. I had found a new friend.

I caught up to Grandad in the Men's Shoppe. He was staring at a gold lamé jumpsuit with a wicked gleam in his eye. I pulled him away, saying that it wouldn't go with his red bandana.

19

At dinner that night I told everyone about Ingrid and her party plan and asked if it would be O.K. Everyone was up for it.

"That's marvelous," said Mom. "I really like that idea. But Ingrid doesn't have to pay for it. She can contribute, of course, but let's make it a real open house and invite everybody we know and everybody we've ever wanted to know. That way it will be fun for all of us. There are some people I know with kids that I haven't seen in ages. And Jim's friends and their kids. Wow! What fun. Why don't you call Ella, Ingrid, and Charlie and the kids that Ingrid was talking about and have a party-planning party. Then you can ask for their help with the leaflets and posters, too." She was in a fabulous mood. "I've changed my mind about your campaign. It is a good idea. At least it's better than having you roam the streets again, and I understand how you feel about losing the creep. I especially like warning the kids themselves."

There was such pride on her face. I thought what a neat person she was, especially after hearing about Ingrid's and Janie's situations. Mom and I had had our troubles, but there was never any lack of love between us.

I called Ella right after dinner and explained the whole thing. When I got to Janie, she said sarcastically, "Oh, Miss Black America." But after I told her what Ingrid said, her attitude changed.

We decided that Friday night would be the best time to have our planning party, since I would get the printed matter back from Harvey in the morning. If Ella was surprised at my involvement with the anti-creep campaign she never said anything and she seemed enthusiastic about it because of Annie.

Then I called Ingrid and she said she would call Janie and Lois. Then Charlie called me and I told him everything. Then I called Ingrid again and after what seemed like hours on the phone we had it all set for Friday night.

Grandad and I picked up the leaflets and posters on Friday morning. I was so pleased to see my work in print that I kept looking at them all day, while we put together the food for the pre-party party.

At eight-thirty the living room was full. Charlie brought the two friends he'd spoken of—Dick and Calvin. Ingrid brought Lois Good. Ella and Howard brought the captain of our school's basketball team, a tall serious black kid named Bill.

They all had their reasons for being there and for being willing to help with the anti-creep campaign. Ingrid —the party and her sister. Ella—because of Annie and, I guess, to help me. Charlie—as a concerned person, and his friend Dick—who's cousin had been an actual victim of the creep.

Ella, Howard, Lois, Dick, and Calvin planned to meet in the Mount Hope shopping center the next morning, pass out half the leaflets there, then go on to Briarwood in the afternoon. Charlie and I were to con people into putting up the posters and since there were fifty of them, Ingrid and Bill were elected, too.

We finally got around to planning the party. The list of people to ask kept growing. Mom, Wallace, and Grandad joined us and said invite everyone in the whole world! Grandad suggested the possibility of roasting a whole pig in the backyard—something he'd always wanted to do. The kids stared at him in amazement. None of them had ever seen the likes of my Grandad! When they got over the shock, they cheered him and he positively beamed.

I woke up the next morning and hopped out of bed. I felt better than I had for ages and was ready to launch my anti-creep campaign. I dressed to look older again and I was pleased with the result. I was beginning to look my age. Charlie took the day off from the garage and came over for breakfast. Then we went up to the shopping center to meet the others. It went well and the people who received the leaflets seemed generally receptive.

I did get one hassle though. Charlie and I had gone into the library where Annie had been picked up, and we had no problem putting up a poster there, but when we came out I saw a little five-and-ten store nearby. It was close to the grade school I'd gone to, and I knew that kids hung out there. I'd done my share of hanging out there, too. My allowance had gone there every week for six years. We walked in and I spoke to the owner, Mr. White. Everyone called him Whitey and he was shocked about the poster. At first he refused to have anything to do with it. He said it was vile and dirty, and nice people shouldn't have to look at it. I listened to his tirade and almost backed down, but then I remembered Annie. I lowered my voice so that he would have to shut up to hear me and said, "Do you know Annie Duvall?" I had to repeat it several times before he heard me.

"Yes. I know her," he said. "She's a sweet little kid. So what?"

I told him so what. I started with the first encounter and ended up with the attack. When I said, "So you see, Whitey, this poster may be vile according to you. But if Annie had seen it, it might have made all the difference. When the man approached her she would have known to run away."

He turned a rather pasty grey during my recital and then said, "I guess you're right. I wasn't thinking of that. I always want to protect the kids who come in here. I want them to have an innocent childhood. But I guess that's impossible these days. I'll put up the poster." He looked unhappy. "I don't like it. But I'll put it up."

I felt sorry for him but as we left the store, Charlie said, "I really like the way you stood up to him—I couldn't have done it." We went back to the car and headed over to Briarwood. I felt real pleased with myself.

The rest of the day went according to plan. When we left the Briarwood shopping center we were all tired but felt we'd accomplished something. Charlie came home to dinner with me and we just sat around afterward watching TV.

The next day started quietly enough, but things really picked up when we got the Sunday paper. Surprise!

There was an article about us in it. None of our names were mentioned, but the writer was very positive about us. He referred to us as: "A small group of teen-agers who have taken on the job of informing the public to be more aware of the potential danger to the children of our communities."

The whole leaflet was reprinted, the posters were mentioned, and Harvey's name and the phone number of the shop were included.

The phone started ringing then. Ingrid. Then Charlie. Then Ella, and one by one all the kids called. I invited them over to celebrate our publicity and discuss the possibility of doing it again.

Grandad had to go to the store and lay in some snacks for our meeting. He'd been gone for sometime and Charlie had arrived, when Grandad called from the store. The old Buick had conked out again. Charlie went over to help. They got it started but by the time they got home, Grandad was silently fuming. It had just been in the garage for more than a week.

Charlie teased Grandad out of his angry mood. "Honestly, Mr. Williams, the car is dying. Give it a decent funeral and buy a new one."

They looked at the Sunday ads for cars and Grandad finally admitted that Charlie was right. He decided to go to the bank for a loan the next day and then go car shopping. He asked me if I wanted to go along, since I would be driving the new car, too. That was an offer I couldn't refuse and Grandad started looking forward to what he called the "Great Car Hunt."

Ella and Dick brought more papers and we were all rereading and talking about the article, when the phone rang again. This time it was Harvey. He told me the response to the article was tremendous. He was taking almost more orders than he could fill for the leaflets. I

191

asked him who was ordering them. He answered, "The president of the Dormont P.T.A., a Little League coach from Fox Chapel, and even the principal from a grade school over in Shadyside. It just goes on and on, Brina, and I want to thank you."

I was so happy the campaign had taken off like that that I told him no thanks were necessary. Then he said, "How would you like to do some work for me?"

"What kind?"

"Well, I know a lot of small businessmen who get leaflets or pamphlets, sometimes posters and other things printed. Sometimes they would like to have artwork on them but they can't afford the fees an ad agency charges. I think they'd like your work. Would you be interested?"

Was I interested? I jumped at the chance!

When I got back to the kids, I was flying. I had a job! Or at least I would, as soon as Harvey found me one. And I had to study for my driver's test. Help Grandad find a car. Forget the creep. It was time for me to go on to other things.

After everyone had left, I went out to the front porch where Mom was sitting. I plunked myself down on my usual spot and realized she was looking very sparkly. I asked her what she was looking so happy about, and she replied, "You. You've come a long way from that self-involved kid you were such a short time ago. I was so worried about you, then I was worried about this creep-catching business, and now I have very little to worry about. I realize you'll still have problems, but you're handling yourself so well. And I'm enjoying the kind of person you're turning out to be. I think you're just super! And I think you should know it!"

"Mom, I think you're super, too. About the party and having Charlie over and everything."

"That's nothing. I love it. I told you I wanted you to have friends and entertain them here and I meant it. The party will be fun. And I bet your next year in school is going to be fun, too, now that you've found out it isn't as hard as you thought to make friends."

"That's what Paul said—I mean that it was easy to make friends. He said all you had to do was let them know you were interested. I didn't think so at the time, but he was right."

Mom said, "Paul went through it himself. The loneliness and isolation of not having any other friends but you. It took him a lot longer to change though. Yours has been so fast!"

"I had his help. And yours and Grandad's. And Wallace's. And Charlie's."

"Yeah—Charlie. He's really special, isn't he? He's a lot different from Paul. He's probably never had any trouble finding friends."

We sat there for a long time talking. It was a conversation that wasn't earth-shaking, but there was a difference to it from any other we'd ever had. She was accepting me as her equal and I was accepting her as mine.

20

Grandad and I left the house early the next morning, dressed in our look-alike jumpsuits, complete with railroad caps and chain watches. Wallace gave me permission to go; in my jumpsuit and railroad cap, I looked as different from that little-girl, creep-decoy image as I possibly could.

We went to the small branch bank of a downtown bank first. We made quite a stir in our outfits. The people must have thought we were some new kind of bank robber.

The man who interviewed Grandad for the loan took us in stride. He was a real banker type, very conservatively dressed, spiffy and shiny. Especially his head. He was one of those men who insist on covering up their balding heads with three or four strands of hair. I kept waiting for a good stiff breeze to come wafting through the bank and lift the hair up. One finally did, but the hair must have been glued down. It was spell-binding and I wished I had my sketch pad with me.

Eventually I got the giggles from watching the shine on his dome. I guess he knew what I was thinking because he kept looking at me.

By the time we left the bank, I'd remembered Harvey's toupee and I was laughing hysterically. As we got back to the soon-to-be-retired Buick, Grandad said, "What on earth are you laughing at?"

I told him and when I mentioned Harvey's toupee, Grandad laughed, too. But then he said we were being unkind—that those poor men couldn't help losing their hair. I told him, still laughing, that I was glad he had all of his. He promised that if he ever started losing his, he'd get his whole head shaved. That cracked me up even more.

The loan had been no problem, and we started the rounds of car dealers. I really tried to take an interest, not only because I would be driving the car soon, but because Charlie would expect a report on every detail.

We went to Buick dealers, Ford dealers, Datsun dealers, saw new cars and old cars, those slightly used, and some just ready to die. We kicked tires and went on demonstration rides. Grandad said you didn't buy a car all at once, so this went on for a few days. You name it and we saw it.

Late Wednesday we ended up at "Big Richard" Biggle's New and Used Cars over in Heliotrope. There Grandad saw a year-old Mustang—bright red—that he really liked. He thought it would be a good size for me to drive, too. We talked to a salesman, another balding gentleman, who took us on a demonstration ride. After a quick look-see at the car, I didn't pay much attention to it, because I was itching to draw this baldy, too. He had combed his hair forward from what was left of it on the back of his head, and it was flopping all over the place. I considered telling him about the man in the bank, who I was sure used glue, or even giving him Harvey's name and phone number so he could get a wondrous toupee made, but I was good and kept my mouth shut.

After the ride, Grandad said the car needed a wheel alignment, whatever that was, and Baldy said it could be done and be ready by Friday. That pleased Grandad and they started dickering over the price, the trade-in, and what have you. That took so long, I had to ask Baldy if I could use the bathroom. He pointed the way through the showroom, past the switchboard girl, and into the back of the garage.

When I came out of the john, I made a wrong turn and ended up outside a big grubby office. There was a man sitting behind a very messy desk. It was piled high with papers and parts of cars and junk. He was talking on the phone, but he looked at me in the doorway, and smiled a big car-salesman-type smile. I seemed to be having a run on bald men—Harvey, the man in the bank, Baldy outside, and now this one.

Just like the others, his few strands of hair were trying to pretend they were several. His glasses and the top of his head gave him a luminous glow. I made a mental note to try and capture that gleamy look in a drawing. He looked familiar and I would have asked him if I knew him from somewhere, but he was still on the phone. Then I realized I was staring, so I smiled brightly and went outside. I may have been unkind to bald men, but I wasn't impolite.

Grandad was just closing the deal on the car when I got outside. While he went into the office to sign the papers I went back to the old Buick to wait. I patted the Buick's fender and said I was sorry to see it go.

Grandad came out of the showroom with the bald smiley man I had seen at the desk. They shook hands and Grandad came over to the Buick alone. He got into the car and I asked, "Who was that man you were talking to?" At least I didn't say bald man.

"Why?"

"Oh . . . I thought I knew him from somewhere."

"That's "Big Richard" Biggle himself. It's his car lot. You probably remember him from those TV commercials he did a few years ago." Grandad started up the old Buick.

"Oh. Yes, now I remember. The real hokey commercials. He wore funny hats and blew horns and stuff. I've never seen anyone who's been on TV before. That's kind of exciting."

"Want to go back and get his autograph? I just made a pun," he laughed, "auto-graph."

"Ha ha." I stuck my tongue out at him.

That evening Harvey called and said he had a job for me. A local bar and grill owner wanted a new image for his place, and since the name of it was Happy

Times, he wanted a clown. He would use it in ads, handbills, napkins, everyplace.

Charlie knew I wouldn't be concentrating much on him and left early that night. I went straight to work. I worked on this clown and that clown and continued on the next day. After lunch I went out to the front porch and lined them all up. I was surrounded by sixteen rough sketches of clowns. I knew that eventually I'd have to choose three or four to submit to the bar owner. The choice would be crucial to the job, so I took a break to mull it over.

It had been drizzling when I came out and then it started pouring. I watched the water dripping over the edge of the awning, and felt all safe and secure; as you only can when the whole world is wet and you're dry.

I wasn't ready to choose my favorites from among the multitude of clowns, but I still felt like drawing. I picked up my sketch pad and started doodling a face.

It turned out to be the man in the bank with the unhappy head. That started me on a series. The next face was the car salesman. Then came "Big Richard" Biggle, star of television commercials. All the drawings turned out well, and I thought about doing a portfolio of drawings to show Harvey. Maybe he could interest his toupee-maker in doing a poster with a "Before" and "After." But then I'd have to have an "After." I started on that. I took some tracing paper and put it over the drawing of Biggle. I started sketching in some hair, a whole head full. The kind he probably dreamed about. I chuckled; I was really amusing myself.

Then something about his face caught my complete attention. I added a mustache. Then I drew a cap with a visor turned down low on top of his head. I lifted the tracing and carefully erased the glasses on the original drawing.

No wonder Biggle looked familiar.

He was the creep.

He'd been wearing a wig the day I fought with him. A good wig, not like Harvey's. And a phony mustache.

I gasped aloud, "Now what?" I didn't have an answer. Suddenly the rain stopped and the sun started its struggle to come out. It was warm there on the porch, but I shivered.

I stared at the drawing with the tracing over it until it was blurred in front of me. But that just made it look more like the creep.

I wondered if anyone else would see what I saw, especially any of the girls he'd attacked. It all seemed to fit so well together. He would be able to get any kind of car! He would be able to leave his business anytime. He owned it.

I stared at the drawing for a long time—the shape of the eyes, the mouth, the nose. Everything was so similar to the drawing the police artist and I had put together. But I didn't know what to do.

When I realized I was driving myself crazy, I got up and went into the house. Grandad was asleep on the couch—his usual rainy day activity. I stood and looked at him snoring peacefully and figured he would be out for another hour or so, until his subconscious told him it wasn't raining anymore. Then he'd be up and running around again.

I went into the kitchen and looked at the phone. I checked the watch around my neck. It was almost two-thirty. What to do? I shrugged my shoulders and picked up the phone . . . I had to do something. I called downtown police headquarters and was put right through to Wallace. I told him as quickly as I could what I'd done. And that from my drawing it looked like Biggle was the creep.

He listened all the way through. When I was finished, he said, "C'mon, Brina. He's a respected businessman and I know him. He's a volunteer for the Police Athletic League. He's on the Pittsburgh Chamber of Commerce and he's on the board of whatever that hospital is out in Heliotrope. He raises money for charity, all sorts of things. It's impossible."

"I'm telling you it could be him. The shrink's report said that the creep is a nice guy. Is Biggle a nice guy?"

Long silence. "I know the report said that and Biggle is a nice guy, not exactly quiet, but charming and friendly."

"Have you ever seen him lose his temper? And he can get all those cars. . . ." My voice trailed off. By this time I wasn't sure and I guess I sounded it.

Wallace said, "I just can't believe it's Biggle. You might be right—I'll think it over. No. It's impossible. And we have absolutely nothing to go on. We can't even haul him in for questioning, at least not on the basis of a drawing." Another long silence. "Are you sure it's not just because you have the creep on your mind? Are you sure you're not seeing something that isn't there because you want to catch him so much? You've been through a terrible strain this summer and I know you want this over and done with. Can you say that you're absolutely positive?"

I thought it over. I looked at the sketch from all angles. I couldn't be absolutely sure. Maybe Wallace was right and I was wrong.

Wallace was still waiting for an answer. "No . . . I can't be positive," I said in a small voice.

"Well then . . . don't worry about it for now." His tone was even kinder than usual. I had the feeling he was getting ready to commit me to the looney bin and I resented it. "Look, Brina . . . I've got to run. I'm due in the Wizard's office for a meeting. I'll ask him home to dinner and we'll take a look at it. Bye." He hung up before I could say anything else.

He hadn't believed me at all. He'd just humored me. That hurt.

I wanted to do something to prove that I was right to Wallace. And to myself. I couldn't go back to drawing clowns. I couldn't just wait around for Wallace and the Wizard to show up. I'd had enough talking. And I knew when Wallace and the Wizard came home we'd talk endlessly about it and I'd have to try to convince them. How would I convince them when I wasn't sure myself? I had to do something.

I picked up the yellow pages and looked up the car lot. Maybe if I heard his voice I could tell. I dialed the number and when the switchboard girl answered I asked, "May I speak to Mr. Biggle please?"

"I'm sorry. He's gone for the day. May I ask who's calling?"

"It's not important." I hung up quickly. A new thought gripped me. He might be out attacking another little girl! What if it was Biggle and he was right this minute raping a little girl. I couldn't just stand there.

I looked through the white pages. Biggle, Biggle, only one in the book.

Biggle, Richard. 305 West Washington Street.

That was up on Mount Washington, where the inclines run. It was probably one of those new apartment buildings, all glass, so the people living in them could see Pittsburgh all spread out below them.

The phone practically jumped into my hand. I dialed his number. After three rings he answered.

"Hello . . . hello. Who is this? Hello *Hello!*" He hung up and I wasn't any farther ahead.

I thought maybe I could recognize his voice, but I couldn't. "Damn!" I muttered.

I picked up the phone and dialed the garage where Charlie worked. I thought if I talked it over with him, I would come to some constructive conclusion. He was out, delivering a car.

Right next to the phone were the keys to the old Buick. I picked them up and toyed with them. Without thinking any more, I went into action. I went upstairs quietly, so as not to wake Grandad. I twisted my hair up in a knot, put some money in my jeans pocket, scrutinized myself in the mirror, and hurriedly put on eyeshadow, blusher, and lipstick. Not bad, but not good enough. I went into Mom's room and put on her best pair of designer sunglasses. They were older looking than mine. I looked in her mirror. I certainly didn't look like that little kid I was when Biggle had attacked me.

I tiptoed downstairs and peeked in the living room. Grandad was still fast asleep. My watch said a quarter to three when I let myself out of the house.

I ran over to the old Buick and got in, moved the seat all the way up, started the ignition, and was on my way.

I didn't have any plan. I just thought I'd go over to Mount Washington and check out his building. Maybe I'd catch a glimpse of him and be able to decide if I was right or not. With any luck at all, I'd be back before Grandad woke up. Even if I wasn't, I'd tell him I was just taking the old Buick around the block for a good-bye drive. At that point I didn't care if I got into trouble; I just had to do something.

I was a little nervous driving by myself for the first time. But Grandad always said I was a good driver. Besides, if I got stopped and the cops found out I was driving with only a learner's permit, would they put me in jail? I doubted it. Besides, Wallace would get me out.

It got really scary when I turned onto Banksville Road; all that traffic, and Pittsburgh drivers are all crazy. Grandad says it's because of the steep hills and winding roads. I gripped the wheel and forced myself to relax. I was Bionic Brina again.

Right before the Fort Pitt tunnel, I turned off onto Saw Mill Run, then turned left on Woodruff, another left on Merrimac and right on up to the top of Mount Washington. There I turned right on Grandview Avenue and stopped by the stone lookout. I took the street map out of the glove compartment and walked over to the lookout.

There weren't many people around and I couldn't help noticing the view. It was beautiful. Most people don't think of Pittsburgh as a nice city, but from up there it is.

The sun was poking its way through the clouds and the Golden Triangle was beginning to look golden. Skyscrapers reflected the misty sun. It was quite a sight. The rivers looked shiny, all three of them.

"The Monongahela and the Allegheny meet at Pittsburgh and form the Ohio," I mumbled to myself. That's drummed into every school kid within five hundred miles of Pittsburgh—maybe all over for all I know. I looked over the wall of the lookout at the old McArdle Roadway winding its way down the hill below me. Of the million hills around Pittsburgh, Mount Washington is the steepest, so the roadway was a little like a roller coaster. It was the only way down that side of Mount Washington, except for the inclines. To my right the Monongahela Incline was busy going up and down, down and up. There were two sets of tracks and two cable cars. When one was at the upper station on Grandview, the other was at the lower station on West Carson Street. They would start from each station at the same time and pass each other en route, at a halfway point on the steep hill. It was fascinating to watch them and I sort of wished I could take a ride, but I wasn't there to enjoy myself.

I checked the street map and found West Washington Street was exactly where I thought it was, right behind me, running parallel to Grandview. I got back in the car and drove to the end of Grandview and turned right. I made another right at the next corner and I was on West Washington. 305 was about halfway up the street on my right. I'd been right about the building, too. It was one of the new apartment buildings. Mount Washington was becoming an "in" place to live and that building was one of the in-est places I'd ever seen.

I turned right off the street and drove down to the back of the building. The parking lot jutted out over a slight hill and the backyard of an old house, whose front yard faced on Grandview, was below me. Then there was the station house of the incline and the beautiful view of Pittsburgh below in the distance. I put on the brakes and was almost hypnotized by the view again. I turned the car around and looked up at the back of the building. I envied Biggle; it was a neat place to live. Each apartment had huge picture windows and a large balcony. If I had my way though, there would be a vacancy soon.

I took my foot off the brake and eased into a parking place next to a blue Ford. With all my running around with Grandad I was getting more familiar with cars. I could even have a reasonably decent conversation with Charlie.

I got out of the Buick and went around to the back

of the Ford. It had dealer plates on it and a big sticker saying "Big Richard" Biggle's Cars. It had to be his car. I took a good look, as if it could tell me something. I could see that Biggle wasn't very neat. Just like his office, it was a mess! There was an old blanket, a suitcase, all kinds of loose papers, car advertisements, and pamphlets crammed in the back seat and strewn on the floor.

I decided to drive up to the street and watch the front entrance for a while. Then, if nothing happened, I'd go home and face the music that Grandad would make if he'd discovered I'd taken the car.

As I opened the car door, I looked up at the building again. Then I realized how dumb I'd been not to park in the street in the first place.

For there, on the third floor balcony, was Biggle. He was gripping the rail and looking down at me. His glasses reflected the hazy sun and he whipped them off and squinted down at me. I said an instant prayer that he wouldn't recognize me, but I stood there paralyzed with fear, and really gave myself away.

I was sure just from the way he stood and stared that he was the creep.

I got slowly in the Buick, thinking I could fool him into believing I hadn't been looking for him—that I wasn't the decoy, that it was quite by chance I was in his parking lot. I was fooling myself.

I turned the ignition key. The damn old Buick turned over. Turned over again. I hit the gas. It coughed and died. I felt sick all over. The fear got worse.

How stupid I'd been! Even if he didn't know me with my hair up and Mom's sunglasses on, he'd remember the car. Cars were his business and he'd just accepted this on a trade-in. He would have to wonder what this car was doing in his parking lot. Maybe I could pretend I was delivering it? Stupid idea. Cars get delivered to car lots, not to homes. And then he'd get a real close look at me. This was the third time he'd seen me. If he didn't know who I was by now, he was pretty stupid. And I didn't think he was stupid. Not with all he'd gotten away with.

I tried to think straight. I remembered all the mystery stories I'd read, where the heroine heroined herself right into a corner. I'd always put them down. Now here I was, cornered myself. I thought about staying in the car, locking the doors, and blowing the horn until someone came. But it was so deserted around there, and for all I knew he might have a master key to car doors or some other way of opening the door. I just didn't know that much about cars.

I couldn't sit there any longer; I decided to make a run for it, to get somewhere where there were people. I looked up at the balcony again. He was gone. Ten to one he was on his way down to me. I got out of the car and went to the back of the parking lot. There was the stone ledge. I climbed over it and ran to the backyard of the old house. I stopped there and hid behind a tree. I poked my head around it enough to see Biggle coming out the door of the apartment building. There he was, trying to figure out which way I'd gone. He looked in the Buick. I was frozen behind that tree. He came over to the stone ledge and stared my way. I couldn't wait for him to come any closer. I had to keep going.

When I ran past the house, I thought about banging on the door. But it looked so silent and if no one was home, I'd really lose time. If he was right behind me, he'd get me.

I was too scared to look back to see where he was. I kept on running, through the front yard of the house.

There was Grandview and I ran straight across it. No traffic at all. I got to the incline station on the other side.

I decided to go into the station and phone Wallace. First sensible idea I'd had in what seemed like years. Ran in, got my bearings. There were a few people just going through the turnstile for the ride down the hill. I looked wildly for a pay phone and saw one on the wall to my left. I was on my way to it when I remembered I didn't have any change.

I went over the middle of the station where the change booth was and dug in my jeans pocket for a dollar. I glanced outside. I saw the blue Ford pulling up at the curb. Biggle had driven over instead of following me on foot. That made him more mobile than me. But he couldn't drive onto the incline.

I made up my mind in a hurry. I went to the man in the booth and handed him my dollar. "Change, please." It came out in a croak.

He gave me four quarters and I thought irrelevantly, "Wonderful . . . now I have to spend a quarter on a phone call. If I ever get to make one."

I stood there looking wildly at the man who had given me the change and he said, "You'd better hurry, the car is leaving in a second."

I darted a quick look over my shoulder. Biggle was peering into the station. He wasn't sure I was in there. I said to the man, "Please call Detective Wallace at police headquarters downtown. Tell him Sabrina Randall will be at the bottom of the hill."

"What are you, kid? Some sort of juvenile delinquent? Go away kid . . . you'll miss your car. Damn practical joker." He turned away from me! He was still mumbling as I threw my quarter in the money box and pushed through the turnstile. I ran down the steps to the last part of the car and jumped on. The doors clanged shut with a big shiver and the car started down the hill.

Only a short time ago, I'd wondered if I'd still get a kick out of the ride. But now all I could think about was Biggle.

If he asked the man in the booth about me, then he'd know where I'd gone. I figured it would take about two and a half to three minutes to get to the bottom of the hill by the incline. By car down the McArdle Roadway, it would have to take at least four to four and a half minutes, depending on traffic, which should still be light at that time of the day. He would have to go under the incline tracks, through the traffic light—which I fervently hoped was red—at the Liberty Bridge, make a U-turn to go up West Carson Street, which was parallel to the McArdle Roadway, to reach the station at the bottom of the hill.

I took that journey in my mind and hoped he'd run into a lot of traffic. That the car would break down. That he'd fall over the roadway embankment. And several other things. I also hoped that the man in the booth would have a change of heart and call Wallace. But I doubted it. I must have looked like a lunatic. My hair had fallen down and was all over the place. I'd lost the sandals I was wearing somewhere and I was barefoot. I vaguely remembered kicking them off so that I could run better and I'd lost Mom's sunglasses. She'd kill me if Biggle didn't. If nobody killed anybody and I got out of this alive, I planned to come back and punch the guy in the booth.

I was all alone in my part of the car, and all I could see were the tops of people's heads. The cable car itself was built on a slant, with three parts. Each one was partitioned off from the rest with the steps outside the car, in the station. There was no way to get from one part of the car to another except over the partitions. I didn't know why they were built that way, but I thought I'd figure it out another time.

I sat there and told the car to hurry—as if that would help. As we passed over the McArdle Roadway, I looked up it but didn't see the blue Ford. The trip seemed to be taking an eternity.

Finally the car screeched to a stop and I was at the bottom. The doors slid open and I jumped off.

I groped in my pocket for one of the quarters and headed for the payphone on the far wall of the station. Whoops. There was a sign on it: OUT OF ORDER. I looked around at the other people. There were two middle-aged ladies and one old man waiting for the "Next Car" sign to flash on, so they could board the car I'd just gotten off, for the trip back up the hill. They couldn't be much help to me. I was more capable of beating up Biggle than any of them.

I decided to get out of there and try for the bus stop outside. I knew that buses ran regularly by the station, straight over the Liberty Bridge and up Grant Street right to the front door of police headquarters. I started out the door, then had second thoughts. Maybe the man in this booth would believe me. It was worth a try. I walked boldly over to him and said, "Will you please call the Pittsburgh police and tell them to send a squad car over here. There's a man following me."

"I don't see no man, kid. You tried this up top, dint ya? Ole Benson, he called down on the intercom, tole me about it. Dint like it much. I don't either. Run along. Go play in traffic. Ha ha heeeha."

"Please believe me."

"Go 'way. Before I get mad."

People are so stupid sometimes. I wished I could

squeeze out a few tears and make a crying scene. He'd probably be a sucker for tears. No tears. I gave up. And ran out of the station.

I ran through the parking lot, feeling the dampness left over from the rain on my bare feet. There was a bus just pulling away from the curb. I ran for it and shouted for the driver to stop. It was no good and I cursed myself for stopping at the booth. I looked wildly for a cab. None in sight, but there was another bus on the opposite side of the street. I watched for an opening in the traffic, hoping I could run across and catch it. There was a lot of traffic coming from town now and they were whizzing by too fast for me to cross. They weren't going to stop for me either—it would cause a real smash-up.

When I looked to my right, I caught a glimpse of a blue car making the U-turn at the bottom of the McArdle Roadway onto West Carson. I wasn't going to stand there and find out if it was Biggle. I ran back into the station.

He wouldn't expect me to get back on the incline and go back up the hill again. Maybe I could ride the incline all day and if I timed it right, he'd never catch me.

Of all the mistakes I made that day—that was the worst one.

I ran back over to the turnstile and threw my quarter in. The man in the booth saw me and grinned a toothless grin, "You are some kid. You'll wear out the incline. Up and down. Down and up. Ho. Heh—ha."

I glared at him. Another one I'd come back and take revenge on. I swore it.

"Call the police!" I yelled as I ran through the turnstile. I stopped at the bottom of the stairs, outside the incline car and turned around. I took a peek outside.

The blue car was just pulling into the parking lot. I was sure then—it had to be Biggle.

I charged up the stairs to the last compartment. The only place for me to hide was under the seats on either side of the compartment. I picked the one next to the partition and scrunched down under it. He wouldn't be able to see me from outside and I hoped he'd think I took the bus into Pittsburgh. I was sure he hadn't seen me outside the station.

I could hear the old man and the two ladies from the waiting room getting on. It was their first trip in the incline and they were giggling nervously. I hoped they'd enjoy it. I hoped it wouldn't be my last. Then I heard a voice.

"Did any of you see a young girl get on?"

One of the ladies answered, "No, I didn't."

My heart was in my ears, banging away. I'd been pretty cool until then. There had been an unreal feeling about the whole thing, like a movie I was watching, but now I was terrified. The car doors closed and the car lurched. We were on our way. Back up the hill.

I kept hiding for a few seconds. Then I peeped out from under the seat. There wasn't anyone else in my part of the car. I didn't want to give up my semi-safe position but I knew I'd have to move eventually—to run off the car. I decided to take a chance and come out from under the seat. I didn't know whether Biggle was in one of the other compartments or not and I had to find out, so I would know how fast to move when the car got to the top of the hill.

I'd been lying on the floor under the seat and it was filthy. When I crawled out and was on my knees, I unconsciously brushed myself off. I listened for his voice, but I couldn't hear anything over the squeaking of the cable car.

I figured I was safe because of the partition. I crawled up on the seat and crouched there, working up my nerve to take a peek over it. I stood up. A half foot away on the other side of the partition, a head appeared. Biggle. I stared into those crafty-crazy brown eyes and couldn't move.

He reached over the partition—almost casually—and grabbed my hair. He pulled my face forward and said, "Well, here you are after all."

I had this strange desire to scream—"No, I'm not!" But all I could do was stare at him. He had me, and my head hurt where he was tugging at my hair. I made another vow. If I came out of this alive, I would cut my hair.

He pulled even harder. Now that I didn't need them, tears came to my eyes. "Climb over the partition . . . dear." He cooed. I couldn't believe I heard him right. "Now!" He tugged again at my hair and I reached up mechanically and started pulling myself over the partition.

He had to let go of my hair to help me over. I got one leg over and he grabbed it. I got the other one over and was standing on the seat of the other compartment. He was just climbing down when I kicked him. I'd aimed at the crotch, but I missed it and got him in the stomach. He doubled over in pain and I plopped myself down next to one of the ladies. My bare foot ached, but I'd gotten him!

"Please help me! That man is. . . ." He recovered enough to grab me. My kick wasn't that strong. I planned another one.

"You'll have to excuse my daughter," he gasped, "She's been trying to run away from me. You know how children are these days. . . ."

The car was almost up to the top now. "I'm not his daughter!" I screamed.

"You see how she is?" Biggle shook his head sadly, really acting his part. "Now, dear, you know who I am." He had the nerve to pat my head, then he grabbed my hair again.

The car lurched to a stop. "He's not my father. He's going to kill. . . ." He clamped his hand over my mouth and dragged me to my feet, pulling my hair at the same time. The pain was unbearable.

"Shut-up!!" he yelled. The car doors started sliding open. "I guess this is the only way to handle her. I really hate to do it!" He smiled his toothy car-salesman-type smile at the lady. "If she doesn't behave, I'll just have to spank her." He was enjoying himself!

The car doors were standing open. The lady got up and looked from me to Biggle and back to me again. The rest of her group had moved as far away from us as the compartment would allow. They made a rush for the door.

The lady joined them, but just as she got to the doors, she turned back to us and said, "I know what you mean," to Biggle. "Children are so disrespectful. My very own daughter ran away from me when she was only fourteen. We had a very good home in Donora, and what did she do? She ran away and ended up on the streets."

And then, to me, "You take my advice dear and go home with your father."

She smiled sweetly at Biggle, who still had his hand clamped over my mouth, stepped through the doors, and walked up the steps. Of all the people in the world to ask for help, I had to find a lady whose daughter was a runaway. Some luck.

We were alone in the car then. Biggle growled, "Behave yourself now," and took his hand off my mouth. I kneed up and into his crotch. The pain must have been excruciating. The tears welled up in his eyes. But he never let go of my hair and pulled it even harder. We stood there, suspended, both of us in pain.

He got over his faster than I and he was still pulling that damn hair with one hand. With the other he reached into his pocket and pulled out a switchblade. He must have had it for years, because there was a law against them. But with all the other laws he'd broken I guess one more didn't count.

He snapped the blade out. I stared at it. "I'm going to throw up. I'm really sick," I could hear myself whining. I hoped it would catch him off guard.

"Go ahead, but you'll be wearing it!" He leered at me, all signs of pain gone now. It had almost been true. His aftershave was enough to gag a maggot.

He poked the knife in my side and we walked off the car, sort of sideways. "We are going into the waiting room," he hissed, "and we will wait for the O.K. to get back on this car. Then we are going back down to my car. You have had it, little girl. It's time you were punished."

It didn't take too much imagination to figure out what he meant. I'd seen the little girl in the hospital, but I didn't think he'd let me live to go to a hospital.

"I called the police." It was worth a try.

He prodded me in the side with the knife. "Little girl . . . I don't care what you've done. You tried to fool me before at the park. Keep your damn mouth shut. As long as I have you, nobody is going to do anything. Everyone in this station thinks you're a runaway. You made quite a stir up here and down below. They all think you're quite mad. And, my dear . . . I do not see any policemen."

But I did. As we came up the stairs and into the station, I saw Wallace, examining the post cards and souvenirs of the famous Pittsburgh incline.

I'd never been so glad to see anyone in my life! I wanted to scream and scream loud. But I felt the knife in my side. If I screamed, he'd kill me right here! He'd be caught . . . but good Lord, I'd be just as dead.

As we walked over to the booth, Wallace turned away. I figured he was waiting for a chance to grab Biggle from behind and I mustn't blow it. His knife was still in my side, and I was sure my hair covered it completely. I could feel it all tangled up and I was afraid it would slice up my hair. Of course, that was the least of my problems and I was going to get it cut anyway after I got out of Biggle's grasp. Now that Wallace was on the scene I was sure I'd get away.

The "NEXT CAR" light flashed on and Biggle said, "Throw two quarters in the box, dear." He smiled that tooth-filled smile at the man in the booth. "You see? I've found my little girl."

He'd really covered himself everywhere. The man in the booth, my best friend, didn't say a word. Now that it was too late, he probably knew that I really was in trouble. Wallace would have told him.

"I said put the money in the box, dear," said Biggle again.

It was bad enough he had me lock, stock, and barrel . . . now I had to pay for the ride. I fished in my jeans pocket for the last of the change from the dollar. Unfortunately, I found it. I knew he couldn't put the knife down to get his money, but he would have figured out something.

We walked back through the turnstile and back down the stairs and onto the very front compartment of the car. We sat facing the view of Pittsburgh. I was sick of the sight of it. How was Wallace going to get me out of this? I turned around and looked up to see if Wallace was on the car. Biggle pulled my hair again and I had to look at him. I hadn't been able to see anything above the partition, but Wallace had to be there.

The car doors clanked shut and the car started down the hill. Of course he'd noticed my frantic glance up toward the rest of the car. "What were you looking for, dear? No one is going to help you."

Somewhere I found the courage to say, "Shut up! You've got me—so shut up!" At least that got his attention and I didn't have to sit there thinking how stupid I'd been.

He smiled that awful, awful toothy smile again, "What is your name, dear?"

It's amazing how much strength you can muster up during harrowing experiences because I actually answered him, "Sabrina."

He nodded, "That's a very nice name, dear. Is that Sabrina Williams? That old man isn't your father? The one at the car lot—is he?"

How dare he call Grandad an old man—my grandfather, who I might never see again. Tears of anger, rage, and frustration started blurring my eyes.

"You creep!" I yelled.

"No, he isn't your father," Biggle leered, "because from now on I'm going to be your father and you have to do everything I say. Everything." His voice had gone back to that high-pitched whine I remembered from the conservatory park. His eyes seemed to get wilder and crazier while he stared at me, as if taking inventory.

I swore a few choice swear words at him.

"Oh, my!" Again that awful smile and that awful whine. "Those aren't very nice words to say to your father, my dear Sabrina."

My name sounded like a dirty word coming from his mouth.

"You're going to have to be punished. . . ." The car crunched to a stop and we were at the bottom of the hill again. His crazy eyes darted from me to the door, then back to me. "Up and no nonsense, Sabrina. Listen to your father, dear." The TV smile again. It was a wonder his face didn't hurt from it. He was really insane.

As we moved toward the door of the car I saw Wallace passing by. Why didn't he wait and jump Biggle from behind? Then I felt the knife prodding me again and I remembered that Wallace would have no way of knowing whether Biggle had a knife or a gun or what on me. But Wallace knew me well enough to know that if I weren't being threatened by something I would be fighting back.

Biggle was really hustling me right along now. We were through the turnstile and in the waiting room quickly. There was Wallace staring at more postcards. As we passed him, I hesitated and Biggle prodded me with the knife. I swore at him again, trying to remember every curse word I'd ever heard.

"Now don't say such things to your father." He was convinced he was my father.

"My father is dead! He's dead and I wish you were dead, too!" The tears were really coming now.

Biggle remained absolutely unruffled, "No, no, I'm not dead and I'm your father. . . ."

Why didn't Wallace do something? There were a lot of people in the station now. They were all staring at us, too, and then turning away and trying not to get involved. They wanted to go to their nice peaceful homes and not think about anyone's troubles. I wanted to go home, too. And I couldn't even turn around to see where Wallace was.

Biggle shoved me out the door of the station. We crossed the parking lot and headed for the blue Ford. We got to the driver's side of the car. He said, "Open the door, dear Sabrina."

I resisted and I felt the knife scrape my back; my skirt tore, my skin would be next. I opened the car door. Wallace—please. I prayed.

Biggle pushed me in and climbed in right behind me. He had an even stronger hold on my hair, if that were possible, so any idea I had of jumping out the other side stopped before it started.

He had me strapped in with the safety belts—one around my shoulder and the other across my lap with my hands under it, before I even knew what he was doing. Safety belts! Some safety! What a nightmare.

He said, "You sit quietly, or I'll punish you right here."

I sat quietly. He put the key in the ignition and turned it. The engine started right up. I felt doomed, abandoned by Wallace and terrified all at the same time.

Suddenly there was a great heaving in the back seat! All the papers and stuff were flying all over the place. There was a glint of gold! When the papers and junk settled, I saw that Biggle was being strangled by a gold chain.

I strained around and looked in the back seat. There was Grandad! His gold watch was in his left hand, the end of the chain in his right, and the middle was choking Biggle's neck. Papers and junk were dripping off him. His hair stood up in angry spikes, his eyes were furious, his whole body stiff with rage.

The door to the driver's side opened and Wallace had his gun pointed at Biggle. "Ease up, Harry," he said, almost gently, to Grandad. "We don't want to kill him."

Grandad jerked, tightening his grip. Biggle was turning purple and struggling for air. Both his hands were up, trying to get the chain off, his eyes popping. "Harry," Wallace said softly. "Harry, let go."

It seemed a monumental effort, but Grandad finally sagged a little and let go.

Wallace hauled Biggle out of the car and threw him over the hood. Grandad jumped out of the car, too, and rushed to my side. He had me unbuckled quickly and pulled me out of the car. He held me very tightly and when I could look up at him, I saw tears falling in great big drops down his cheeks.

"Oh, Grandad, don't cry," I whispered. But I was crying, too. He took out his bandana handkerchief and wiped my eyes, then his own.

After we had our tears wiped and our noses blown and dry, we walked hand in hand around the car where Wallace had Biggle cuffed. Biggle seemed confused and disoriented. I wanted to go over and kick him, to hurt him, but he was caught, disarmed, and subdued. There was no point to it.

I stopped looking at him, feeling nauseated. I looked at the Wizard and Perky standing by the car. Amazed to see them, I asked, "Where did you come from? How did everyone get here?"

The Wizard actually grinned and said, "We've been here ever since you came out of the station. We were ready to block the exit to the street. But we didn't know you were in the back seat, Mr. Williams."

"I did," said Wallace. "I saw him get into the back of the car while we were coming down the hill on the incline. I imagine you and Biggle were too busy to notice him."

"There's time for explanations later. Let's get this creep downtown and book him." He handed me a little white card. "Brina—read him his rights."

It was over. I'd finally caught the creep. But I hadn't done it alone. I said to Grandad, "You read them with me."

We stood in front of Biggle. He was no longer the monster, just a disheveled, pathetic creep. We read from the card together, "You have the right to remain silent. . . ."

21

Right after Grandad and I finished reading Biggle's rights to him, three squad cars came screaming into the incline parking lot. The scene began to look like something from an old movie—all sorts of uniformed cops bumping into each other. We drew quite a crowd of rubber-neckers. The Wizard gave orders rapidly and Biggle was loaded into one of the squad cars with Perky riding shotgun.

We were to meet at headquarters and Wallace got into the Wizard's car to go back up the hill to his own. He said he'd had enough of the incline on that one trip to last him a lifetime.

Grandad and I went to the street where the old Buick was parked. The squad cars left and so did the crowd. The parking lot was peaceful again.

We got into the car and I sank gratefully into the front seat on the passenger side. Grandad started the engine and I suddenly remembered, "How did you get it started?"

"Is that why you left it? It wouldn't start?" Grandad asked.

I told him of my attempt to run from Biggle in the car. He listened, then said, "You must have flooded it. It started fine by the time I got to it. It's touchy, you know, but I've been driving it a long time."

"Was I scared! How did you know where I was? How did you find the car?"

"Well, that's a long story. I knew where you were because you left the phonebook open to the page that had Biggle's address. I'm almighty glad you did, too!" He laughed a little and the tension eased on his face.

"Wallace called soon after you left. He said it had been only about ten minutes since he'd talked to you. There were the sketches lying right there and the phonebook. I'd have to have been a real bimbo not to know what you were up to. Especially when I saw the car keys were gone. I told Jim to hang on and I went and checked out front for the car. It was gone. Jim was fit to be tied.

"I got him calmed down enough to tell me what he was fussing about." By that time we were heading over the Liberty Bridge, toward Pittsburgh. "He told Perky what you said about the drawings and everything. Perky's a lot smarter than he acts sometimes, you know. He remembered when he was in "Missing Persons" back about fifteen years ago, he was assigned to a case involving a runaway wife. She'd taken her two little girls with her, ages ten and twelve, and the husband reported them missing. The police looked into it quite thoroughly when they found out from the neighbors that the man had been beating the wife and kids. For a while, everyone thought he might have done away with them, but they couldn't prove anything. And the husband was away in California when it happened. So, he had an alibi."

"It was Biggle's wife and kids?" I asked.

"Yep. When they ran away they changed their names and there was no trace of them until a little over two years ago. You see, Biggle never gave up. He hired a friend of Perky's, a private investigator, to run periodic checks on their whereabouts. Then two years ago the P.I. found out they had been killed in a train wreck, in Canada, only a few years after they left Biggle."

"Whew! That fits in with the shrink's profile. At least some of it does. A traumatic event triggering him off. But why do you suppose he picked that particular way to strike out?" Now that it was over, I could be interested in the whys instead of the whens.

"Beats me," said Grandad. "We may never know. Anyway, Wallace called you back to tell you that. He was sorry and felt he'd been a little rough on you. While he was on the phone with me, Perky called up the parents of some of the girls that the creep—I mean Biggle—had attacked—the ones he'd called by name and known where they lived. And sure enough, Perky got hold of three of them; all three had been over to the car lot buying cars.

By the time Jim had told me the story, Perky had told him about the phone calls and Jim told me, well, you'd been gone for about twenty minutes, near as we could figure."

"I was probably up at the lookout on Grandview then. I stopped to get my bearings and look at the street map."

"You should have stayed there. You should never have gone in the first place. . . ."

"I know. I know only too well!"

221

"I guess maybe you do at that. Well, I'm not going to yell at you. I'll let Diana do that."

I winced. All that positive ground-breaking with Mom and I was back to being a bad little disobeying kid.

We pulled into the police garage. Grandad parked and we sat there in the safe dark car, talking.

"I called the Mount Hope cab company and told the dispatcher that there would be twenty dollars in it if a cab got to the house in five minutes. In three and a half, I had a real speed-demon honking his horn as he got within a half a block of our house. I was out on the street waiting for him. I jumped in and told him there would be another twenty for him if he got me to Mount Washington in ten minutes. And he did it. I almost got killed on the way, but he did it!"

"I was probably just pulling into the parking lot of Biggle's apartment house when the cab driver was picking you up."

Grandad nodded, "We must have just missed you by a few minutes at Biggle's place. Wallace met me there. He came by himself, leaving Perky and the Wizard to get a warrant. We were going to go up and break into Biggle's apartment, without the warrant, when a woman came out on the second floor balcony. When she found out that Jim was the police, she told us she'd seen you from her kitchen window. She'd been really worried, because she saw you run off toward the incline and saw Biggle looking for you. She saw him take off in his car and then saw him over at the incline. Good thing that building is higher than anything around it. She could see everything and she got very concerned but she didn't know what to do."

"I sure wish I'd known she was around! When the car didn't start, I just ran!"

"That was the right thing to do, because Biggle could probably charm his way out of a snake pit. That woman was so worried, she would have believed any story he told her." Grandad shook his head. "Yep. A charming, sneaky creep. Well, after she told us where to look, I got in the Buick and it started right up. I have the right touch, you see." He patted the steering wheel lovingly. "Jim got in his car and we both drove over to the incline. After we parked outside we went in and asked that guy in there if he'd seen you. He told us you went down the hill on the incline and that your father had followed you in his car. Jim got real mad then. He showed the guy his I.D. and said, 'She's my kid! Now you get on that intercom and find out where she went when she got to the bottom.' Scared that guy half out of his wits!" Grandad chuckled.

Then it hit me what he said Wallace had said. "Wallace really said that? Well, what do you know."

"Yep. You should have seen how mad and scared he was at the same time. Anyway, he told the guy to call down, but I wasn't going to wait around to find out. I ran out, jumped in the car and went on down McArdle. When I got to the parking lot I saw the Ford with the dealer plates and knew it had to be Biggle's. I went inside and talked to that guy in that booth. He was just hanging up the intercom and he said you'd gone back up the hill with the man claiming to be your father following you, but your real father, who was a cop, was waiting for you up there and that you were all back on the incline car, waiting for it to start. Went on and on . . . never heard a grown man talk so much in my life. Then the intercom rang again and the guy up the hill said the car had started down. They must talk to each other all day long. He started apologizing to me. . . ."

"He should apologize to me . . . him and his friend on top!"

"Want to go back and get their apology now?" He said it with a perfectly straight face.

"No, thanks!" I yelped. He laughed.

"If you could have seen your face just then . . ." He kept on laughing until I finally joined in. It was a relief to laugh again.

We laughed ourselves out and he went on. "When my talkative friend in the booth told me you were on the way down, I knew what to do. I ran outside and hid in the Ford. Whew . . . it's been quite a day so far and Lord knows when we'll get out of the Wizard's office. We'll have to go through a lot of red tape. We'd better get up there."

He started to get out of the car, but I stopped him. "Grandad, I have to thank you for what you did today." I looked at the face, the blue eyes, the spikes of hair, and was so glad to see what I was seeing. I would never forget the raging anger that had taken possession of those familiar features when he was strangling Biggle. I would never forget it but I hoped I'd never see it again. I loved him too much to ever want to see him go through such agony again. "Remember how afraid you were that you might let me down?" He nodded. "Well, you didn't and you never will and I love you very much." I'd never said aloud before that I loved him and I remembered what Mom had said at the beginning of the summer—that you should always tell people you love them when you do.

He hugged me and said, "I love you, too, you little whippersnapper."

22

We got out of the car just as Wallace and the Wizard pulled into the garage in their separate cars. We all got in the elevator and jabbered excitedly at each other until we got to the Wizard's office. We spent the rest of the afternoon there going over the whole thing. I found out that my friend in the booth on top of the hill had finally called police headquarters, after Wallace told him to and told them to radio the Wizard's car to meet us at the bottom of the hill. I decided to forgive those two booth men. I wouldn't forget in a hurry, but now that I was safe, I could be nice and forgive.

I dictated a thing called a deposition—a statement of what happened—and signed it. The creep was really and truly booked.

Wallace called Mom and told her to come over to the office and to pick up some shoes for me on the way. Poor Mom. By the time she got there, they had a full confession from Biggle. He'd broken down and was a ranting, raving maniac. I was glad I didn't have to see it, because seeing Mom was enough. She was almost a ranting, raving maniac, too.

She arrived with another pair of shoes for me, just sandals, no clogs, and immediately started yelling at me for stealing the car, for going after the creep single-handed, and for almost getting myself and Grandad killed. I told her it wouldn't happen again.

She said, "Of course it won't happen again. The creep's been caught!" That made sense.

Wallace calmed her down by reminding her that Biggle would have come hunting for me. Sooner or later, he would remember where he'd seen me before. Just as I remembered him. Once he did, he would have had to get rid of me. That was scary.

By the time we went to our separate cars to head for home it was almost seven. We'd asked the Wizard and Perky to stop by and Perky called Charlie to tell him to meet us at our house, too.

Grandad and I were on the way home in the old Buick, when we remembered food. He was in no mood to cook anything! We stopped for two pizzas with everything. Celebration pizzas, Grandad called them.

We got home and Mom was surprised to see the pizzas. She'd told Wallace to get some Chinese food, and she'd picked up one of those ice cream cakes. Wallace got there with the Chinese food; Perky and the Wizard weren't far behind. With buckets of fried chicken. They thought they were doing us a favor!

It was some sort of hysterical food scene. When Charlie showed up he said he wished he'd known, he would have brought some fish and chips. I helped Mom set everything out on plates and when she saw it all laid out on the table, she started laughing. Big gulping laughs, like she couldn't get enough air. She was still laughing when the tears came. I grabbed her and took her out on the kitchen porch. Somehow I knew that we should be alone. Through the tears and the gulps, she shivered, "It's over, oh, thank God, it's over. And you're still alive."

I said the only thing I could think of to say. "I love you, Mom, I love you." She held me and rocked me back and forth until we were both O.K. Then I said, "I'm hungry."

"I'll be damned. So am I!" We got up and went into the kitchen and it was a good thing we had all that food. Neither one of us could stop eating.

I eventually got around to asking the Wizard if I could tell Ella what had happened. He said I could tell her, but no one else because if the news media got hold of it, I might become the target of every kook in the Pittsburgh area. I didn't need that! And as long as I could tell Ella, and Charlie knew, I didn't care about anyone else.

The Wizard said that I would probably get some sort of commendation from the mayor in a private ceremony. Grandad said, "That old stick in the mud!" He'd never liked our mayor, but he was pleased all the same when the Wizard told him that he would get one, too. I asked if the mayor would give me my fare back from the incline. Everyone howled at that.

In the midst of all the confusion I remembered something that I'd been meaning to do, so I slipped away from the crowd and went up to my room. I was just putting some things into a shopping bag, when Wallace knocked on my open door.

I turned around and he said, "Are you all right?"

"Sure."

He looked relieved. "I thought maybe you were having some sort of nervous reaction."

"I already had it with Mom downstairs. At least I think that was it."

"What are you doing?" He looked at the shopping bag.

"I'm giving those dresses and that dumb red purse to the Salvation Army now that I'm out of the decoy business for good!"

He laughed a big booming laugh. "You are something else! Only you would think of that at a time like this. I didn't have a chance before to tell how great I think you are. You're a brave, stupid, wonderful, awful kid."

"What a testimonial!" I laughed right along with him. Then I remembered what he'd said to the man in the booth about me being his kid, and I asked him about it.

He stood there for a moment, all the laughter gone, and then said seriously, "Brina, I've never had a kid and you're as close to it as I'll ever get. But I couldn't imagine having a better one."

Suddenly my good old tears came back. "Then you're going to stick around?" I whispered.

"Do you want me to?"

"Yes," I answered quickly, but I meant it.

He sat down heavily on my bed and looked relieved. "Sometimes I've had the feeling, that you resent me a little. Interfering. Taking Diana's time away from you. Changing your life and hers and even Harry's."

"I did at first. I didn't know it showed."

"I was looking for it. You see, any change like that is upsetting. And taking into consideration all you were going through, you'd have to have some reaction. I'm just glad it wasn't worse."

"Always the psychologist, aren't you?" I grinned.

"You bet! Listen, the lease on my apartment is up soon. So you want to help me move in here permanently? I thought maybe I'd pack up my stuff this weekend and we could. . . ."

I interrupted, "But what about Mom? Do you think you'll get married?"

"Diana isn't sure she wants to make the commitment. She went through an awful lot with you being a police person, worrying about your safety. She hasn't realized yet that my safety is always in jeopardy. When she does, I'm not sure how she'll take it. She's already lost one husband. I guess we'll have to wait and see." He was silent and from downstairs I could hear the others making merry.

I'd never thought about his safety either. And at that moment I prayed that nothing would ever happen to him. I almost told him to quit the force. But that would be his decision and Mom's. I reached over and took his hand and pulled him up, "Let's go down and get some of that cake."

"Haven't you had enough to eat?" He laughed again.

"Never." And I hugged him. I hugged him so hard, I would have broken his ribs if he weren't so big.

23

Things really settled down around our house after that. The next three weeks before the party were quiet, but happy. I had done my job and I guess there's nothing like having done a job well. Before I had caught the creep, I had decided to go on to other things. After I caught him . . . I was ready to go on to other things.

My friendship with Ingrid, Lois, and the others became stronger. I did tell Ella the whole story. She said, "Well . . . I thought there was something peculiar going on with you. I'm glad to find out it was that and not that you were flipping out!"

Her church group had their recital downtown and her solo went so well, she was even mentioned in the Pittsburgh paper.

I was mentioned in the paper, too. But not by name. I was: "An unidentified girl accosted by "Big Richard" Biggle on the Monongahela Incline, leading to his arrest and subsequent confession to several attacks and rapes of little girls in the Pittsburgh area."

I finished the clown for Harvey, and the owner of the bar liked it, too—I think because it had crossed eyes and looked drunk!

Grandad decided to pass on the Mustang. He thought just having it around would remind us too much of the creep. He was right. I, for one, do not want to remember the fear I had. I want to enjoy my life.

Charlie found a cute little blue Datsun and Grandad bought it.

It was just the right size for me and I was driving it almost more than Grandad, because he had found a chauffeur. He had decided with all the entertaining I was doing, to take a cooking class. Chinese cooking! What else! And not being anyone's dummy, he started dating the teacher after the very first class. On the third date, he brought her home . . . to cook a twelve-course Chinese feast for us.

She was a short, plump, merry little lady, with sparkling brown eyes, and one streak of white in her black hair. Her name was Elizabeth and she was born in Hong Kong, part Chinese, part French, and part English, but she had lived in Pittsburgh since before World War II. She was a little younger than Grandad and, just like him, she had a youthful attitude. She drove a huge white Cadillac, and would pick Grandad up and bring him home from their dates.

The first time we met her, she arrived at our house, covered in more jade jewelry than I had ever seen outside a jewelry store . . . rings, bracelets, gold chains with jade stones, and earrings you could die over. I hung around the kitchen to watch her cook the feast and the first thing she did was to take a jewelry box out of her purse and methodically remove every single piece of jewelry and store it in the box. Then, after everything was ready, she put every single piece of jewelry back on. Fascinating.

Watching her prepare the feast was fascinating, too. And the feast . . . wow! Everything from soup, through spare ribs, a beef and mushroom thing, a fish course— I did not enjoy the squid—shrimp, it seemed endless . . . all the way through to the fortune cookies. My fortune said: All things are within your grasp. Exactly the way I felt.

So there we were. Instead of the three of us in the house, it was four, but somehow we didn't seem to bump into each other as much as we used to.

The day of the party, everyone came over to help— Ingrid, Charlie, Ella . . . all of the kids. We had a houseful before the houseful. Then everyone went back home to dress up and come back.

The party began at eight o'clock. We must have had a hundred people in our backyard . . . tons of kids, adults, friends of Wallace's, friends of Mom's, friends of Grandad's, and friends of mine. All kinds of people. All sizes and shapes. Perky and his wife, Elinor. The Wizard and a date! Harvey and his wife. Mrs. Fiona and her husband and kids. . . . Everyone I had had anything to do with that summer, but the creep.

After it had been going strong for about an hour and a half . . . I had the strangest feeling of being watched. I turned around and saw a shadow over by the garage and at first I was almost afraid again. I couldn't help thinking the creep had come to the party after all. I shook myself and crossed over to the shadow, no longer afraid . . . just curious.

It was Paul. He grinned down at me and said, "I almost didn't recognize you. You cut your hair!"

I reached up and felt it.

"Oh, my hair!"

I'd forgotten my trip to Goodhugh's Beauty Shoppe. I was so comfortable with my now shoulder-length hair, my pierced ears, my higher heels, and my new image altogether that it had never occurred to me how different I would look to Paul—or to anyone else who only knew the old me.

I reached out and grabbed his hand. "Come and join the party."

"No . . . it's your party. I don't know any of those people."

"You're the one who told me how easy it is to make friends," I said lightly.

"You really have changed. What happened to you this summer?"

I laughed, "It's a long story and I'll tell you all about it, just as soon as I get . . ." I started to say permission, but stopped.

"Get what?"

"Never mind. But I will tell you about it someday. Will you join the party?"

"No . . . I can't. I have a date. I just wanted to see how you are . . . and I can see you're just fine. I'll come over sometime before I go back to school and we can talk then." He leaned over and kissed me on the cheek, then walked away.

I watched him disappear into the darkness and all

sorts of thoughts rushed around in my brain. One of which was that I had sworn I would be surrounded by masses and masses of people when he came back. And there I was, surrounded by masses and masses of people . . . but it meant a whole lot more to me than it did to him.

Then I remembered that I was supposed to help feed those hungry masses. And you know, I was getting hungry myself! I hurried back to the party.